For my bestie...
Whether it's Rockers, Navy SEALs or ridiculous hot
British men, you've always been there. Our journey started
with a particular book and a simple request for a magazine.
I'm beyond thankful I volunteered. Love you to pieces,
Yvette.

SEXCATION
HEIDI MCLAUGHLIN
© 2017

COVER DESIGN: Letitia Hasser ~ RBA Designs
EDITING: SJS Editorial Services

❀ Created with Vellum

SEXCATION

New York Times and USA Today Bestselling Author

HEIDI MCLAUGHLIN

ONE

Jade

----

*P*aradise.

That is where I am. The pink sandy beaches of Bermuda have been calling my name for months, ever since a few of my clients raved about visiting. I wanted my best friend to come along, make a girls' week but she was adamant that I do this alone. This being what she refers to as a life-changing vacation. I'm under strict orders to not be my usual self, to get out there and be free. None of which I can see happening. I'm rather content to sit by the pool or by the ocean, and people watch or read one of the novels I brought with me. That is definitely not life changing, except for the sandy beaches. The only thing different from my day to day is that I've shut myself off from the outside world. My phone is off, and my laptop didn't make the trip.

The weather right now in Bermuda is perfect. It's not too hot, at least by my standards. As far as I'm concerned, it's perfect. I'd live here if given a chance. And maybe I can someday. The resort isn't even close to capacity, which is nice considering that I'm alone. So very alone in all the ways that matter. The last thing I want to see are couples constantly cuddling on the chaise lounges, kissing, and making 'come fuck me' eyes at each other while I try to get a tan. And I so desperately need a tan.

My room has an ocean view, which was well worth spending the extra money to walk out on my balcony and sip my early morning coffee without having other guests mingling around me. I need those small moments after I awake. My only gripe about my room is that it's adjoining, and honestly, that freaks me the hell out. It also slightly pisses me off that I have to share my balcony. What if, whoever is staying there gets the sudden urge to knock in the middle of the night? Or, God forbid, they lose their key and want to use my room to get to theirs? I shudder at the thought.

The sliding glass door for the shared room opens, and I find myself holding my breath in anticipation. I was hoping that the room would be vacant to save me the curiosity of wondering who is staying there, but that wouldn't be my luck. No, my luck is having the man that I was checking out earlier when he was checking in as my neighbor. It was his suit and the way he spoke to the receptionists. His voice was smooth and British. So very British that I found myself rubbing my thighs together and mentally cursing myself because where there's one, there's plenty, and I don't know if I can handle that. Who would've thought an accent could elicit such a tantalizing effect on me?

And now that man is standing in the shared balcony space as I am, and for the life of me, I can't take my eyes off him. He was and still is dressed in a black suit and white button-down that I saw him in not moments ago, but now his eyes are hidden behind mirrored aviators, and I only know this because he's staring at or through me. He's returning the penetrating gaze that I gave him earlier, at least I think he is. When his head cocks to the side and his tongue darts out to wet his lips, I turn away quickly, embarrassed that he caught me gawking, but I couldn't help it. There is something about a finely dressed man in paradise.

Stepping back into my room, I pull the heavy curtains shut and turn up the air conditioner to try to curb my overheated skin. Even as I stand in front of the mirror, which happens to be next to the adjoined door, my heart races, wondering what the man on the other side of the wall is doing, or who for that matter. A man like that doesn't come without a woman or have an entourage waiting to worship at his feet.

"Snap out of it," I tell my reflection, who seems to mock me.

I'm here to clear my head, not fantasize about the other guests at the resort, and that's what I'm going to do. Clear my head. I change into my swimsuit, apply sunblock to every visible body part, and slip my cover-up over my head before grabbing the stack of magazines that I bought at the newsstands outside the airport terminal, my sunglasses, and hat before heading down to the pool. I'm cautious though when I open my door, checking first to see if he's coming out as well, and only when the coast is clear do I speed walk to the elevator, praying that my mystery neighbor stays locked inside his room.

Unfortunately, by the time I actually find the pool, it seems like I'm not the only one who decided to take advantage of the early morning calm, yet thankfully I still have my choice of chaise lounges. I choose one across from the obvious harem that is happening at one of the cabanas.

Once I'm situated, I pull my sunglasses down just a bit, knowing that my oversized hat will keep my staring a secret, and watch the three women across the pool from me chat up my picture-perfect bad boy with his heavily tatted arms, blonde hair, and very nice torso. Each time he turns, the muscles in his back flex, creating the perfect ridge for my nails to dig in deep. I lick my lips just thinking about the animal he must be in bed. Men like that, you know they know what they're doing between the sheets. Not that I'd know anything about that considering I attract the boring number crunchers and only fantasize about being with someone dangerous.

"Get a grip," I tell myself as I try to read the words on the paper in front of me. I don't know what's come over me, but first, my neighbor and now this man has me yearning for unadulterated passion. I suppose if I were comfortable with my sexual prowess or lack thereof, I wouldn't have to resort to wondering what it'd be like to have a toe-curling orgasm that left me breathless, achy, and totally sated.

Except, I can't stop watching the women and how they act, and find that I'm taking mental notes. If I'm going to have to see gorgeous men while I'm here, I might as well try to have some fun, to live a little and not be so inhibited. The women seem fond of him, touching him unabashedly even though he tries to thwart each attempt. And they laugh like damn hyenas when he says something funny. At least, from where I'm sitting, it seems like he's humoring them. I can't imagine he's a jerk, but one never knows. He looks around and runs his hand through his hair while he continues to stand there. If I had to guess, I'd say he doesn't know any of them, and they're trying to pick him up. Each time one tries to touch him. He shies away.

I finally tell myself to stop, that I'm not learning anything from them, and that I'd probably have a better chance at picking up a man if I'm myself and not handsy like the ladies on the other side of the pool. Yet, I continue to peer over the top of my sunglasses every so often but making sure to look away when he turns to see who else is around. I make up the conversation they're having in my head to pass my time. Their laughter grows louder and their touching of the tattooed man more forceful.

My magazine is suddenly boring, and the drama unfolding across the pool is so much more entertaining, but I don't put it down for fear they'll notice me. They haven't a clue that I've named each of them, Tuffy, Buffy, and Muffy, and his name is Romeo. I'm not fond of the name Romeo, but it fits perfectly. He's making these women swoon, and they're all planning for an orgy. He turns and looks in my direction, and I swear I can feel him staring at me. As coyly as possible, I slide my glasses back up the bridge of my nose and pretend I'm interested in the magazine that's causing my legs to sweat.

There's a splash in the pool and some more laughter, forcing me to look up. He's in the pool, and he's walking toward my side with a beer in his hand. When did he get a beer and where can I get one? He sets his beer down on the edge of the pool and climbs up the ladder ever so fucking slowly, making sure that anyone within easy eyesight can see the ridges of his torso flex as he pulls himself up. Each step is almost methodical, giving the water ample time to pebble and drip down his tanned skin. Once again, I find myself rubbing my thighs together, praying that he hasn't seen me.

He shakes his hair, letting water spray in every which direction. A drop lands on me, and I leave it on my skin as something to remember this moment by. Romeo bends over to retrieve his beer and I quickly look around for the closest bar or waiter. I need to quench my thirst or at least occupy my mouth before my voice says something incredibly stupid. After watching Romeo, my mouth is parched, my tongue is eager, and I'm tempted to finger the droplets of water on my leg to keep my focus on anything but him.

He walks by, blocking my sun and before I can say anything, he sets his beer down on the table that separates my chair from the one next to me. I look up, even though I can't see much of him through the rim of my hat, and prepare to ask him what the hell he's thinking. There are many other seats he can park his glorious physique at. Seats that are across from me that would give me the perfect view of him.

Oh, maybe he needs some lotion rubbed on his body?

Except I never get a chance to ask since his lips are on mine and when I gasp, his tongue enters, causing me to moan. His hand caresses my cheek as our lips move softly against each other's like they belong together. Like they haven't met in hours, not ever.

And before I can even blink, he's gone. Well, not gone, he's now sitting on the chaise next to me, acting as if it's an everyday occurrence to kiss a complete stranger. And that is when I see his face and the realization hits me square in the chest. He's my suit-wearing-sexy-as-fuck neighbor, my balcony sharer who under that dark suit, hid his bad-boy image.

"What was that?" I ask, stupidly. I know it was a kiss and aside from it being one of the best kisses I have ever experienced, I need to know why he kissed me and if he's planning on doing it again. I'd like to be a bit more prepared. And rethink my quest for a beer. I'll need something fruity and inviting.

"I told those women over there that you're my wife. It's the only thing I could think of when they wouldn't stop asking me to go back to their room," he says in the most amazing British accent that I have ever heard, and I've heard a lot. Living in New York City, I hear everything, but the way this man just spoke to me has sent shivers down my spine. And I knew it! The women across the way wanted to have an orgy, not that I could blame them. His voice is enough to make me want to join.

"I see, so you think you can just waltz over and kiss me?"

"Technically, I swam. Water was involved, dancing was not." He rests his head back, but I can see the smirk play across his very kissable lips.

So Romeo is a smart ass. I think I like it.

"How do you propose you keep them away? Won't they figure out we're not married? I'm sure they'll happen to see you sitting alone later or me flirting with another man. They'll question you. Us even. What if they think we're swingers?"

He looks at me like I'm Medusa and shrugs as if he doesn't have a care in the world. Hell, maybe he doesn't, and this is a game to him. I'm just the lucky player this week.

"When do you go home?" he asks.

My head should be yelling stranger danger, but it's not. There's something about him, something that makes me comfortable, which makes me want to tell him everything. "Seven days, I arrived this morning."

"Same here, so I think that we should hang out with each other. Unless you're not single."

"I'm single," I blurt out far too easily and way too eagerly sounding. Whatever happened to playing hard to get and allowing the man to chase a little? Unfortunately, the minute I laid eyes on him at check-in, I realized that getting laid was high on my priority list.

"Well, would you look at that! I'm single as well. So what do you say? You, me, the next seven days in each other's company? We'll have fun, I promise you."

"What if you meet someone?" Not what if I meet someone. I mean I planned to meet at least one someone. He just so happened to be the one until I realized he was my neighbor. But now that I've seen him without his suit on, he has a better chance of getting laid every night and afternoon if he chooses. Just by looking at him, I'd spread eagle if it meant I get to touch him.

This guy moves over to my chaise and picks up my legs, putting them over his. I pull my sunglasses off so I can get a good look at him. I swallow hard as I take in his crystal-blue eyes, which are a striking contrast with his blond hair and tanned skin. Back home, he would never be my type, but here in Bermuda, who gives a shit about a type?

"What's to say I haven't already met her?"

"Oh, you're smooth," I tell him. "Okay, what are the rules?"

"Rules?"

"Yeah, rules? I mean obviously we have separate rooms, but what if one of them decides to follow you and realizes you're alone."

"Easy, they're adjoining rooms. What's your next rule?" His thumb is gently running up and down my leg. The sensation has my heart beating a bit faster.

For a brief moment, I'm speechless, forgetting that our rooms are adjoined. I thought for sure I had found a hole in his little plan. "Right, okay," I say, without adding another rule. I completely suck at this game.

"You want some rules, huh? Well, here are mine for starters. Kissing is a definite. And holding hands, maybe even some flirting when we're out and about in public."

I feel like a girl back in middle school when she got her first boyfriend and had to lay down the ground rules. Except I like his guidelines. Kissing is fun, especially if he's kissing me. I have a feeling that I'm going to end up following all of his rules when having them was my suggestion, to begin with.

"Your turn," he says, catching me off guard.

"My turn?"

"Yep. For a rule. Remember? You were laying down the law."

Short of demanding sex, which I won't do, I can't think of anything. I shake my head, telling him I have nothing.

"Excellent, so we have a plan. So, what's your name?" he asks.

That's when the light bulb goes off for me. I'm on vacation, away from my life and responsibilities. I can be whoever I want to be, and he'll be none the wiser.

"Okay, here's my rule. We lie to each other."

"Pardon me?" He looks confused and dare I say, hurt. I suppose I would be too.

"Hear me out. I'm on vacation, and I'm assuming you are too. The last thing I want to do is talk about home or work. I'm single. You're single. So we have nothing to worry about there, and no one here knows us, so let's fake name each other, actually fake everything. Make up the most outlandish story you can about yourself. We're not trying to impress each other and since we're acting like we're married, why not?"

"You're crazy," he says, laughing. "I'll fake name you as long as you promise not to get all clingy and expect a relationship when the week's over."

I extend my hand, and he shakes it.

"My name is Jade," I tell him, creating the most

islandesque name I could. I've always wanted to be someone else, and now I get the chance. It's acting, but without the cameras following you around and the people telling you what to do.

"I'm Jackson."

Jackson is far better than Romeo, and I find that I like the way it sounds in my head. Jackson. I like it. Too bad it's fake.

"It's nice to meet you, Jackson."

"You too, Jade. So, now that we have that settled, what shall we do with the rest of our day?"

"I don't know. I haven't made any plans, but I'm up for suggestions, or you could continue with what you were going to do."

"Nope, not now that my wife is free for the day, we should do something together. Besides, we have to keep up our act. I don't want us to get found out straight away," he says, nodding toward the women that he left with broken hearts.

"It is almost lunchtime. I suppose we ought to eat."

He reaches for my hand and easily slides his fingers between mine. Together we walk hand in hand back to the resort. I figure we're heading into the restaurant, but instead, he takes us toward the elevator. We stop on our floor and head toward our rooms.

"What are we doing here?" I ask.

"Getting changed into something more suitable for lunch. Unless you want to go out with me dressed like this?" He rubs his hand over his torso, causing my mouth to water.

"No, clothes would definitely be good."

"Go and unlock your door between our rooms and I'll do the same." He disappears behind his door, leaving me to catch my breath.

As soon as I slide the lock, he pushes the door open, and I step back until the back of my knees hit the bed, and he's standing in front of me.

"I think I'm really going to like this game," he says. I think I am too—the way that he's kissing me right now with his hand pressed into the small of my back and his other caressing my cheek really has my lady bits jumping for joy that they might get some action from this man. And when he presses into me, showing me that yes, my imagination was not lying to me and that he's definitely packing, my body zings with electricity and anticipation of what's to come. Even behind closed doors, he kisses me deeper than he did outside, leaving me breathless and having to remind myself that this is just a game with a one-week expiration date.

TWO

Jackson
_____

I'm buying a fucking lottery ticket. I don't even know if they sell them here on the island, but I need one. A guy can only get lucky so many times in his life and right this minute, by my count, it's been three times in one bloody day.

First, I see her standing there in the hotel lobby, looking all sweet and innocent, like butter wouldn't melt. There was something about the way she was clutching on to her bag, as if it were her lifeline. Her shoulder-length, dirty-blonde hair was pulled back into a small ponytail and every time she would look at me, her eyes would immediately divert away in another direction. That didn't stop her cheeks from turning a beautiful shade of red. I could tell right there and then that she was single. Call it instinct, the male version of female intuition. It was the way she stared at the ground, then back at me. If she had been waiting for a man to walk through the doors, I wouldn't have registered on her radar, especially if her other half treated her right.

Then, when I stepped outside on my balcony, there she was, staring at me, like she was waiting for my arrival.

Thank fuck I had my aviators on, otherwise she would've seen that I was ogling, that I was taking in every inch of her before I bordered on stalker territory. Christ, she was beautiful, standing there, gazing right back at me. My head tilted to the side and my tongue darted out to moisten my lips. And that's when she fucking gasped and hotfooted it back into her room, which gave me a good ole chuckle. But knowing that the woman I saw in reception was staying next door to me, and the only thing separating us was a wall, drove me to distraction.

At this point, I couldn't get out of my room fast enough. I needed to get myself as far away as possible from the temptation on the other side of the wall. I needed to drown my agony in booze and loose women. And that's what I thought I found when I spotted three lovely ladies in barely there bikinis. Every guy's dream, right? Take a holiday. Participate in an orgy with beautiful women who all have fake tits, job's a good 'un. As far as I was concerned, I was quids in and then I turned around and spotted *her*. How I knew it was the same girl from before, my hotel 'neighbour,' if you will, and the one who literally took control of my body just with one look, is beyond me. My cock sprang to attention in no time. It hadn't even made a twitch with these other women. In fact, it pretty much deflated when they asked me what I do for living. Which is such a massive turn off.

I told them I had to go, because my wife had finally made it down here. To be honest, they were sad. I, on the other hand, was fucking elated and wasted no time swimming across the pool, carefully holding my beer up so I didn't spill any. My body may be in someone else's control, but I still have some priorities.

My neighbour wore sunglasses and a huge sun hat, which blocked the sun from her face. I hoped and prayed that she was watching me as I climbed out of the pool. I may have shown off a little, but it was all to get her attention. I needed it for what I was about to do. I've seen enough of those deodorant ads and thought why the hell not, and promptly shook my head back and forth, letting the water spray everywhere. It felt bloody amazing.

I walked towards her and put my pint down on the table between her sun lounger and the one next to it. I didn't even hesitate. I leaned in and kissed her. Smack bang on the lips and waited for the moment that took her breath away. When it happened, I swiftly slid my tongue right into her mouth. The surge of energy hit me like a ton of bricks. I wanted to mount her and claim her right there and then. I have never been so attracted to a woman in my life before. I had to touch her, but didn't want to get kneed in the nether region. Instead, I let my hand caress her cheek, eliciting a sigh from her in return.

I had to get off her before she felt my hard dick press against her leg. I didn't want to scare her any more than I already had. So, I sat next to her while observing her body. Her creamy-white legs disappeared under the white dress she wore, which I assumed hid a bikini. I glanced quickly across the pool where the triplets shook their arses to the music playing over the speaker and could easily understand why a woman would want to stay covered up. Most of them think men prefer that fancy crap, but I don't. I want a woman who is natural—flaws, beauty marks, and all.

"What was that?" she asked. I was tempted to point out that it was a kiss, something that happens between two people who are attracted to each other, but I didn't. Instead, I told her about the situation I was in and how I had to lie to the three women in question.

We bantered back and forth and I loved it. She made

me laugh and to be honest, that's hard to do when you first meet someone. Except when she asked me about the situation I put us in and we ended up with a dilemma on our hands. My only solution was to become her fake husband for the rest of our holiday.

Most of the time, I'll admit I'm a smooth bastard, but that idea was bonkers to say the least, and I kicked my own arse for being such a moron. Even more so because she went along with it, like it was the most brilliant idea she's ever heard. I mean, really?

But there's more. She told me that she's worried that I would meet someone and then what will happen to her? That right there is a warning sign that this girl has been hurt before, so being the nice guy that I am, I moved over to her and pulled her lovely legs on top of mine, because I'm charming like that, and told her, "Who's to say I haven't met her?" Because let's face it, maybe I have. This girl gets everything going with one simple look.

And then there were the rules. I fucking hated rules when I was growing up. I mean, for the best part of my life, I've been told I must abide by them. 'Do your homework.' 'Don't talk back to adults.' 'Don't speak with your mouth full.' Blah, blah blah. So, it surprised me, to say the least, that I came up with a rule of my own, which was kissing is a definite. It leads to other things so it must happen. The next rule, we lie to each other. Now that one completely caught me unaware, but it made sense. We're on holiday and the last thing I want in my life is a fling that turns clingy once the trip is over. FlingCling is *so* not a good thing. So, I'm up for this game. She tells me her name is Jade. It's hot. I tell her mine.

We ended up back in her room, where things turned around. After we both unlocked the adjoining door, I walked into her room. Jade's sunglasses and hat were now on the bed, and I knew I was a fucking goner just with one look from her. I backed her up until her legs pressed against the mattress. Thank fuck she's strong because if she had fallen over, I don't know if I would've been able to stop myself from pressing into her.

But I kissed her. Deep and passionate with my hand pressed to the small of her back, where only the slip of material she wore stopped me from feeling her skin against my palm. I pushed into her, showing her that she was turning me on, that I could have her now and be satisfied. Something deep inside told me that once that happened, I'd be coming back for more, and more.

Now, we're sitting at a table for two at a little café , which happens to be a short walk from the hotel, with people walking past us while we eat sandwiches. Somewhere along the street, calypso music plays, setting the right mood.

"Why did you agree to my game?" she asks. Well, ain't that a loaded question, but she deserves the truth. I would want to know the same thing, if this was my idea.

"I have a problem with people who say, 'what do you do for a living' to start a conversation, especially if they've already been hands on with me. That's normally a sign that they're only after one thing."

"It's rude. I saw how they manhandled you."

I laugh and find myself tempted by her hand, which sits on the metal table. After our impromptu snogging session, Jade put on a nice little sundress which has my imagination running wild and some strappy sandals. Her toes are painted a turquoise blue. I found it a little weird at first; normally I see reds or pinks on toes, but rarely a blue colour.

I quite like it. I like it a lot. In fact, I've yet to find something about this woman I don't like.

"And yet, you didn't. I came over and kissed you. You could've punched me, kicked me in the nuts, or groped me. I'm grateful you let me kiss you the way I did."

She blushes again. "Why did you? I'm sure there are other, more beautiful women at the resort that would've been happy to oblige you."

"But then I wouldn't be here with my pretend wife, trying to get to know more about her."

Her eyes don't waver from mine as she takes a sip of her cocktail. "Do you really want to get to know me?"

"The fake you, yes. I don't want to get cornered by one of the triplets and not know my facts."

"Are they in fact, triplets?"

I shake my head. "I haven't got a bloody clue, to be honest with you. Fake tits all look the same at the end of the day."

Her mouth falls open into a sexy little O and images of other ways I can make that happen pop straight into mind. "I named them Muffy, Tuffy, and Buffy. The names seemed fitting," she says with a shrug.

I crack the fuck up. "Then that is what we'll call them until they leave."

"Do you know when that is? Or what room they're in?"

I lean over the table and pick her hand up. "They leave after us, and no, I don't, thank goodness. I don't care either. I made you a promise and I always keep my promises." I bring her hand to my lips and let them linger against her skin until a passer-by makes a comment about us being in love.

Not love, lust though, and I couldn't be happier that I

chose her to be my distraction this week. When I finally let go of her hand, she picks up her drink and finishes it.

"Want another one?" I ask, already standing by the time she nods. I lean down and kiss the top of her head, inhaling the scent of her shampoo. The smell of grapefruit assaults my senses, making my heart race. I groan as I walk into the restaurant. I could've easily waited for the waitress to come back to us, but I needed to step away from Jade for a minute. She's fucking deadly with her innocent façade and I have a strong reason to believe I'm going to fall victim to her and love every minute of it.

When I walk out, there's a bloke talking to her as if it's an everyday occurrence. I have never been jealous of any man until now. The pure rage I feel, watching him talk to my pretend wife almost takes over my body, yet I find the will to let it go. Who am I to stand in the way of her potential hook-ups?

Her bloody fucking husband, that's who I am. I slide between them, pushing my shoulder roughly into the other dude as I put our drinks down. With both hands, I cup her cheeks and lay one on her. It's an opened mouth kiss because I know this bastard can see our tongues dancing against each other. Once again, she fucking moans and the sounds go directly to my dick.

"Sorry, mate," I say after I pull away. "It's our honeymoon."

He looks at me with a confused expression and I want to punch him in his face. What can't he understand about my statement? It seems clear to me. He pulls out his wallet and drops a pile of cash onto the table. "Buy her a ring," he says before walking away. I flip a finger at him, but he's right. If we're going to pretend to be married, she needs to have a ring on her finger.

"Do you think that was necessary?"

"Did you fancy him?" I ask. "I can run after him, give him your room number."

She shakes her head. "No, but more tact would be nice."

"Uh-huh, so I can't be jealous about some bloke flirting with my fake wife?"

I can see the sparkle in her eye. She likes pretending, which in turn makes me hope that she'll like taking our little game into the bedroom later. The sexual chemistry is there and I can't understand why we would wait to explore all options of our fake marriage.

"What's your favorite color?" she asks, changing the subject.

"Blue," I say, winking. "Yours?"

"Blue."

I pretty much guessed this by the colour of her toes, which is why I said it. "What's your favourite song?"

"*Total Eclipse of the Heart*," she tells me.

"Do you turn the volume up full blast and sing it as loudly as you can."

She laughs and nods. "Every single time. Then I play it again and again. What is your favorite?"

"I like the Kicks, and *Hotel California* is a good one, but I also like to throw a little Marvin Gaye into the mix every now and again. You know, *Let's Get It On*."

Jade blushes and it's fucking incredible. I think I found my new hobby in life. How many times can I make Jade blush?

"Favorite movie?" she asks.

"*Die Hard*. Yours?"

"*Dirty Dancing*."

Her choice in film has me wondering whether she likes to dance too. Women either love it or hate it. Personally, I enjoy it. There's nothing like having a little preview to what could happen behind a closed door. Jade and I should go out tonight, and maybe, just maybe I can show her what I can offer her between the sheets.

"If you could be anything, aside from what you do now for work, what would you be?" Jade asks.

"Oh, that's easy," I say, leaning forward. "I'd be a teacher."

"Really, why?"

"My mum was a teacher and everyone loved her. It's nice to be loved." By the look on her face, she realises that I'm telling the truth. "What about you, what would you do?"

"I'd be a princess," Jade says, laughing.

"Well, even I can't compete with the royal family."

"That's okay, you've already made me feel like one." Her words trail off, but I hear her loud and clear. Since the moment I walked into the resort and spotted her, luck has been on my side, and it is now. I plan to treat her like a queen while I have her, then I'm buying a bloody lotto ticket.

THREE

Jade

---

*T*oday has been a whirlwind. I'm on vacation. I should be out meeting people, having fun. Yet here I am, walking hand in hand back to the resort with the most gorgeous man that I have ever laid eyes on. I didn't have to reach for his hand. He took mine as soon as we were done with lunch, sending my heart into an unknown rhythm. I knew we were pretending when we were at the hotel, but I had no idea he was planning to extend the charade to the outside world. Granted, any one of the girls could've walked by, but it was his aggression toward the man that had stopped to talk to me, that really put our game into perspective.

Now, don't get me wrong. I love every second of having his lips pressed to mine, and how he subliminally demands I submit to him with one simple brush of his tongue. It is easy to give in even though I have never been a fan of public displays of affection. With Jackson by my side, I have a feeling I'd screw him in public and not think twice about it.

But I *am* thinking twice about sex and wishing I had added that to the list of requirements. He added kissing so why not sex? It's because I've never been this forward in my life. My ex accused me of being frigid in bed, telling me that I lacked the emotion needed to get him off. My best friend tells me that it was all my ex, but I'm not sure how she knows this unless she secretly slept with him. The thought disgusts me. I know she would never do something like that. She did insist that I take this trip. I begged her to come with me, but she said I needed to find my groove. She also gave me a going-away present—condoms—enough to last someone a lifetime. I told myself that I would donate them or hand them out as I took walks along the beach, you know spreading safe love and all that stuff, but maybe now I'll get to use one or two.

There's no denying that Jackson and I have chemistry. It was evident from the minute we came face to face on the balcony. I thought it was one-sided, with me being the one desperate for a sharp-dressed man to make me his. My mouth watered as he stood there, looking at me as if he wanted to devour me, through his aviators. I know I panicked when he licked his lips, but only because I didn't know how to react. I have never had a man do that to me before. It was hot, confusing, and I wanted more. Then to find out that underneath the designer suit is a tatted bad boy that my parents would never approve of, drove my libido crazy. For me, it's the best of both worlds, except there was no way a man like that would give a woman like me the time of day.

Don't get me wrong there isn't anything wrong with me. I see myself as plain. My hair isn't fancy, my clothes aren't designer made, and I give myself home manicures. I live in an apartment with my best friend, my parents own a struggling business, but worked hard to put me through college. I will never be the one to visit the high-end stylists, make two-week appointments for my nails, spend my Saturdays in the spa, or shop at Bergdorf's. Even walking into that store gives me anxiety. The sales people know right off if you can afford anything in their store and their smiles quickly turn into sneers. Places like that are definitely not good for one's self-esteem.

I like the idea of lying to Jackson, knowing that after this week, I will never see him again. There's something magical about creating a whole new persona, especially one that is better than the original. I get to be whomever I want without any consequences.

When we started playing the short version of twenty questions and he asked what I would do with a different life, I told him I wanted to be a princess when I was a little girl. Honestly, what little girl hadn't dreamed about being that? But it was my answer, and telling him that he already made me feel like one, that was the slip of the tongue. I hadn't meant to say that. I don't want him to think I'm falling for him, given that we had only just met.

We arrive back at the hotel and walk past the clerk at the front desk. He eyes us warily, likely remembering that he checked us both in, separately. By the time we're in the elevator, I've broken out in laughter.

"What's so bloody funny?" Jackson asks. "Have I got something stuck in my teeth?" He smiles wide and shows me his pearly whites.

I shake my head. "No, but the desk clerk gave us a look. It was the same man who checked us in."

Jackson smiles and nods quickly. "He probably wants to know my secret. Maybe I can give him some lessons later."

"Be sure to charge him. The knowledge on how to pick up unsuspecting women and turning them into your wife in the matter of minutes probably has a high price tag."

"You're right, babe. I could make us millionaires," he says, throwing his arm around me, just in time too, as the elevator door opens and one of the not-triplets steps into the car.

"Oh, hey," she says, making eye contact with Jackson, and ignoring me. Not that I expected anything else. My stomach tightens when she doesn't press a button to take her to a different floor. I'm willing to bet that she'll follow us off and watch which way we go, maybe even follow us to our room. It's too late now to press another button; that would look suspicious. Fucking lovely.

The ride up is incredibly awkward and she keeps glancing over her shoulder to look at him. Each time, her eyes light up, like she's trying to tell him something, I lean into Jackson and press my lips to his neck, which I can only reach if I'm on my tiptoes, and slide my hand under his white, fitted shirt that accents his tanned arms and tattoos. It's been giving me butterflies since he came out of his room with it on. But it's the feel of his abs against my fingers and the smidgen of hair that disappears into his shorts that has me nipping at his neck.

"Let me help you, love," he says as he bends slightly to pick me up. My dress bunches around my hips as my legs wrap around his waist, feeling exactly what I'm doing to him. Jackson isn't shy about where he sets me and flexes his hips so I know that he's hard right now. He holds me up, with my back pressed lightly against the wall. I continue to kiss a path from his ear, neck, and along his strong jawline, not giving a shit that *she* is watching us. In fact, it turns me on even more.

By the time I make it to his mouth, the elevator dings. Jackson isn't deterred though and crushes his lips to mine. His kiss is hungry. Strong lips push mine apart so he can taste me. I open and meet his tongue as my hands thread into his hair. He carries us out of the car and pushes me up against the closest door, grinding into me. My eyes roll back in my head at the sensation.

I barely hear the door shut, but he does. He pulls away and looks over his shoulder, verifying that the door is closed. "Well, now that she's gone, let's hope she got the message and thinks that this is *our* room," he says, pointing to the sign next to my head. I don't miss the emphasis he put on the word 'our,' nor the tingles that sentiment sends down my spine. He steps back and lets me down. My legs are wobbly and we didn't even do anything except make out for a few seconds. Yet, I felt him, the desire that he has. I want to believe that it's because of me, but I'm not that confident in my skills.

But Jackson, fuck me if I didn't wet my panties when he called me love. Earlier, it was babe and I was like eh, but love—that was one I haven't been called before and I like it, a lot. Once my dress is fixed, I head toward our rooms. He catches up and takes my hand in his. I know it's because he's afraid that woman is lurking somewhere, and that's fine. This time he opens his door and holds it for me so I can walk in first.

I step through his room and into mine and eye my bed. I'd like to collapse and take a nap and maybe pleasure myself, but I can't do that with the adjoining door open. The last thing I want is for him to hear me and know he's having that much of an effect on me.

Jackson doesn't leave me any time to decompress. He comes into my room and plops down onto my bed. "What's the bet she's already told her friends what floor we're on?"

I shrug. "I don't think it matters. We put on a good show for her. If that doesn't prove that we're married, I don't know what will." *Sex!* Except that will only complicate things.

"Yeah, I think we were pretty convincing."

"So... now what?" I ask, fiddling with the hem of my dress. This hot-as-sin man is lying on his stomach with his arms under the pillow and looking at me, tempting me to do something brazen.

"Dinner and dancing," he tells me. He sits up and stretches, showing me the hair that my fingers brushed against earlier. I thought I had memorized his torso from earlier, but clearly, I didn't do a well enough job—this I would've remembered.

"All right. I'll change."

"Me too," he says. He heads back to his room and rummages around. I grab another dress out of my suitcase and lock myself in the bathroom. I turn on the radio, hoping to drown out what I'm about to do. With my dress off and my panties pushed to the floor, my hand instantly goes to my pussy. I'm wet and horny, and hating the man next door for doing this to me. One press onto my clit has me almost toppling over from the sensation of being touched. I insert one, then two fingers and work in a frenzied motion, moaning into a towel until my orgasm takes over. This is the fastest time I've ever gotten myself off, and I know it's because of *him*.

I'm in need of a shower and step in quickly, washing away the grime from walking along the streets. I forgo washing my hair because it takes too long to dry and I can style it easier the way it is. I dry off and work on my makeup when there's a knock on my door. I turn the music down and swallow hard.

"Yes," I say with a shaky voice.

"How long until you're ready?"

"Only a few minutes. I had to take a shower."

"Does that mean you're naked?" he asks. I look down at my body and nod, knowing that he can't see me.

"No, I thought I'd save on laundry and took a shower with my dress on." Especially my panties because they're definitely in need of being cleaned.

Jackson laughs. "Very funny, I like your humour, love. I'll be watching TV until you need me to help you get into your dress."

I grip the side of the counter. Where the fuck did this man come from? Everything he says is perfect, and yet I can't keep him. In one day, he's ruined me for others. I finish applying my makeup and run my straightener through my hair, curling big chunks as I go. When I unlock the door and open it, he's standing there in a royal-blue, button-down shirt with the top few buttons undone, semi tucked into a pair of black slacks. I inhale deeply only to realize that wasn't the smartest thing to do. He smells divine.

"You look beautiful," he says. By the look in his eyes, I know he means it. He's not lying right now and that sort of scares me. I look down in my black sheath dress and feel like I'm underdressed even though I know I'm not.

"So are you."

"How about we go turn some heads tonight?"

"After I put on some shoes," I say, pointing to my bare feet. He laughs and steps back, giving me space to move toward the closet. I pull out my favorite pair of heels and step into them.

"Heels are sexy, but thank fuck you're still shorter than me, because there's something I'm quite fond of."

"What's that?" I ask as I head toward the door. He pins me against it with his arms on either side of me. He bends down so were eye level.

"I like bending over to kiss you." Jackson brushes his lips against mine and pulls away too fast for my liking. He's left me stunned and at a loss for words. It's only been a few hours since we made our agreement and I feel like we're way past what is acceptable for a fake marriage. He reaches for my hand and pulls me along behind him and back toward the elevator.

It suddenly dawns on me that it's rather early for dinner. "It's a little too early, don't you think? I mean I guess we could get a drink in the bar."

"We could, if I hadn't already made us a reservation."

"We have reservations?"

He nods, but doesn't say anything else. In fact, he just smiles while I continue to stare at him. When we step out of the elevator, he leads us through the lobby toward a waiting car. The driver holds the door as I slide in with Jackson following.

"Any clue at all?"

"Do you trust me?" he asks as his eyes bore into mine. I don't even think about it and nod. "Good. Then no more questions."

The ride takes about five minutes and we pull into the parking lot of the pier. There are boats everywhere and vendors line the sidewalks selling their goods. The driver stops, and as soon as we're out of the car, we're beckoned by the merchants.

"Keep walking," Jackson says as he places his hand on my back to push me along. He guides me down the pier and turns me toward one of the yachts. Of course, it is massive and an instant red flag goes up, stopping me dead in my tracks. "What's wrong?" he asks.

I shake my head. "I... uh..."

He laughs, which only increases my anxiety. "You're

either afraid of boats or you think I'm going to kill you. I can promise you that the latter won't happen when there are other people on board. This is a dinner cruise with other couples. I thought we'd have a nice time and we won't need to pretend. We'll just enjoy each other's company."

Everything inside me melts. "How are you single?"

"By choice, except for this week, that is. This week, I'm well and truly *not* single."

Jackson helps me on board where we're greeted by the captain and shown where to go. The top of the yacht is intimate with white lights strung from pole to pole, giving off a romantic ambiance. A waiter leads us to our table, but I choose to stand and look out over the ocean.

"How far will we go out?" I ask, turning in time to find Jackson handing me a glass of champagne.

"Not that far. We'll actually stay fairly close to the shore."

I take a sip from the flute and close my eyes as the bubbly settles. "Thank you for this." I reach up to fix a collar that doesn't need to be adjusted.

"Thank you for saving me. You have no idea how much I appreciate it."

I'm starting to think that maybe I do and that maybe Jackson has saved me as well.

FOUR

Jackson

$\mathcal{I}$ hadn't planned this until I saw the advert in the hotel reception as soon as we came back from lunch. The only drawback was that it started early. I had planned to go on the dinner cruise later during the week, but our day had been going so well that when she hopped in the shower, I quickly popped down to reception and made the booking. If anything, I owe her one for saving my arse earlier today. The more I think about it, the more ridiculous my actions were. She could've easily made a complaint about me and had me kicked out for assaulting her.

There are about twenty or so other couples on board, all mingling along with each other. Each time someone asks me what I do for a living, I tell them I work in the textiles industry. It's not a far cry from what I actually do, but since Jade and I are keeping secrets, I don't particularly see the need to go into any detail.

The bell chimes and we all take our places. Each table is set for two, with some artificial votive candles between us. Being a gentleman, I hold Jade's chair out for her and wait until she's comfortable before sitting myself down. The boat moves slowly, drifting over the waves amongst the huge cruise ships that are currently in the port.

Jade tilts her head as far back as possible and looks up at the monstrosity of the cruise ship. "Have you ever been on a cruise?" I ask her. I've always wanted to go on one, but haven't had the chance. In all honesty, I've never really made the time to go on a holiday until now. Taking care of my mum was always my priority because my dad was always at work. Now that he's retired and she's in remission, they're off taking well-deserved breaks. They've recently returned from Greece, and I know my mother has a number of other trips planned while I take charge of the business and continue to build my father's empire.

"No, I've never really thought about it. Honestly, I didn't want to come here but my best friend forced me to."

"May I offer you some wine?" the waiter interrupts us.

"Yes of course," I say, pushing our glasses toward him. It dawns on me that I should've asked if she liked wine before I answered on her behalf. Jade gives a small smile when her glass is full and doesn't hesitate to take a sip.

"Why's that?" I ask. "About you not wanting to come here?"

"Oh, well... things are complicated back home. I didn't want to leave, but I needed the time away."

"Boyfriend trouble?" I can't stop myself from asking, even though I know we're supposed to be lying to each other, and even though I remember her telling me she was single, I don't want to be caught up in some twisted love triangle with some crazy boyfriend hunting me down and doing me some grievous bodily harm. I don't care how many lies we tell, if someone wants to find me, the internet can give him access to anything he wants.

She shakes her head and leans a bit closer to me, almost

as if she's about to tell me a secret. "Okay, here is one truth about me."

I hold up my hands. "Are you breaking the rules?"

"A bit, but I won't give details."

"Glad we've got that clear; please, carry on, then."

"Right, so I had this boyfriend. We were together for a while, but it wasn't anything... like over the top."

"What do you mean?" It's a known fact that sometimes American phrases have different meanings to English ones, and having lived in England all my life, there are undoubtedly some American slang words that I have yet to come across.

"This is embarrassing," she says.

I must reach only a few centimetres to touch her hand. Her skin is so soft it gives me an urge to feel the rest of her. "There's no judgment here, I promise you."

Her teeth slowly pull at her lower lip as she nods. "You know we've..."

"Snogged?"

Jade blushes, which is another victory for me. "Well, it took us months before we even French kissed. That is what I mean by over the top."

How can any bloke pass up a good snogfest with a gorgeous girl? I find it bloody hard to sit here and not kiss her. The way she feels against my lips is bloody fucking amazing to say the least.

"Anyway, the relationship was just there. We got along great, but we were boring. I'm actually very boring back home."

"I very much doubt that," I tell her.

"My ex called me frigid."

I can fix that, I think to myself but don't say the words out loud. I don't want her to think that I expect to get a shag because of our agreement, but one can put money on it I'm going to try my hardest. It will be my mission this week to get between her legs, if, or when, she's willing.

"Maybe your ex didn't know the right buttons to press." My thumb brushes over the top of her hand. The insinuation is there unless she's oblivious to my charm. The pink tinge on her cheeks and the sparkle in her eyes confirm that she's not.

Jade pulls her hand away and clears her throat, sitting up straight, which increases the distance between us. I don't care if our table is small, I want her as close to me as possible. "Anyway, I thought we could take a vacation to liven things up. I mentioned a cruise, but he gets seasick. He refused to fly over the ocean or any large bodies of water so that limited where we could go. He doesn't like humidity, areas that are prone to natural disasters or have a wildlife infestation."

"What *does* he like?" At this point, I assume he lives in a plastic bubble.

"His apartment."

"And let me guess, it's bright white, immaculately kept, and you absolutely, categorically aren't allowed to wear your shoes inside?"

Her eyes widen with surprise when I correctly guess the kind of place her ex lives in, but I haven't finished yet. "And yet your place has non-matching furniture, second-hand goods that you found at the local shop or flea market, and you don't give a rat's arse if your friends wear shoes indoors because you want them to be comfortable?"

Jade picks up her glass of wine and finishes it. "Are you some sort of telepath or something?"

I shake my head. "No, but it's obvious that you are a

complete opposite of your ex, going by the way you've just described him."

"And what about you?"

Now it's my turn to pick up my wineglass and drink every drop until it's empty. I'm in two minds whether to lie to her or tell the truth. "My home is very welcoming." It's a complete lie. Right now, my flat is at the top of some newly refurbished building with a load of boxes piled up against the walls. My furniture is brand new with the price tags still on, and I'm almost certain my mattress is still in the plastic protective covering that it arrived in. To be honest, apart from the photos sent to me by the estate agent when I bought rented it, I don't know what my flat looks like. I have yet to meet my neighbours and have my fingers crossed that they're all lovely and aren't cooking fish stew every day and smelling up the place, aren't drug dealers nor running a brothel. I think of my flat in London and how the area I live in is convenient for everything I need. It's a short journey to work on the Tube, meaning I don't need a car, which is a godsend given that parking is an absolute nightmare. Luckily, I also happen to live very close to some highly rated restaurants and when I'm not able to pop in for a quick meal, I can order a takeaway and have it delivered by my new best friends, Deliveroo, who offer a door to door service.

Thankfully, our starters finally arrive. It's minestrone soup. Hot liquid on a moving yacht. Whoever thought that was a good idea must've had their head in the toilet. I make sure to place my folded cloth napkin on my lap, covering my groin. As I look around, I can see that I'm not the only man on board doing this.

Jade and I eat in silence. Maybe she feels like she said too much or I did with my speech about her place. To be honest, it was an easy guess. Her ex sounds like a complete twat, and Jade deserves better. She may be shy and reserved, but deep down she's outgoing and looking to explore the world and everything it has to offer. I can see it in her eyes. She's adventurous, and wants to try new things, even if she's apprehensive about it. There's little rebel in her somewhere, I'm sure. I mean, she let me kiss her without any forewarning and now look at us.

I could easily see myself with Jade or someone just like her. It's only been a few hours and already I hate that we've agreed to lie to each other. But I don't do clingy and that's what I'm afraid this could turn into. The rules are in place to protect both of us from what lies before us at the end of our week together.

Our main course is served. I took the executive decision of ordering everything on the menu because I didn't know what she likes and dislikes, so it tickles me when the waiter must set up a separate table just for our food.

"Are you hungry?" she asks. Beside us is a feast of lobster, steak, and chicken together with various steamed vegetables, some rice, and two different kinds potatoes (roasted and fried), not to mention all the sauces and condiments added on top.

"Er... I wasn't sure what you liked so I thought it best to ask for one of each. I figured we could share."

"Share? As in you'd let me eat off your plate?" she asks as though this is a ridiculous idea.

"I'll even feed it to you if you'll let me." Jade licks her lips and I know I've scored brownie points with her. "Tell me, love. What would you like?"

"A little of everything."

I get to work on cutting the tender piece of filet mignon, putting half on her plate and the other half on mine. The chicken is next, but it's the lobster tail that I save for last. Once our plates are full, I look down and laugh. "This is so much food."

"You won't be mad if I don't eat it all, will you?"

"Not at all, but you have to save room for dessert." Unless we decide to skip the dessert course and head back to the hotel so we can fuck like rabbits. That thought gives me the idea of asking for a doggy bag to take back with us; we'll need food to restore our energy.

"Open up." I load my fork with lobster and move it towards her mouth. Her tongue darts out, teasing me before her lips close around my fork. My cock springs to attention, making damn sure I know he's still hanging around and waiting for some action. *Me too, mate, and it's only been a day.*

"That's delicious," she says, before covering her mouth with her napkin. I reach for more, but her fork is there, knocking mine out of the way. She returns the favour, letting me take a bite of the succulent meat. Of course, my dick strains painfully against my zip, probably trying to find a way to make an appearance. I have no doubt he'll knock against my trousers to make sure he's fully awake.

"That's the best lobster I've ever tasted." It's true, because she fed it to me and that alone puts her leaps and bounds above anyone else I have ever dated.

We continue to eat, sharing food with each other even though we both have the same thing on our plates. From the outside, I'm sure we look like we're ridiculously in love. The other couples stare at us, and quite honestly, I don't mind at all.

Once our plates are taken away, the volume of the background music becomes louder. "Would you like to dance?" I hold out my hand to her, waiting and hoping she'll take it.

"Of course."

After taking a few steps onto the makeshift dance floor, I spin her around in a twirl. When I was a young boy, my mum made me take ballroom dancing. Of course, many parents went above and beyond for their children in the hope that we'd marry a lord or a lady. My mum wanted me to be prepared even though my father's profession pretty much sealed my fate and left me ineligible by the time I was fifteen when everyone found out what he did. I didn't care. It was always my intention to take over the family business anyway.

Jade is in my arms as we sway to the music. Other couples join us. Some go all out and do the waltz across the floor, but I'm content to hold Jade in my arms, and find out the truth about her through her eyes. As far as I'm concerned, she's an enigma and the best damn thing that could've happened to me on this holiday. I don't even want to think about how my day would've ended up if I hadn't been such a daredevil earlier.

We stay on the dance floor with our eyes locked until the boat is docked. I don't want the night to end and as soon as we're out of our taxi, I pull her away from our hotel and towards the beach.

"Take your shoes off," I whisper to her as I take mine off. I reach for her heels and somehow managed to place them in my shoes, enabling me to carry both pairs. Our hands find each other as if on instinct. The sand is cool against my feet as we trudge toward the water. There are very few people out here, which is nice.

"Wanna go in?" she asks, letting go of my hand. She's ankle deep by the time I get the hems of my trousers rolled up.

"This feels amazing." The water is perfect, and maybe

it's because she's standing here, in it with me. She splashes me and takes off running. I follow behind her, catching her easily and pulling her into my arms.

Jade kisses me. It's soft and demanding. If her ex thought she was frigid, he must've been a block of fucking ice; there isn't anything wrong with this woman. My hands are everywhere as our mouths move against each other's. They tangle in her hair, they grip her back and they cup her face while hers pull at my shirt, with her nails gently pressing into my back, and finally she pulls on the ends of my hair, causing my eyes to roll to the back of my head in sheer lust-filled delight.

I want to lay her down on the sand and bury my cock deep within her. I want to hear her scream my name and feel her arch her back as I enter her for the first time. None of this can happen here. Reluctantly, I pull away after hearing whispers from the few people on the beach with us.

"Wow. I don't know what came over me?"

"I can assure you, I'm not complaining." I steer her toward the hotel, stopping only to pick up our shoes that I had put down so I could follow her into the water. I look down at my trousers and notice that they're wet and covered in sand.

"I can wash those for you," she tells me. I frown and shake my head.

"That's what the laundry services are for. I'll send them there tomorrow." Only I won't. I'll take them down to the front desk and ask that they be cleaned and that I'll pick them up the next day.

We leave a sand trail right into the hotel, which Jade finds funny and laughs. She's also worried that we're going to get into trouble and I tell her that we won't be the first, nor the last people to do it. The lift is empty when we get in. I could stand to the side and give her some space, but I don't. I stay right next to her, as any man should when his woman is close by.

I open my door and she follows me in. She stands between the two rooms, eyeing the beds. With a deep sigh, she looks at me and says, "Good night."

My mouth drops open but she's already disappeared into her room and shut her door lightly, leaving only a small sliver of visibility into her room. I've been completely cock blocked. Not that I expected to get lucky tonight, but the thought was there.

I quickly take off my clothes, leaving them in a pile on my floor, and collapse onto my bed in frustration. I can hear her moving around in the other room... her room. By now, I've decided that she's changed her clothes, removed her makeup, and maybe even tied her hair back so that it doesn't get all tangled while she sleeps.

I pull back the duvet and switch off the lamp providing the only light source between the two rooms. Sleep evades me, and I think that maybe I should start counting sheep. I try but it does nothing to help me fall into a slumber. I'm halfway there when I hear the air conditioner turn off and then there's nothing except a deafening silence. I feel like I can hear her breathing on the other side and can only imagine her soft inhales and exhales of breath, shifting from one side to another and even a possible sigh—all of which are made up in my head.

The clock on my bedside table tells me I've been at this for two hours, and I'm tired as fuck. It's been ages since I've had a decent night's sleep, probably the night before my mum was diagnosed with cancer. Since that day, I've been on high alert and with the added pressures of taking over my father's company. The stress just weighs on me.

Maybe that's why I like Jade so much, why I'm willing to put myself out there. Well, at least most of myself. The only lie I've told her is about my flat, and it really isn't a lie. I expect my place to be welcoming... someday.

Knowing that she's on the other side of our dividing wall leaves me awake, and not thinking straight. I'm about to do something ridiculously risky and probably extremely stupid, but I don't give a damn. Carefully, I make my way to her room, and push her door open as quietly as possible. Thank God this is a new hotel because the hinges don't even squeak.

Jade lies on her side with her naked back exposed, causing me to believe that she's naked under the covers. I look down at my boxers, thankful my dick is staying under control. Before I know it, I'm at the side of her bed, pulling her blankets back and climbing in beside her. Jade shifts, and I freeze immediately. I'm afraid to even breathe, thinking I should probably take my stalker arse back to my room and hope that she'll speak to me in the morning, but instead, her movement has pushed her backside against my leg and the only logical thing to do is roll onto my side and spoon her.

As soon as my arm lies across her stomach, she sags into me. I close my eyes and pray to God that I'm not dreaming.

FIVE

Jade
———

The blankets that I have intertwined with my legs
go flying about as I kick them away, thinking this
would be the best way to get rid of the offending object
suctioned to my boob. My breathing picks up as fear runs
through my body. I'm afraid to look at my chest, fearful of
what I might find. I thought my room was high enough off
the ground and far enough away from the ocean that there
would be no risk of sea urchins getting in. But I'm wrong.
One must've hitched a ride on the bottom of my dress or
came in on Jackson's pants because there's an octopus or
starfish stuck to my breast and I don't know what to do.

Thankfully, a small slither of sunlight peaks through my
blinds, giving me enough light to see, even if my eyes don't
want to register that I'm being attacked by something from
the *Little Mermaid's* family. Wait, did she have an octopus?

It doesn't matter because I have to look. I turn my head
slowly, letting the massive scream that I know is coming
build up, and as I shift, the tentacles squeeze, almost as if it's
groping me. All I can think of is when Robin Williams
played *Popeye* and he had to fight that massive squid to save

Olive Oyl. Sadly, unless Jackson hears me scream, I'll have to save myself.

My eyes are closed and I hold my breath by the time my head has turned in its direction. I'm not prepared to see beady eyes and a massive forehead staring back at me. I open my eyes, just to a squint and see flesh. I open wider to find that it's Jackson. He's next to me in bed, in a deep sleep, and holding my boob.

He's holding my boob.

My heart races with both sheer panic and elation because this man, this gorgeous, sexy, beautiful man should scare me. I should be pissed that he's crawled into my bed, my private space and made himself comfortable, but I'm not. I'm happy and relieved that it's him and not some ugly, smelly blob trying to molest me.

Now that I've rolled over, his hand is no longer on my boob, and honestly, I sort of miss the feeling. It's been far too long since I've been felt up, groped, and manhandled. My ex... ugh, that he's even present in my thoughts pisses me off, but I can't help and compare the two. The word opposite doesn't come close to describing him and Jackson. Besides the obvious differences in appearance and accent, Jackson isn't only manly, he's also determined. He's gorgeous, polite, and he smells like his cologne was made specifically for him. He's the type of guy that women drool over, believe me I was doing just that before he came over and kissed me. He doesn't seem to be afraid to take what he wants, and has that take-charge attitude. I have no doubt he's strong, not only physically but mentally as well. He's like the full package when it comes to building my own man. I used to think my ex was this way, but the only fortitude he had was to succeed at his job and while that is noble, it wasn't enough.

And yet, he's the one who broke up with me because I was "frigid." It's true I wasn't adventurous mostly because I was afraid he'd tell me that he wasn't interested. Something tells me Jackson would never tell say no or ask me to stop. If I suggested he take me up against the wall, he'd happily agree and make me forget that I was the one asking.

I roll back onto my side and position myself so that his hand is firmly on my breast. I like the feel of his hand there. It's neither rough nor soft. His hand doesn't allude to what he does for a living, but, given the lack of callouses on his palm, I can rule out a construction worker or fireman, although seeing Jackson in suspenders with a hard hat or helmet on would likely send me over the edge. I'd toss all my manners out the window and catcall him like there was no tomorrow. And I'd own it. I have no shame.

Speaking of no shame, I wiggle my ass into his groin, curious about what he's packing. I know I shouldn't, but he violated me first and it's only fair that I check out the goods too. If he didn't want me to, I don't think he'd be here.

He moans and pulls me closer, allowing me to feel his erection. Earlier, behind the cover of clothes, I felt him get hard. Knowing that I was doing that to him energized me, but now... now that I can feel his penis resting against my backside, anxiety creeps in. What if my ex was right? What if I'm too timid to be intimate with someone the way they need me to be?

I refuse to believe that especially after the way Jackson has been making me feel. In the hours I've known him, I have never felt so sexy, admired, and well... desired. He looked at me tonight like I was something to eat, to savor like a delicate dessert.

Adjusting, I put a bit of space between us so I can get my arm behind me. His cock twitches when my palm brushes against him, and I smile, trying not to make a peep. I don't want to wake him, yet I sort of do. I'd like to see how far he's willing to take this fake marriage of ours. We agreed to kiss in public, especially when the triplets are around and to keep the adjoining doors open. That's it. We didn't agree to fondle each other while the other sleeps.

Except my finger is trailing down the length of his cock and the farther it goes, the wider my eyes become. I repeat the process, going up and down his shaft, pushing the flap of his boxers out of the way when I get to the base of his groin. Fuck me, he's long.

Jackson's hips thrust toward me. I don't know if it's because he's waking up or if it's pure reflex. I'm praying that it's his natural reaction to being touched. If he were to open his eyes, I would probably scream and run into the bathroom and hide. But he doesn't make a sound other than shallow breathing.

With all the courage I can muster, my hand wraps around his phallus. My mouth drops open with the realization that not a single one of my fingers can touch my thumb. Long and thick is a combination I've never had in my life. My ex was average. Same as the boy I dated in college that I lost my virginity to. But Jackson, everything with him is different. He's not shy or unabashed.

I pull my hand away, anxious that he'll wake up and ask me what I'm doing. What *am* I doing? I have a ridiculously hot man lying next to me, and I'm battling between what's right and wrong when I could be pleasuring and learning about him. I should be throwing caution to the wind by putting myself out there, showing him that I don't care how the week ends as long as he and I have the best time of our lives.

We're pretending, right? So feelings shouldn't matter

when our time expires. I can do the no-strings-attached-friends-with-benefits-sexcation thing just like the next person. That's why I came here. Well, beside the fact that my best friend pushed me to take this trip. I told myself that I would let loose. That I would flirt a little, and that's what I'm going to do.

Twisting my arm back behind me, I reach for him, shocked to find that he's still hard. It dawns on me that this could very well be his morning wood and not because he's attracted to me or because I had been touching him earlier. No, I refuse to believe that. I have firsthand knowledge that he's turned on when he's with me. I felt him last night when we were dancing and before, in the elevator. The allure is there, and before I can second-guess myself and freak out about my looks and how Jackson could get anyone on this island to look his way, I grab a hold of him with a soft grip and slowly move my hand up and down his hard-on.

With each stroke, I pray and fear that Jackson will wake up. What happens if he does? Will he tell me to stop? Will he want sex? Will he placate me until I've finished what I'm doing?

What am I doing? That seems to be the question plaguing my mind as I feel my bud swelling. I'm in an awkward position, lying on one arm while my other is behind my back; otherwise, I'd give myself some relief. I could move my legs back and forth, create some friction, but for some reason I love the idea that Jackson is still sleeping or at least pretending to be.

His erection hardens in my hand and every other pass or so, his hips flex and he moans. I sneak a look over my shoulder and find that his eyes are still closed, but there's a concentrated look on his face, making me believe that he's dreaming. This could very well be the real-life version of a wet dream. Only mine is playing out in vivid color as the ache between my legs grows. I'm half-tempted to shut my eyes and roll over so I can mount him just to relieve the pressure.

My thumb brushes over the head of his cock, spreading the pre-cum as I go. Jackson hisses and mumbles something unintelligible. I freeze for a moment and my heart beats rapidly, waiting to see if he'll wake up. His response is to move his head closer to me so that we're sharing a pillow. He releases the hold he has on my breast, only to rub my nipple. My eyes roll back as my nipple becomes erect and wetness pools between my legs. Fuck, I love the feeling of his hand there, of my hand on his cock, and the way I feel deep within.

I want him.

I need him.

I'm going to have him.

My hand sets a steady pace, moving up and down his rod. His dick is hard like cement. I'm not naïve to think he won't fit, but it might hurt a bit. I'll welcome the pain and the fullness that I'll get when he enters me.

I close my eyes and imagine what it will be like to have him take me. Will it be on the bed first? That seems the logical first step, but there isn't a damn thing logical about what we're doing. If my parents knew that I was sharing a bed with a man who swam across a pool and kissed me not even twenty-four hours ago, they'd both have heart attacks and disown me.

Everything about him is dangerous, and yet the thought of fucking him is so exhilarating that I don't think I care. I want this man more than anything, and by the feel of his rigid cock, he wants me too.

Jackson's hips thrust, faster than they had been before.

He mumbles words like 'yes' and 'love' between grunts and deep throaty groans. He nuzzles my hair, inhaling deeply while his fingers pinch my nipple. That alone sends a shockwave through me, while the ache in my pussy thunders for some sort of attention.

Surely, if he comes while he's sleeping, he'll wake and know that I've been taking advantage of him, and I'm not sure I can face him right now. I let go, while his hips still move back and forth, and slip out of bed. I reach for my robe, only to realize that I never brought it to bed with me. A quick look over my shoulder tells me that his eyes are still closed, but the movement of his hips hasn't stilled. He's going to come on my sheets and I won't be here to witness it.

I hightail it to the bathroom and shut the door quietly. My heart pounds in my ears while my imagination runs rampant with visions of Jackson and me fucking. I'm so stupid for not finishing, for leaving him hanging like that. Maybe this is what my ex referred to as me being frigid. His terminology may be wrong though. Right now, I feel more like a tease who left a man on the brink of an orgasm.

There is something seriously wrong with me.

SIX

Jackson

I rub my hands over my face. Sweat dampens my fingertips and my heart races as fast as it can. I still can't believe my dream. It was so vivid. I've had plenty of wet dreams in my life, but this one? It was like something I've never experienced before. The desire to have sex grows (pardon the pun). No, it's not that I need sex. It's more. I *want* it. With Jade. I shake my head, trying to clear the scenario, but it's there, tempting me. Laughing at me. In some parallel universe, I'm a lucky bastard getting shagged six ways to heaven, while the real me must make do with the fantasy.

Everything seems normal as I check my surroundings. The only thing that strikes me unawares as I get my bearings is that my bed is facing the wrong way, and my suitcase isn't next to the TV where I left it. In fact, it's not even there and I know for a fact that I didn't move it last night. Speaking of last night, I can't spy the clothes I left in the pile on the floor when I undressed. I sneak a look at the clock, wondering if housekeeping has come and gone, but it's barely after seven in the morning.

Lifting my head, I glance with amusement at the tent in the sheet, courtesy of my erect dick. That bastard is hard and strong, as is proven by the fact that he isn't only single-handedly tenting the sheet, but the duvet as well. My hand reaches underneath to ease the burning desire before it explodes. As soon as I touch my dick, images of a hand wrapped around my hard-on bursts vividly into my mind. I quickly replay the dream, causing me to look around the room frantically for fear of getting caught in the act.

That's when it hits me. I'm in Jade's room. I came over last night because I couldn't sleep. But as soon as I got into her bed, I flaked out. As the memories come slowly back to me, I get the distinct impression that I may have slept through a rather fantastic hand job. What kind of loser does that kind of thing? Oh yeah, this one, because, the longer I sit here and think, the more I remember that last night was the best bloody night of sleep I've had in ages. Normally, I'd get two or three hours of shut eye at best, before my mind kicks in and I'm wide awake. I've tried pacing and that doesn't help. I've tried counting sheep, and that's useless. I've exercised, switched on my laptop and sent a few emails to clients and employees. I've looked at various online prop-erty websites to see if there is anything suitable I could buy to continue my father's business, and while working like a night owl until the crack of dawn does wonders for clearing my excess workload, it does fuck for helping me catch up on some much-needed sleep.

Last night was different though. I walked into her room and took the liberty of climbing into bed next to her, managing to fall asleep instantly. I also distinctly remember grabbing her boob and holding it in my hand like it was some kind of lifeline that would prevent me from drowning. Odds on, I'd say that my sneaky actions resulted in me falling asleep with a bloody huge smile on my face and to be honest, it was totally worth it.

Still, I must admit to being a little confused about why Jade didn't finish the job in hand. Could it be that she was dreaming too? If she was, that's damn hot. I mean, to be involved in a wet dream with my fake wife? Pretty bloody fantastic. Speaking of, I look around the room to see if I can spot her, so I can get her take on last night, but see no trace. Where the bloody hell could she be?

"Jade?" I call out her name and listen to see if I can hear movement. She could be in the bathroom, but I don't hear any water running. I get up and quickly rush over there with my hand covering my modesty.

I half-expect her to be in my room, but it's empty. I glance towards the bed and imagine us lying there together, taking part in every sexual position known to man. Of course, the very image of that goes straight to my dick and he promptly stands at attention again. Yeah, he wants her too, and clearly, he's almost as desperate as I am.

Pushing my boxer briefs down, I spit into my hand for some lubrication before grabbing hold of my junk, which elicits a sharp hiss on contact. I rub up and down, but my hand isn't nearly as good as hers from what I can remember, and neither is the pathetic excuse for a lube job that I've given myself, but it'll have to do until I can get the real thing. My eyes are closed, and I imagine that it's her mouth, pussy, and even her tits wrapped around me. The building sensation makes my knees buckle and forces me to move towards the wall for support.

I moan loudly. "Fucking yes! I'm almost there," I cry out to the empty room as my balls tighten and the pressure builds. I have not come this hard in a long time, and it's all because Jade got shy before she could finish the job.

Although, taking into account what I've now learned about her, It wouldn't surprise me if she surprised herself by touching me. I'd admire her for taking the risk. I have a feeling she probably tried to talk herself out of it. Thank Christ she didn't, although I wish she was here with me now to help me with my little problem.

A problem I bet she's having too. I've never known a woman to give a man a handie or blowjob and not feel the urge to be touched in the same way. It's nature's reaction, a natural turn on. If she had awoken me, I would've made her feel pleasure in ways she's never felt before. Her ex thinks she's frigid. I say that's bollocks. I think she hasn't had a real man show her how to fuck and get fucked.

The door opens and in she walks. Our eyes meet for only a second and then I look at the tray of food in her hands and she looks at my dick in mine, but I'm too far gone, there's no stopping me now. She stands there, completely frozen. Her mouth opens and closes with no words coming out, before it finally settles on the shape of a lovely little O.

Yeah, that right there? It's the perfect spot for me to put my dick. But I don't want to ask her if she wants to suck me off. I should though, just to see where I stand with her. Maybe she's hoping I don't remember what happened last night. It's fine if that's how she wants to play it, but that's not my game.

I angle myself perfectly so she can watch my hand move up and down my shaft. My grip changes from firm to lax, alternating back and forth. I'm waiting for her to either put the tray of food down or drop it, whichever works so that she can place her hands on her body and she's using them to touch herself.

The fucking sight of her erect nipples pushing through her skimpy top makes my balls tighten again. "Fuck," I say, hissing out the word as my hand moves faster while my mind conjures up images of her grinding on top of me with her tits bouncing up and down. What I wouldn't give to see that. I'd let them spring around freely until I couldn't stand to not touch them. I'd take them in my mouth, sucking and nipping at her sensitive flesh. My backside slaps against the wall as my hips meet my every stroke rapidly. I fucking love the sound of sex. The moans and gasps, skin slick with sweat slapping together and my balls spanking against the warm flesh of a beautiful woman.

"I'm going to come," I tell her. I don't know why I say it. It's going to be the result no matter what. It's not as if I'm going to stop what I'm doing, walk back into my room, and hide myself from her. I don't even search for a tissue or something else to ejaculate into. I want her to watch me as I come. I want her to see exactly the reaction I have to her, how hard she makes me, and how much I want her. I want her to put down the godforsaken tray, get on her knees, and put her mouth around me, deep and hard. I want her to allow me to weave my fingers into her silken hair and fuck her mouth until my cum drips down her throat. If she did that, I'd pick her up and put her on the bed, spread her legs as far apart as possible, and I'd go to town eating her out. I know she's wet and hungry for my dick. I can tell by the way her legs rub against each other, trying to get the friction she needs to ease the tingle her clit feels right now. Jade can't fool me, and I have a feeling we both know that before the day is over, I'm going to be balls deep in that pussy of hers.

I fight to keep my eyes open as the heaviness sets in. The low growl accompanied by deep moans has my dick pulsing. The pure ecstasy of release isn't lost on me. I sigh heavily, and slump against the wall while I continue to stroke my dick through each stream of jizz that's spurting anywhere and everywhere, into my boxers, down my legs and onto my hand.

Everything goes quiet except for my rapid breathing. To be honest, I'm a little scared to look at Jade, for fear that my sexual act may have scared the crap out of her. I flex my hand, trying to ease the cramp that has built up in it, while my stomach makes itself known. I'm all sweaty and in desperate need of a shower, and my cock still has some life left in it. I don't know how that could possibly be, though. I'm fucking spent.

"I brought breakfast," she says, walking carefully into the room. She walks past me and puts the tray down onto the small table in the corner. I wait for her to turn around and look me in the eyes, but she doesn't. I'm left with no choice but to pull my boxers up, make my excuses, and make a swift exit.

"I'll be back," I tell her as I leave her room, and walk back into mine. I doubt myself. Maybe I should've done the deed in the safety of my own bathroom, instead of standing in full glory in the middle of her room, with nowhere to hide. I couldn't help myself though. Being there, being in close vicinity of her bed, made me lose all my self-control, and knowing that only a few hours ago, we were lying together under those sheets, and she had shed her inhibitions while she allowed herself to touch me, had me growing erect in no time. The memories of her caressing me are seared into my mind, and I had to relieve the tension somehow. Have I pushed her too far in my assumption that she wants to be intimate with me?

No, I don't think that I have. I think she's scared and nervous. She expected to find me sleeping or in my room, not being held up by the wall while I gave myself a hand job.

My dick becomes uncomfortable as the stickiness covers it and the inside of my boxers, and the only way to avoid what could be an unpleasant feeling is to have a shower. I think about telling her I'll only be another few minutes, but words fail me. I let the pent up sexual tension between us play out singlehandedly and I should've known better than to let her see that. Although, now that she knows, there is no doubting how much I want her and how much she turns me on, maybe there is hope something will happen between us.

I have a quick shower and put on clean clothes. I don't know what her plans are for today, and quite frankly, I haven't made any. One thing is for sure, I do plan on spending the day with her as much as possible and am happy to do whatever she wants. When I walk back into her room, I hesitate a little, but only for a moment. The sliding glass door, which leads to the balcony, is open and she's put out all the food on the table. From where I stand, I quietly observe her. She's reading a book and her feet are propped up against the railing, showing off her pretty turquoise toes.

She turns around and looks at me. The sight of her makes my knees go weak. I don't know if it's because I'm so besotted by her or the fuck-me spectacles she's got on. Right now, she's taken on the role of sexy librarian, and it seems I have a thing for them judging by the feeling of pure desire running through my body.

I'm hesitant in the steps I take towards her. Jade follows my movement with her eyes until I bend down and hover over her. I kiss her lightly on the lips, letting them linger there for as long as possible, before pulling away to stop things from getting intense. Right now, I think we're both unsure about whatever happened earlier and it's probably for the best we cool ourselves down for a minute or two.

"You look extremely sexy in those glasses," I tell her as I sit down. She blushes at my comment, as I knew she would. Jade lifts off the metal cloche, which covers the plate in front of me. "How did you know I love French toast?"

"I didn't," she says, shaking her head. "But it's my favorite and I had hoped..."

She doesn't have to finish what's she saying. I have a feeling we're on the same page. Yesterday started off this weird holiday fling for the both of us after I kissed her out of the blue, and this morning the page has turned. It'll be hard as fuck to keep my feelings to myself, but I made a promise and I will not go back on my word.

SEVEN

Jade

I froze. There is no other way to explain what I did. I went frigid. That's likely my nature, and unfortunately for me, my make-believe marriage will be over before it's hardly begun. I suppose it's for the best; this way neither Jackson nor I develop feelings for each other that will only leave us heartbroken when the week is over.

Except the feelings have already started and I'm not sure I can turn the switch off and look at him like he's a friend. Hell, he's not even that. He's a stranger that I let kiss, touch, and grind against me. Who I fondled while he slept, which makes me look and feel like a complete psycho trying to take advantage of him. It doesn't matter that he was in my bed. Granted, he was clutching my boob, but I think that was all by accident. He's probably a sleepwalker and didn't think to tell me to shut and lock my door last night.

In my life, I have never seen a man do that, continue to pleasure himself after being caught. One would think that they would pull their drawers up and run into the other room, but not Jackson. No, he made sure I watched him while he finished. He never broke eye contact with me until it was time for him to go clean up.

He was offended by my lack of response. I could see it in his eyes. I think that maybe he wanted me to join him, but I couldn't get my legs to move. My fingers strained, holding onto to the tray as my eyes took in the scene before me. I had felt him in my hand only an hour or so before, but seeing him in the flesh, watching him stroke his erection was another sight. My mouth watered at the thought of having him fill me, at the idea of dropping to my knees and sucking him off. I've never been a big fan of giving blowjobs but I anxiously wanted to taste Jackson. The throbbing I felt earlier was back and stronger than ever. I could've easily set the platter down and made myself available to him, but instead, I stood there like a frigid prude.

When Jackson excused himself and disappeared into his room, I wanted to cry. I created the tension between us, when all I had to do was ask if he needed help. I don't think he did, but in my mind, that was the perfect question to ask. Now I wonder if he would've said yes or would he have told me that he was okay and finished anyway? It's something I'll never know.

I refuse to look at the floor, not wanting to know if any of his jizz landed on the floor. I feel sorry for the house-keeper when she comes in later, if that's the case. There isn't a doubt in my mind that the staff will make up any type of story to describe what happened in here. Too bad I won't be around to hear them, as they'd likely be comical.

Setting the tray down so I can open the door, I set our breakfast up on the patio. As soon as I hear his shower come on, I decide this is a good time to catch up on some reading. Making myself comfortable with my book and a cup of coffee, I try to get lost in the world of Nora Roberts. Only her character seems to be experiencing a rough time in her life and for some odd reason, I feel guilty. Here I am, enjoying the perfect weather of Bermuda with a drop-dead sexy man while this made-up woman can't figure out her own life.

This is how I normally feel when I'm home. Like I'm lost and muddling through the concrete jungle that I live in. I've thought about moving, but the idea of being away from my parents is unsettling. It's not because I'm a homebody, but more so because I have a hard time meeting people and am afraid of being alone.

Take Jackson for instance. I would've never had the courage to speak to him if he hadn't come to me first. I would've been happy watching from afar, dreaming about what could be if I had the courage to put myself out there.

I continue to get lost in the written word until my senses are overtaken by the manly smell of Jackson. Peering at him from over my shoulder, he's dressed in khaki shorts and another white shirt that details the muscles in his arms and makes his tattoos stand out. I hope that I can get up close and personal with the ink and ask him what they mean, although I know some people like to keep the story behind their designs to themselves.

Jackson comes closer, and the aroma of his cologne envelops me instantly. I inhale deeply and let the scent settle over me. I don't know what it is, but I love it and want to smell it on me. He grips the back of my chair, hovering, before kissing me chastely. I want to deepen the kiss, but he pulls away, smiling as he does.

"You look extremely sexy in those glasses," he says, causing my cheeks to flare. I've never been one to blush, at least not as frequently as I do when Jackson is around.

He sits down across from me and lifts the lid off his

food. There is only so much one can do when staying in a hotel and living off restaurant food and room service.

"How did you know that I love French toast?" he asks, with a big grin on his face.

"I didn't," I tell him honestly. "But it's my favorite and I had hoped..." My words trail off as we make eye contact with each other. Something in the air shifts. It's hard for me to pinpoint what or what the dynamic will be. At the end of the week, we go our separate ways, never knowing a thing about each other.

I realize my mistake. I've given him a small glimpse into my life over the past twenty-four hours. I told him a story about my ex and now he knows my favorite breakfast food. We're supposed to be lying to each other, making stories up as we go. That's not what I'm doing.

"Um," I say, looking down at my covered plate. Jackson's hand reaches out and pulls off the lid, revealing my breakfast. It's all there, everything I ordered, and matching his.

"Would you like some syrup?" He holds up the small jar of amber liquid.

I shake my head. "I've never been a fan."

"Neither have I." He sets it down and hands me a few pats of butter.

"Powdered sugar?" I ask, showing him the extra bowl of sugar that I requested.

"Yes please." He takes it from me. "It's like you read my mind when you ordered our breakfast."

"I took a gamble."

Jackson cuts into the bread and slowly brings the fork to his mouth. My tongue darts out to wet my lips. Watching him eat has to be the sexiest thing I've seen when it comes to food.

"You know, we should go to Vegas and test out your luck." He winks. I like the idea of Vegas, but know it'll never happen. Once I leave here, Jackson will be nothing more than a memory.

"Maybe in another lifetime." Jackson must catch the underlying meaning in my words. He nods and quickly stuffs his face with food. I do the same, wishing I could start the morning all over again. I don't know how much I'd do differently, but if I had to change one thing then we'd be eating breakfast in bed instead of on the balcony, and maybe we'd feeding each other instead of letting awkward silence build between us.

Jackson finishes long before I do and each time I look at him, he's watching me. I feel like I'm under a microscope, only he's smiling, and not in some creepy way.

"So, what are we doing today?" He picks up a strawberry that I pushed aside.

"Honestly, I didn't make any plans outside of staying at the resort. I'm here by myself and I came to relax. I didn't really want to be a tourist without a friend. I didn't want the judgment," I tell him.

"Makes sense. I was planning on doing the same thing, but now that we have each other, I think we should do some exploring. You know, check out some of the sights?"

I'm intrigued. I do like the idea of exploring the area. Besides, if I get home and tell my best friend that this hot hunk of a man and I sat by the pool every day, she's going to whack me upside my head for even leaving my room. At least, this way I can share our adventures and create some memories.

"What do you propose we do?"

"Everything we can without tiring ourselves out. I at least want to finish the night with a nice dinner somewhere." He reaches across the small table and takes my hand. "What I would really love to do is to take you all over Bermuda. Be a tourist with you. Sit on the pink, sandy beaches and swim in the turquoise water, which matches your toes." Jackson waggles his eyebrows, making me giggle. "But maybe a different day. Today, however, I think we should head over to St. George's and do a little shopping, buy some souvenirs, be tourists, that kind of thing. We can walk around, eat lunch, have a few drinks, and just play it by ear."

"Sounds like a plan." I stand and pile up our dishes until he reaches for my hand.

"Leave that, housekeeping will clear it up for us." Tugging me into the room. "I'm going to clean my teeth." Jackson walks briskly toward his room while I head to the closet and pull out one of my swimsuits before ducking into the bathroom to freshen up. I quickly put my suit on and redress, brush my teeth, add sunscreen, and pull my hair into a small ponytail.

When I open the door, Jackson is standing there with his arms hanging from the doorway. The veins in his arms pop out from the strain he has his arms in. I swallow hard at his closeness.

"I have a feeling that we're going to have a great day."

"I agree." I'm tempted to kiss him, to see where it could lead. Everything that happened earlier today was way too fast and we were unprepared for how the other would feel. Our rules indicate that kissing is allowed. We never talked about sex nor has either of us suggested we alter the rules. I don't know if I'm strong enough to bring it up.

Jackson leads us out of the hotel, thankfully missing any sign of the triplets, although it would be comical to see them again. I'm sure we will in due time. He tells the valet that we need a taxi. The man whistles loudly and within seconds, one pulls up. Jackson holds the door, climbing in after me. I expect Jackson to sit close to the door, but he scoots as close as he can to me, putting his arm around my back, and sets his hand on my lap.

The driver pulls into traffic and Jackson points out different things along the route for me to look at. The nearness makes it seem like we're more than friends. I have half a mind to tell him that we're not at the resort so he can stop acting, but I like it. I love the attention that he bestows upon me. Everything feels like we're a real couple and not two people making up things as we go.

Jackson asks the driver if he'll take us on a mini tour of the town and he does. Most of the houses are pastel in color, making the area seem like we're trapped in one of those bubble gum machines that come in an array of color. They're cute and whimsical. The driver points out who is rich by the style of the home and who isn't, and tells us what restaurants we need to eat at, and what other sites to see. And when he asks how long we've been together, Jackson looks at me and pushes a strand of hair behind my ear.

"Not long enough," he says.

I try to hold his gaze, but I can't. I half-smile, half-grimace, and continue to look at the passing scenery. This man will wreck me at the end of the week and I don't know if I'll ever recover. Maybe it's best we end the charade now instead of waiting until we're in too deep to call it quits.

EIGHT

Jackson

---

*A*fter what started out as being a potentially rocky day, everything seems to have worked out quite nicely. I was afraid that the connection we had earlier had been ruined by us not knowing how to act after our little 'incident' this morning. We each did something that we probably shouldn't have, especially after the first day. Ideally, it'd be clever of us to treat this as a one-night stand, but we both know it's much more than that. At least it is now. It didn't start off that way. I thought I was being a smooth operator when I kissed her. Little did I know what I was in for.

I really had no plans or venue in mind when we got into the taxi. I mostly wanted to get out of the hotel and hang out with her. It's dangerous territory, I know, but I can't seem to stop myself from wanting to spend every moment together. Maybe by the end of the week, we'll have been in each other's pockets for so long that we'll be sick of the sight of each other and saying, 'au revoir' at the airport won't be such a bad thing. At least, that's what I keep telling myself.

One week of lies and playing make believe and then we'll never see each other again.

Everyone that overtakes us as we drive along are on scooters, which gives me a brilliant idea. "Hey, mate, can you take us to the scooter rental?"

"You got it," he says as he switches on the signal to leave the road. Jade looks at me with wide, expectant eyes.

"What?"

"I've never driven a scooter," she tells me.

"Do you want to learn? I can teach you." In fact, it would be my pleasure to show her how to drive one.

"No thank you." There's a shyness in her voice as she replies.

"Perfect, that means you won't mind if I drive us around then, right?"

She nods, but it's hesitant. I'm tempted to ask her where she lives, but that's crossing the line into personal information that we agreed not to share with each other. If she told me, the chances are that I would pay that area a visit and see if I could track her down. It'd be a game to me, and one that would come at a price.

The driver pulls up in front of a yellow building resembling a banana ice lolly. Jade reaches into her purse, but I quickly stop her from pulling out any money.

"What are you doing?" she asks.

"Not letting you pay."

"Yes, I am, at least my half."

I shake my head, rolling my eyes playfully as I take out my wallet and hand the driver some money to cover the fare. "When you're with me, you don't have to pay." She opens her mouth to protest, but I give her a stern look. I'm all for women empowerment and being equal partners, but sometimes a man should play the gentleman card. Sometimes he needs to show the beautiful woman he's with that she's worth his money.

I also pay for the hire of the scooter after giving Jade yet another warning look. In my mind, I'm preparing myself for a fight later, but it'll be worth it. I want to hear all the reasons why she should be allowed to pay for herself and not be pampered. I'll remind her that it's she who's doing me a favour, one which has so far, moved far beyond anything I could possibly imagine.

"You'll look adorable in this helmet," I say after she slips it on her head. With mine on, I sit on the scooter and wait for her. I have one back at home; it's the easiest way to get around London. Sometimes, on the weekend, I even give myself the freedom of riding it down to the coast; albeit to get a real thrill, I should probably upgrade my Vespa to something more hardcore. For the most part, though, I find myself weaving in and out of traffic, cursing like a sailor at the kamikaze drivers who like to encroach on my lane. "Use my shoulder to steady yourself."

She does so immediately and without any prodding from me, secures her arms around my waist, and because the scooter is small, Jade must slide as close to me as possible. I'm not complaining in the slightest. I like the feel of her touching me.

We take off down the road at a slow and steady pace. She squeezes me tightly a few times as we go over a few bumps in the road. She's probably scared, but I convince myself that the squeezes are her way of reminding me that she's there. As if I'd forget.

I was a young boy the last time I was in Bermuda. We came here for a family holiday, but I can't remember any of the sights. We had a chauffeur that took us everywhere and there are a lot of things one misses when sitting in the back of a limo. One also misses out on doing anything fun being a kid on holiday with his parents and stuck in the hotel room with a child-minder.

We cruise through the streets until I see the sign for the botanical gardens. When I pull in and park, Jade claps her hands joyfully. "Are we going in?" she asks.

"Yeah, why not?" I make it sound like coming here isn't a big deal, but it's obvious to her that it is. Inside, I give myself a high-five for making the right decision. She hops off the scooter and puts down her helmet next to mine before walking toward the door. It only takes a few steps for me to catch up with her and she jumps a little when I take her hand in mine.

Jade stops walking and looks down at where our hands are joined together. "I can't imagine the triplets would come to a place like this." She points towards the door. Jade has a point, but I can't seem to let go of her hand.

I shrug my shoulders and walk towards the entrance. It takes me a second to understand the implication behind her words, that she thinks I'm holding her hand in case we happen to run into Jo, Flo, and Mo, but the truth is, I *enjoy* having her hand in mine. It's got nothing to do with who I may or may not be trying to avoid.

Once we've got our tickets and are inside, Jade starts oohing and aahing at the different flowers. She says something about the shrubs, but all I can think of is the Harry Potter stories and that ridiculous maze he had to run through to win the tournament. The only difference here is that the maze isn't trying to attack us, and it barely comes up to my waist and I can easily see the way out.

With that said, each time she tells me about a flower or asks me to smell it, I bend down and do so. Most of them smell pretty good, but I'm a guy and it's a flower. What else can I say? I know that giving them to a girl (or a boy for that matter, because hey, it's the twenty-first century and I'm all about gender equality) makes them happy, and at the end of the day, that's why I'm here, because the smile on Jade's face is completely worth it.

"That was beautiful," she says.

"So are you." The words fall out of my mouth before I can stop them. She blushes before tilting her face away from me to hide her shyness, which endears her to me even more. All I want to do is get her back to the hotel and hope she'll let me undress her. Kissing her senseless right now is also top of my priority list. One thing's for sure, though. I wouldn't be acting if I were kissing her. No, it'd be one hundred percent the real deal and that thought doesn't scare me in the slightest.

"Jackson," she says my name breathlessly and fuck me sideways if I don't feel myself getting hard right at this minute. I quickly look down at the ground and smirk.

"Let's get out of here and see what else we can do." I walk us briskly back to the scooter and hand her helmet to her, which she slips on her head before taking ahold of my waiting hand. As soon as she climbs on, I pull out into traffic and follow the signs to the beach. This is different from the one we went to last night, and if I remember correctly, it's the one my nanny took me to, the one with the pink sand.

Jade continues to point at the magnificent pieces of art as we drive past. Everywhere we look, there are multi-coloured houses and buildings, and there's art painted freely on walls. The vibe here is both amazing and welcoming. I continue driving to Southampton and Horseshoe Bay. Thankfully, it's not packed when we arrive. Tourism, like any place, can be hit and miss, but we're in luck.

We park the scooter and head towards the beach. This

time I don't hold her hand. My mind has decided to play some tricks on me, and I can't decide whether I should or not. Putting some distance between us would probably be the best thing. I don't want her to get the wrong impression and think I've gone back on our deal. That I want to carry on whatever we have between us and become some long-distance thing.

We come across a booth and pay for a couple of beach towels. As we walk towards the beach and onto the sand, I'm relieved to see that my theory is correct and the beach isn't crowded. I'm not entirely sure how we are so lucky, but I'm not going to complain. I follow her towards the water, and put my towel down before taking off my shoes. Jade takes off her shorts and shirt and yet again, I find myself getting hard.

"Shall we go for a swim?" I ask her, but I don't wait for an answer. I must get into the water and try to control whatever is happening in my shorts. I'm not ashamed of the attraction I have towards her, but it's a public beach and after this morning's events, I don't want to come on too strong and scare her off. Maybe a part of me is also running away from her, to curb the growing attraction I feel towards her. I dive under and revel in the warm waters of Bermuda. This is a small piece of heaven. I stay under for as long as possible, wondering if she'd like to go snorkelling tomorrow or the day after. My head is torn in two. Part of me wants to go full on romance and woo her into falling for me. The other part though knows that whatever we have going on between us will end in a few days. We made an agreement, a pact. We've got rules that we agreed to follow and I can't go changing that, especially as it's only been one bloody day. I need to either just get over it and make the best of this situation or call the whole thing off. Although, if I saw her around the resort with another guy, I'd probably lose my head.

I resurface and find Jade wading in knee-deep water. She's looking around, and she seems a little lost. A feeling of guilt washes over me, because I know I put that there. I've been leading her on with my touchy-feely crap and now I've gone stone cold on her.

"Hey, love," I call out, getting her attention. When she looks in my direction, I beckon her over. She walks towards me as much as she can until the water is too deep and she must swim the rest of the way. As soon as she's within arm's reach, I pull her to me, and her legs wrap around my waist.

"Yes, Mister..." she trails off, not knowing what to call me. I'm more than tempted to tell her my last name, but the chances that she'd believe me are slim.

"Smith," I tell her.

"That's the most common name in the United States."

"Well, it's lucky for me that I'm from England." Not that it matters. Smith is the most common name wherever you go. I move us deeper into the sea, which guarantees she must hang onto me unless she wants to tread water. "Tell me one truth."

She looks at me warily. "That's breaking the rules."

"I know," I say, shrugging. "But look at it this way. If we tell each other one thing a day until we leave, it'll make our story so much more outlandish when we tell our mates about our holiday."

Jade's hands push in and out of the water. I can hold her easily because she doesn't weigh a ton, but now she's almost weightless.

"One truth?"

I nod. "One today, another one tomorrow, and so on.

Surely you can think of six things about you that won't give away your identity."

She tilts her head back towards the sky as if she's looking for her truth there. "My best friend's name is Jackie."

"See? Easy. So, Jackie. That's a nice name. Is it short for Jacqueline?"

"No, she was named after her father," she says simply. "Your turn."

"Okay, mine... Let's see." My mouth is doing a great job at putting me in awkward situations. I know what I want to say, that I want to fuck her, but something tells me my actions will speak louder than words. I need to *show* Jade what I want, not tell her. "Back in England, I drive a black scooter like the one we have here." I nod towards the shore even though ours is parked nowhere near us right now. She looks back, as if she could see it from here.

"You are like one of those yuppie men that Jackie and I make fun of."

I smile, but she's so far from the truth it's not even funny. I'm a homebody. I prefer to go to work, grab some dinner, and take it back to my place. Occasionally, I'll go to a bar for a few pints with my mates or to find a woman to take home, but it's not an every night thing for me. I know it's not the norm for men my age, but it's what I like.

"Probably," I lie. "And I have a feeling you're the geeky librarian of every man's fantasy."

Jade blushes and shakes her head. I'm pretty sure that I've just uncovered a truth about her she doesn't want me to know. Instead of prodding some more, I walk us back toward the beach where she reluctantly drops her legs from my waist. Before she can get away, I tug her towards some rocks where I think we can find a place for us to make out.

NINE

Jade

---

*P*art of me wonders what type of relationships Jackson has had in the past. There are times when it seems like he wants to forget the game we're playing and tell me his life story, and I'd love to hear it, but I'm not so sure I want to share mine in return. It's not that I'm embarrassed about who I am, but growing up in my household with my father's profession—I was always the kid that others couldn't play with, especially the older I got. Jackie has been my only true friend while growing up and that's because her mother worked for my dad, so her parents understood.

Jackson lays on his stomach. His eyes are closed and his face is turned toward me. He seems to be asleep, which is why I'm staring at him. I suppose if he were awake, I'd still be looking because I can't seem to keep my eyes off him. He's perfect, at least to me. It's hard to explain but he's everything I've been seeking in a man, but never had the courage to go out and get. It's the way he carries himself. He's confident and self-assured. When he looks at me, I feel alive, sexy, and desired. When he's near, my senses are heightened. I love his accent and want to hear him talk non-stop. If he were reading the dictionary aloud, I'd sit and listen just so I could hear his voice over and over again. And when he calls me "love"... well, that's when I lose my wits and wish we weren't playing this game.

I'm not naïve enough to think if I weren't his hotel room neighbor and if I hadn't been at the pool at the right time, I wouldn't be here now. Our paths crossed for a reason. What that reason is, I don't know, but I'm thankful. I don't want to imagine what my vacation would be like without Jackson.

I prop myself up on my elbow and study the tattoos on his arm. They extend from his shoulder to his wrist and around to the inside of his arm. I'm not sure if there's a spec of non-inked skin left. I would've never guessed the man at the check-in desk was the man across from me now. He looked so businesslike the other day, yet so much the bad boy when I saw him at the pool.

My eyes follow the muscles of his arms, taking in the array of tattoos that I can see. One arm seems to be a combination of different designs whereas his other arm's a full-on scene. I haven't been able to tell exactly what that is though.

I start at the top of his shoulder and study the design that represents London. The London Eye is at the top of his shoulder with Tower Bridge right below it, followed by a double decker bus that looks like it's driving over the Union Jack flag. Anyone who looks, like I am, can tell that Jackson is proud of where he's from. The rest of his arm is made up of flowers, birds, a couple of colorful koi fish, and two tattoos that pay homage to his parents. I wonder if he's close to his parents like I am?

I turn my attention back to his shoulder and the scene from London. I have always wanted to visit England, but have never had the courage to go, at least not by myself.

Jackie, won't travel, which is why I'm in Bermuda without her. If she hadn't bought my ticket, I would've never gotten on the plane. But she insisted, telling me I need to escape reality and get over my break-up. Thing is, I have been over it for a while. I just didn't want to go out and meet anyone, and I've consumed myself with work.

I don't even know what I'm going to tell Jackie when I get home. I still have a very long week with Jackson and things could change. Our dynamic could shift and we realize that our game is stupid and don't want to play anymore. Although, I can't imagine I'd be the one saying that. I feel lucky he's even spoken to me. He, on the other hand, won't have an issue picking up another woman.

But what do I say to my best friend? Hey, guess what? I met this amazing man who treated me like a queen, but we fake named each other and lied about everything in our lives because we thought it would be funny? Somehow I'm not sure that will go over very well with her.

Switching positions, I lay on my side, still facing him. I'm tempted to close my eyes, but this is the perfect time to memorize every feature I can see so when I'm home, I don't forget him. Not that I ever will. If today were the only day I got to spend with him, would be enough to make this trip worthwhile.

When he opens his eyes, I don't startle. It's almost as if I expected him to know I was staring. He smiles though, which I happily return. I'm tempted to make a move, to lean over and kiss him, but things have been a bit off between us today. I know I shouldn't expect affection, although he did say kissing was mandatory. Part of me hoped that yesterday's kissing fest would play into today as well. Of course our morning was awkward.

Jackson rolls onto his side, mimicking my position. He

rests his head on his bicep, his own personal pillow. "Like what you see?" he asks with a smirk.

"Are you fishing for compliments?"

He shrugs. "Sometimes it's nice for a man's ego to be stroked."

Stroked. I try not to let the images of him pleasuring himself pop into mind or recall how I felt when I had him in my hand. I wish I had the courage to do more with him this morning but the thought of him telling me no or waking and asking me what I was doing scared the shit out of me.

"I think your ego is just fine."

"Yeah?" he asks, moving a bit closer to me. Now he's on his elbows and leaning my way. "Do *you* think I'm fine?"

"Sexy," I tell him. I have nothing to lose by being honest with him about his looks or how I'm feeling. Everything else can stay bottled up.

"Sexy, huh? Sexy enough to kiss?" he asks, shifting closer to me.

I nod slowly as I try to keep track of what he's doing. My eyes move from his crystal-blue orbs to his lips and back until he's so close I have no choice but to close my eyes, and when I do, I feel a jolt of electricity and passion as his lips move softly over mine. In one swift move, he's right next to me with his hand on my hip and his arm under my head, cradling my body to his as if he's protecting me from someone or something.

I curl into him and open my mouth to deepen the kiss. I don't care if we're out in public, among others. We're on vacation and this is what people do. It's not like others aren't doing the same or people will remember who we are.

Our legs tangle together, with mine hitching over his while his thigh pushes between my legs. He pulls away and caresses my cheek with the back of his hand and gazes into my eyes. "You're so beautiful," he tells me again. I've been told I look nice when I dress up, but can't remember a time when another man paid me a compliment regarding my beauty, and Jackson has done it multiple times.

"Only in your eyes."

He smiles. "I'd like to think that's true, but unfortunately, it's not. I had to scare that bloke away from our table earlier and there are plenty of men here have been checking you out ever since we got here."

I'm tempted to look around, to see if he's being honest, but I rather like the position I'm in. "I could say the same about you."

"You could, but I can tell you right now, in the past twenty-four hours, you have well and truly put me under your spell. I'm captivated by you."

"I feel the same."

Jackson kisses me again, but something has shifted. There's a need, a deeper desire, behind his kiss, and it's the same for me. I pull him closer, needing to feel him against me, but he doesn't budge. He pulls away and buries his face in the crook of my neck and his arm and groans.

He sits up slightly, but doesn't pull away from me. "Jade, I promise you now, if I moved on top of you right now, I'd find every possible way to push your bikini bottoms aside and fuck you."

My mouth drops open as I say, "Oh."

"Is that something you want, Jade? Do you want me to fuck you right here so all these men can see you're mine?"

I'm tempted to say yes, but instead, I freeze. I don't know if there's an adequate response to a question like that because yes, I want him to fuck me, to show me what it's like to be with a man who makes me weak in the knees, but to do it in public, surrounded by people, I'm not so sure that would be my style.

"It's okay, love. Don't look so scared. I would never put you in a situation you're uncomfortable with." He kisses the tip of my nose, brushes his lips against my eyes and then my forehead, moving up my body slowly so I can feel how hard he is. When he gets to my ear, he whispers, "But make no mistake, I do want to fuck you."

My body sighs and he chuckles lightly. He sits up on his knees suddenly and pulls my flushed body up. His erection pokes through his shorts. "What do you say we take a quick dip?" Jackson doesn't wait for me to answer before he pulls me to my feet and through the sand.

We're almost running as we hit the water. He dives in and I follow right behind him. When I surface, he's nowhere to be found. I spin in circles, wondering where he could've gone. I squint and look back toward shore, but don't see him.

"Looking for me?" he asks, scaring the shit out of me. He's behind me, standing a few feet from me. His chest is exposed with the sun glistening off his skin. I swim over and stand in front of him. While the water flows over my breasts, it barely covers his chest.

"I thought I was dreaming," he says.

"About what?"

"About the hand job I was getting this morning. When I woke, I thought I had just had the best fucking wet dream ever and I was so pissed off it was over until I realised you were doing that to me."

"Oh."

Jackson kisses my neck and reaches for my hand. He guides it down his chest and into his shorts. He leaves my hand there, testing to see what I'm going to do. I look him in the eyes and he cups my cheeks with his strong hands. I push further, brushing my hand against his erection.

"This is all you, Jade. You make me feel this way," he says between kisses. "Please, do it again."

My hand moves up and down his shaft. One would think the water would be a natural lubricant, but he feels rougher than he did earlier. My thumb sweeps over the head, feeling the warmth of his pre-cum.

"If you don't want this to go any further, please tell me now, because I am dying to get inside you, to hear you scream my name while I make you come all over me," he whispers into my ear. His words spur me on, they make me speed up. The rocking of his hips is hidden by the waves and I doubt anyone can tell what I'm doing. And if they can, I don't care. This gorgeous man, this bad boy will destroy me by week's end, likes what I'm doing to him. And so do I.

TEN

Jackson

I have never considered myself a man with simple needs. I'm sitting on the beach, with Jade's head resting in my lap while she reads to me from a book she found as she bought us some lunch. After the hand job she gave me in the sea, we needed to get some energy back, and neither of us was interested in going back to the hotel. Luckily, we found some beachside food huts and chose something from there.

This wasn't how I envisaged my holiday turning out. Technically, I should be working on finding a suitable location where we can expand the business. Part of my job spec also includes looking for willing volunteers to test out some new products. The deal was work by day, holiday by night, but right now I can't be bothered to do anything other than spend all my time with Jade, and to be honest, I don't see that changing soon.

As the sun starts to set, we decide to call it a night. We return everything we rented out for the day and climb back onto the scooter. This time when Jade holds onto me, she leans in closer and tries to rest her head on my shoulder.

The helmet gets in the way but I understand what she's trying to do and the meaning behind it.

Everything changed between us when I asked her to touch me. I was being a little selfish by not returning the favour, but I have heard far too many horror stories about women getting all kinds of infections from fucking around in the water and the last thing I want to do is ruin her holiday. Besides, I have bigger plans for her later, and the best part is she knows all about them and is more than ready to be a willing participant.

Planned sex has never been my thing, not even when I lost my virginity. That just happened in a total "what the fuck moment." But tonight, I know it's going to happen with Jade and I know the dynamic of our fucked-up fake relationship will immediately change into one of those clandestine affairs I've read about.

I decide to take our scooter back to the hotel and make some arrangements with the concierge to extend my hire agreement. I might as well keep it for the week so Jade and I can go sightseeing whenever we want without having to hire one out every day or depend on a taxi to get us where we want to go. It's also cheaper to hire it out in one go than on a day-by-day basis, and it's as my father keeps telling me —it's good business acumen to seek out good deals. As soon as we get back to the hotel, I tell her to go back to her room and get changed while I make some dinner plans.

"Excuse me, mate, could I book one of the tables on the beach for dinner tonight?" I ask the man at the concierge desk. He looks at me like I've got three heads and chuckles.

"I'm afraid it's a bit late for reservations, sir."

I shrug my shoulders and slide over five hundred Bermudian dollars, watching as he nods with understanding and his fingers suddenly type a bit faster. He smiles at me every few seconds and finally picks up the phone to make a call. I bite back my grin when I hear him ask for a beach table for two in thirty minutes, telling the person on the other side it's urgent and for a very important guest.

"What name will this be under?"

"Jackson," I tell him.

"Yes, the reservation is for Mr. Jackson."

I don't correct him. It's all part of the act I must keep up so I can play Jade's game. I can't help but wonder what her real name is. Whilst I like the name Jade, in my mind, it doesn't really suit her. She feels more like a Jennifer, Sarah, or a Heather.

"You're all set," he says as he hangs up the phone. "Follow the path until you see the tiki torches. It'll be you and another couple, but you'll have the utmost privacy."

"Thanks, mate, really appreciate it."

"Hopefully she says yes," he says before I walk away.

"Me too," I say, allowing the lie to fall out easily. I'm not asking Jade to marry me. I'm going all out on the romance because she deserves it. There has only been one other time I've considered marrying someone, and that lasted all of five minutes. We found ourselves in a situation we both needed to get out of. After a long talk, we both agreed marriage wasn't right for either of us so we went our separate ways and remained friends. And yet, it's so easy for me to talk about it now. I'm not sure if it's because it's just a game or something else.

But he does give me an idea. Whilst we were at lunch yesterday, some geezer hit on Jade and when I said something to him, he made a comment about my wife not wearing a wedding ring. It made me think if we need to be convincing, then she needs one. Besides, it will also be a thank you to show her how grateful I am she agreed to this little charade.

I walk into the jewellery store in the hotel lobby, the bell ringing out once as I enter, getting the attention of the solitary sales person working behind the counter.

"Can I help you?"

"I'm hoping so. I'm looking for a ring. Something simple, elegant, but not at all flashy."

"A diamond engagement ring?"

I shake my head. "No, it's for a friend, but..." I trail off, looking into the glass display cabinets, spotting a sapphire sparkling under the light. "Could I see this one please?" I ask, pointing it out to the assistant.

"Yes, of course." She takes the ring out and hands it to me. "The band is platinum with two quarter-carat round diamonds and interwoven prongs. It's really the perfect engagement ring."

It is perfect, but that's not the reason why I want it. The blue reminds me of here, a place I don't want her to forget. Plus, it's a present, a token of my appreciation, even though the situation doesn't exactly call for it.

"I'll take it." I hand it back to her, take out my credit card, and we complete the transaction. The shop assistant hands me a bag, tied in a pink bow. I decide I'll give the ring to Jade at dinner, so I take the black velvet box out of all its delicate packaging and put it in my pocket. "Thanks for your help," I tell the assistant as I leave the shop.

Clearly, it isn't my lucky day. I spot the triplets waiting by the lift doors as I walk around the corner. They spot me instantly, meaning I can't turn and walk the other way. I could walk past them on the pretence I'm on my way somewhere else, but that would mean I'd run the risk of being late for dinner with Jade. I still need to have a shower and get changed.

"Lucky meeting you here," one of them says. The names Jade gave them, Muffy, Tuffy and Buffy sit on the tip of my tongue, but I hold back on using them because the last thing I want is to give the impression that by giving them nicknames, I'm showing any kind of interest, when I'm not.

"Small hotel," I say, shoving my hands in my pockets.

"Where's your wife?" asks another one.

I tilt my head up, indicating she's upstairs.

"Is she really your wife?" the third asks me.

"What makes you think she isn't?"

The third shrugs. "You were letting us touch you," she says, stepping closer to me. "And she didn't say anything."

Ah crap, she has me there. "She trusts me."

"No woman who has a man that looks like you trusts them," the one in the middle says.

I'm dreading getting into the lift with them, but I don't have a choice. When the bell dings and the door opens, I do the gentlemanly thing and put my arm out, allowing them to get in first. They press the button for their floor, and quick thinking tells me to get off on the floor before theirs. I press the button for the second floor and wait by the door. The ride up is painless and when I get out, the one who was with Jade and I the other day mumbles, making me smile. I can only imagine she's explaining to the others what she saw so she doesn't sound like she's lying.

Looking left then right, I find the sign for the stairs and head up, climbing a few flights before I get to my floor. I peek around the door to see for any signs of the triplets hanging around. Seeing that the coast is clear, I walk through and go to my room.

As soon as I open the door, I can smell Jade's perfume

permeating through the air. I stay on my side of the wall even though I'm tempted to walk through and see her.

"Give me a few secs and I'll be ready," I tell her.

"Okay," she yells back.

Turning on the shower, I quickly disrobe and hop in, before having possibly one of the quickest showers of my life. I think about dressing in a suit, but I don't want to overdo it with dressing up and be uncomfortable. With my towel tied around my waist, I stand in the doorway that divides our room, hoping to catch a glimpse of what Jade is wearing.

As soon as I see her, I quickly regret my decision. Her back faces me and as she puts in some earrings. Her hair is curled in loose waves and a white dress shows off her sun-kissed skin. I walk back into my room and rummage through my wardrobe, pulling out a dark purple shirt and another pair of tailored black shorts.

Running the towel over my head to dry my hair, I stare at myself in the mirror. My five o'clock shadow is starting to show which means I probably should have shaved, but it's too late now. Instead, I put on some aftershave and put the black velvet ring box into the pocket of my shorts before heading back to her room.

Jade is on the balcony, leaning over the railing. My whole body is overcome with desire to touch her, to press my groin into her backside and say, 'Let's fucking ditch dinner.' But I don't want to be that type of man so instead, I kiss her shoulder and she leans into me.

"You smell good," she says as she nuzzles my neck. If she keeps this up, the pile of cash I gave the concierge earlier tonight will be for nothing.

"We should go," I say, clearing my throat. She gathers herself together and smiles.

"You're right or we won't leave."

My head shakes slowly. "No, we won't."

I have never experienced this much sexual tension before. It's oozing out and teasing us. I'll be surprised if we make it through dinner at this rate. We hold hands as we make our way out of our room and down the hall. I tell her about running into the triplets and the weird questions they asked me.

"They know we're kidding."

They won't after I put that ring on her finger. I think to myself.

"In which case, we should try harder." I pull her in for a quick kiss, only stopping when the lift arrives. Thankfully, the lift is full of other couples, ensuring I'll keep my hands to myself for the duration of the ride.

When we get down to the lobby, I follow the instructions I was given earlier. As soon as we get to the sand, we take off our shoes and hand them to the maître 'd.

"I have a reservation for Jackson," I tell him and he nods and asks us to follow him. There's another couple already at one of the tables, but the concierge was right. We have an ample amount of privacy. The maître 'd pours our champagne and tell us he'll be back shortly.

"I'd like to propose a toast," I say, picking up my flute. Jade does the same, holding hers out towards me. "To an uncommon way of meeting people."

"And doing so with no regrets."

Unfortunately, I have no choice but to tap my glass to hers. I hate she added the bit about no regrets. I'm regretting the whole thing right now because something deep inside me tells me Jade and I would get along very well outside our fantasy world, yet she's adamant we keep on lying to each other. I can only hope that by the end of the week, she's changed her mind. It's been a day and half and I'm already willing to tell her everything.

I don't know if there's a right time to give a present like the one I've bought her, but I take the box out of my pocket and put it in the middle of the table. "I bought you something."

"You didn't have to do that, Jackson."

"I know, but I wanted to."

I hold my breath as I watch her lift the lid of the box. Her mouth falls open and I'm almost certain her eyes glaze over with tears, but it's dark out here and the only light we have is coming from the candles and torches around us. I can't be one hundred percent sure. She covers her mouth with her hand as she looks up at me.

"Jackson, I can't accept this."

I knew she'd say something asinine. I reach for the box and take the ring out, holding it up as if I'm inspecting it. My other hand holds hers and I quickly slip it on her ring finger. "I didn't ask you if you'd accept it. It's a gift, not a negotiation. I saw it and I thought of you. So, I want you to have it." I hold up her hand and admire the ring. It's gorgeous, but it pales in comparison to her beauty.

"Jackson... I don't know what to say."

"Say you'll keep it. Say you'll wear it and you will think about me whenever you look at it."

"I don't think I'll ever forget you," she says. I know exactly what she means. I won't forget her, even though for my own sanity, I'm going to try.

"Thank you." She leans closer to me and I do the same. I wait for her to kiss me and when she does, there's an explosion of want and desire that shoots straight through me. Dinner can't end fast enough and it hasn't even started yet.

Throughout our meal, we flirt with each other. We steal

kisses, hold hands, and play footsy under the table. Our conversation is light. We joke, tell fabricated stories, and feed each other mouthfuls of food from our plates. And every so often, I catch her looking down at her hand, admiring her ring, and all I can think about is having her naked in my arms and the ring leaving an indentation in my back while I move inside her.

On our way back to our room, she presses against my side and places small kisses along my neck. I can't get us to the room fast enough, and when I finally reach my door, I fumble with my key. It takes me two or three attempts before the door finally opens.

We step inside and everything freezes. As the door slams, we both jump and for some reason—nerves maybe—I look over at it, making sure it's shut properly even though I know it is. When I look back at Jade, she's standing in front of me, with the light from the moon illuminating her. That's all I need to spur myself into action.

With each step I take in her direction, I undo one of the buttons on my shirt. Each stride towards her moves her nearer to the wall, which is the perfect spot in my opinion. I throw my shirt onto the floor and quickly unbutton my shorts, giving my already hard cock the freedom it needs to move.

"Do you want this?" I ask, as I push the straps of her dress off her shoulders.

"Yes. Do you?" she throws my question right back at me. I take her hand and brush it over my dick through the fabric of my shorts.

"What do you think, love?" I don't give her a chance to answer. My hand dives into her hair as my mouth meets hers. There are no gentle kisses, to begin with, no peck on the lips. This is determined and dominating, almost savage even. I push my tongue deep into her mouth, tasting the remnants of the champagne we drank earlier. Her hands rest on my chest, brushing over the hard abs of my stomach and reaching into my shorts, pushing them and my boxers down, and releasing my aching hard-on. She strokes me, spreading the pre-cum around my shaft as my hips move instinctively.

She's not wearing a bra under her white dress. Her nipples are in hard peaks and begging for my mouth and hands to tease and pleasure them. Except I don't just yet. Instead, I cup her breasts and brush my thumbs over her nipples as I look at her. Jade's eyes are hooded. Her lips are glistening wet and plump. I glance down at her hand, stroking my dick and then look back at her, keeping eye contact until my mouth finally descends and takes a whole one of her breasts.

Her head slams back into the wall as she arches her back enabling me to get a better angle. I pay equal and full attention to both her breasts, until I can't bear it anymore and must touch her. My hand moves down her side, and she parts her legs, giving me all the access I need, and she desires. I search for her knickers and find she isn't wearing any, causing me to pause for a few seconds and look at her. There's a wicked glint in her eye as she lets go of my dick, allowing me to pull her dress up and over her head. "Naughty girl," I say as my thumb and finger part her lips. She's so wet and cries out as I brush my finger over her already swollen clit. It's safe to say dinner was a ruse. We both used it as an excuse to prolong the inevitable. "Fuck, you're so wet, Jade." My finger slips into her easily. She rocks her hips forward and reaches for my dick. The rhythm of us moving is unbearable.

"Oh, God," she cries out as I slip another finger into her.

I want to make sure she's ready for me. Our first time isn't going to be easy. It's going to be fast, rough, and unforgettable.

"Fuck, love. I want you so badly."

Those words must do something to her because she turns around and leans over the table, showing me her backside. I slap it hard and rub my hand over the burn to ease the sting. Bending over slightly, I part her lips and marvel at her glistening pussy. She's so completely aroused and waiting for me to fuck her right now.

I scramble for a condom and ensure it's firmly in place. "Are you sure you want it like this?" I ask as I line myself up, pushing the head in slightly. "We have two beds we can fuck on," I tell her, pushing in a little more.

"Here." She looks at me over her shoulder as she leans up on her elbows and watches me intently as I enter her. My eyes roll back in my head in sheer delight as I take her deeply. "Oh, fuck," she squeaks out.

My hips start moving, thrusting slowly with the pressure building quickly. My balls slap both her and the table as I grip her hips. Her cries are mixed with my moans as the scent of sex fills the room.

"Ah, fuck, love. I'm going to come." It's a warning I don't think she needs, but I give it to her anyway. I look down and watch my dick disappear into her, loving every minute of her fucking me.

"I'm close." I'll make sure this is the only time she will ever need to tell me this. I make a promise to myself that I'm going to memorise every inch of her body. I reach around and seek out her clit, massaging it until her soft cries become louder and her movements become more frantic. I don't give a fuck if people can hear her right now.

"Jackson! Oh, God!" she screams out my name as we

continue to fuck, waiting for her to come all over my dick. Fuck, I want to feel her squeeze my dick until she's taken everything I have in me.

Her walls clamp around me and her body shudders. That's enough for me to unload into her. Each wave of pleasure is met with a deep, guttural groan. My fingers dig into her flesh as I ride out the last wave of my orgasm.

I collapse on top of her, breathing heavily. I had a feeling sex with her would be different, but I had no idea it would feel like I was having a heart attack.

ELEVEN

Jade

———

*T*he definition of sexcation: when you go on vacation and have copious amounts of sex with strangers. Jackson isn't a stranger and I can't quantify what copious means. I'm not intending on having sex with anyone else while I'm here.

Once we crossed the imaginary line, there was no turning back or stopping for that matter. Not that I want to, although my body may beg to differ. Every part of me is sore —my toes, fingers, knees, jaw, and every piece of flesh and bone in between. This is the first time in my life I can say I have been thoroughly fucked, and know what I have been missing all these years. It's amazing, the way I feel, when I have a partner who knows what he's doing and can do it well.

I think there isn't anything Jackson can't do well. His kisses make me weak. His touch sends shivers down my spine, and the way his body moves while inside of me... I don't think the word has been invented for the way he makes me feel.

And when I think he's sated, he wants more. And when

I think I can't possibly go again, I mount him and take over, showing him I'm not the frigid woman my ex told me I am. As much as I don't want to think about my ex, the thought of him makes me smile in a mocking way. I am not the same woman I was when we were together. Hell, I'm not even the same person I was when I arrived here a few days ago. From the moment Jackson kissed me, I started changing.

Jackson pushes the room service cart into the middle of his room and prepares our lunch. "Do we want to eat on the balcony?" I ask, pushing the blanket away from my bare chest. He pauses and looks at me.

"Not if it means you have to put some clothes on and cover up your glorious body."

"I can't eat naked." I point to the plate in his hand. It's a cheeseburger and I don't want to get hot grease anywhere near my chest.

Jackson frowns and sets the plate down. He runs his hand through his hair, making my fingers itch to do the same thing. "Okay, but only if you put this on." He bends down and picks up his shirt from last night. He helps me dress and only buttons the mid-section, leaving me rather exposed.

"What about you?" I point to the boxers he's wearing.

He smirks and shakes his head. "Shall I put your dress on?"

I laugh and climb out of bed, only to have to sit on the edge for a minute.

"I've worn you out, love." He cups my face and kisses me softly. I'm torn when he pulls away. I want him again, but my stomach needs sustenance.

"It's the best kind of feeling."

Jackson smiles and helps me stand. I follow him out onto the terrace where he tells me to sit while he prepares our plates. Instead, I look out to the ocean and watch the surfers ride the waves. The water looks calm and inviting.

"Do you want to go down there after lunch?" he asks. His hands grab the rail and his lips press against my neck. I can't help but wonder if there's a dual meaning behind his question.

Last night, the first time between us was rushed. The sexual tension had been building from the moment we met and when it finally came to fruition, the foreplay was minimal. Jackson and I both made up for that throughout the night and into the morning, exploring each other greedily in bed, in the shower, on the floor, and up against the wall. I have never been a fan of oral sex and I quickly realized why when Jackson went down on me. My previous experiences were rough and painful, but with Jackson... the way he licked and sucked made me feel like a goddess. As if I was someone who needed to be worshipped.

I chuckle and tilt my head into his. I can feel him smiling against my skin. "Naughty girl," he says, making me believe he in fact left the innuendo hanging in the air. "Let's have something to eat, love."

Jackson takes my hand and leads me the few steps to the table. By now I'm sure our food is cold, but that isn't going to matter. My stomach growls loudly, enough to catch Jackson's attention. I shrug when he looks at me.

"This is decent," I say, after taking a bite. It's not the best, but I'm not complaining. We had ordered breakfast as well, but were busy when they brought the cart to our door. By the time we finished, the eggs were solid rubber and the cold toast was too hard to eat.

"Pfft, I can do a much better job," he says.

"Oh yeah? Do you like to cook?"

Jackson nods. "Yes, I do, if I have someone to cook for. Most of the time, I get a takeaway because it's easier."

"I tried meal planning once, but by mid-week, I was so bored with what I had laid out. I wing it. See how I'm feeling."

"So you go food shopping a lot?"

Wiping my face, I fold my napkin back into my lap. "Every three days or so. Sometimes I'll make a big meal on Sunday and freeze the rest for the end of the week."

"Do you live by yourself?" he asks.

"Is this our one truth for the day?"

He nods. "Yeah, I guess it is, although that doesn't really give me much information about you."

"True, but no I share an apartment with my best friend."

Jackson picks up his water glass and downs the contents. "You can ask me something if you want." He gives me free rein to invade his privacy. There has been something on my mind since early this morning when I could finally see the tattoo on his other arm.

Taking a deep breath, I ask him, "Who is Sian?"

His eyes land on mine. They're sharp and seem to darken. Immediately, I feel like I've crossed the imaginary line we've placed between us. I shake my head. "Never mind, you don't have to tell me."

Jackson sets his napkin down on the table and leans back in the chair. He reminds me of the cocky businessman behind the aviators I first encountered. "It's not what you think," he says. "I don't normally talk about it because no-one really asks."

"It's fine, Jackson." I stand and pick up the silverware and condiments so I can place them back on the tray. He grabs my wrist and pulls me toward him until I'm sitting on his lap. He cups my cheek, pulling my face to his until our lips are touching. It's soft, sweet, and a diversion tactic. It shouldn't matter, but it does. He told me I could ask, I did, and now he's avoiding the question. "I'm sorry for intruding," I whisper against his lips. Surprisingly, he smiles before pulling away.

"You didn't. I said you could ask me anything and I meant it. I just wasn't expecting you to ask me *that*. It's fine, I'm happy to tell you." Jackson adjusts himself, sitting up a bit straighter, while clutching my hip in his hand. "Sian was my daughter."

"Was?"

He nods. "She was stillborn. The cord was wrapped around her neck and by the time her mum realized she wasn't moving, it was too late."

I know I don't know Jackson well yet, but I still shed tears for his loss. He wipes them away with the pads of his thumbs and kisses me lightly.

"Sssh, it's okay; don't cry, love."

"I... I'm so sorry."

"So am I. I really liked the idea of being a dad, but it just wasn't meant to be."

"Were you with her mother for long?"

He shakes his head. "No, not really. When she told me she was pregnant, we tried to make a go of it, but it didn't work out. I was there for her, though. I went to all her doctor appointments. My mum threw a big baby shower for her. My parents were both excited. We... Sian's mum and I were happy. We were adamant we would be the best parents ever even though we weren't together..." he trails off.

There isn't anything I can say to make things different for him. I put my arms around his shoulders and hug him.

His hold on my hip changes as his arms wrap around me. I regret asking him about the name on his arm and wish I could take it back, but the damage is done. Our happy mood is now somber thanks to my nosiness.

"Do you want to head down to the beach?" he asks as his lips ghost over my skin. Goosebumps rise, causing me to shiver. Jackson chuckles. "Or I can carry you back into the bedroom and finish my lunch by feasting on you."

"How is a woman to decide?"

"Simple, let the man make the decision for her."

I squeal as he picks me up. I expect him to toss me onto the bed, but he doesn't. He sets me down gently in front of the closet in my room. "Put your swimming costume on," he suggests. "Let's go and sunbathe by the pool."

Jackson disappears into his bedroom while I scramble to put my suit on. I stand in front of the mirror and look at my reflection. I have razor burn and my lips are swollen. I lean forward and really look at my breast, pulling my suit down a bit to get a better look. I gasp and quickly pull the fabric over to hide the blemish.

"All set?" Jackson appears in the doorway. I turn and glare at him, watching as his face falls. "What's wrong, love?"

"This," I say, yanking the cup over to expose my breast. He licks his lips and smiles.

"You don't like your tits?"

"No, you gave me a hickey!"

Jackson steps into the bathroom and cups my center. "I gave you one here too, but no one will see that one, except me." He continues to rub his finger up and down, knowing he's turning me on. He holds my gaze as he slowly descends toward my breast. His mouth covers my nipple. His teeth pull on the sensitive flesh as my hand pushes into his air. I don't care if I'm sore, or my body aches. I want him and he knows it.

Except, he doesn't give in to what I want. He pulls away and covers my breast. "I'm sorry I marked you here," he says, kissing my flesh. "But not here." He trails his fingers over my now wet core once again. "And rest assured, I'm going to do it again tonight."

"Promise?" I ask.

He chuckles. "I guarantee it, love."

I sigh, wishing we could stay in the room, but I have the impression he wants to sit on the beach for a while. I excuse myself and pull on my cover-up, grab my giant hat and my bag that holds just about everything I need. Jackson waits for me at the door and holds my hand the entire way down to the beach. We're lucky enough to find a nice wide space for us to set up chairs.

"I'm going for a quick swim." He kisses me quickly before jogging toward the water. I can't take my eyes off him. Everything about him seems perfect, and I suppose it should since we're on vacation and playing a stupid game. After last night, I wonder what his reaction would be if I said I wanted to call the whole game off. Would he be willing? Or would that be the end of us, as we both know it? I'm in the situation where I want both. I want to know the real him and continue to live in this fantasy world we've created. Yet the thought scares me that he may not like the person I am. The "me" he sees now is because of him and the game. I can be anyone I want and he'd never know the difference. At home, I am nothing like I am now, and the thought that I have to go back to being her next week really dampens my spirits.

TWELVE

Jackson

---

*M*y hands are tangled in Jade's hair, gripping the fine blonde and brown strands as I guide her while she sucks me off. My head falls back in a combination of agony and desire as Jade massages my balls. The feeling of them being rolled between her fingers is fucking fantastic. My jaw clenches as the pressure builds, preparing for undoubtedly what will be a massive orgasm.

Jade looks up, her eyes full of lust and need. Hopefully she knows that as soon as I get her back to the hotel room, I'm going to take good care of her. I'm to going spread her out on the bed and have an absolute feast on her, treating her as if she was my last supper. We spent most of yesterday shagging and lying by the sea, and I had promised her that today we'd do some more sightseeing. Leaving the hotel was the only way that would guarantee me keeping my hands off her. Since we've consummated our fake marriage, everything she does turns me on.

And that fact scares the crap out of me. I have never felt this kind of connection to anyone before. I can't get enough with Jade. I have no idea if it's her personality or the fact that my heart beats a thousand times faster than normal when she walks into the room. I felt it the second I saw her in the hotel reception, and I cursed the lucky bastard with her until I realised she was alone.

Then to find out our rooms were next door to each other was a bloody blessing. I honestly couldn't have planned it any better. It was then that I knew I would do anything I possibly could to ensure that I could meet her. It was pure fate she was on the other side of the pool when I needed an excuse to escape.

But fuck if she's killing me with this game of hers. Of course, I agreed to play along because it gave me an excuse to spend time with her. After our first kiss, there wasn't a hope in hell I would let her go.

And, four days into our holiday, we aren't letting the other out of our sight. I couldn't have planned this better if I tried. From day one, I was looking to have a little fun, a little bit of action, but now I've found myself too far into this situation and I don't know how to get out of it. I want to call it quits and tell her I don't want to play this game anymore. I want to come clean and tell her exactly who I am, what I do for a living, and learn every single thing about her. I want to say fuck my flat and my home back in England. I'll follow her wherever she goes, but I'm afraid if I come on too strong, I'll scare her off, and quite frankly, I'd rather have her for the rest of the week then have nothing at all.

You can tell me I'm under the thumb. You can say I'm an idiot for having the clichéd holiday romance, but I'm not stupid. I know that once we leave our little bubble of paradise, nothing will happen and we won't see each other again. Not unless, I can find out everything about her and find a way for us to keep in touch.

When she asked me who Sian was, I thought I would

get up and leave. My daughter is off limits. I don't ever talk about her. Even though Sian's mum and I weren't together when she was born, I loved my daughter as she was being nurtured in her mother's belly. I revelled in that I would be a dad and losing her absolutely broke my heart, holding her limp body in my arms tore me to smithereens. I'm ashamed to admit I didn't handle it very well at the time and went on a twenty-four-hour bender, drowning my sorrows and heartache in booze. I begged Sian's mum if we could try again and replace the baby we had lost. Thankfully, she was more realistic than I was at the time and told me in no uncertain terms to fuck off. In hindsight, she was right. Her loss was far greater, more physical than mine. She felt Sian kicking her all the time, where I was just an outsider. I was not the hands-on father to be that you'd imagine. I didn't attend any of the pre-natal classes. And now, the only date we have contact with each other is on the anniversary of Sian's birth. I send her flowers and she calls to thank me. She's married now, and once confided in me that she's scared to get pregnant again because of what happened with Sian. I wish there was something I could do for her that could help her to move on.

The feeling of my balls tightening brings me back to the here and now, to the place where this beautiful woman who I'm enamoured with is sucking me off because she was horny and couldn't wait until we got back to the hotel. There was no way in hell I would've said no.

When she sat next to me at the table, instead of opposite me, I knew something was wrong. We had been sightseeing all day, stopping at some small shops along the way, and when she tried on a new swimming costume, she allowed me to join her in the dressing room. Of course, I took full advantage of the situation and had my wicked way with her breasts. She got me back when we went for a quick dip in the sea, as she grinded against me. It was when we were on the scooter, though, when she really drove me insane with her wandering hands, making sure she pressed them against my groin. I had half the mind to take her back to the hotel right there and then, but we're in Bermuda and it wouldn't be a proper holiday if we didn't at least make the effort to see some of the famous landmarks. That's the story I'm going to keep telling myself, at least.

But as soon as we walked into the restaurant and sat down at our table, she turned up the heat and nibbled on my ear whilst her fingers swiftly undid my shorts. I told her if she wasn't careful, I would take her into the bathroom and teach her a lesson she'd never forget. She told me I was talking crap, or bullshit as she called it.

And now, here we are, with her on her knees, giving me the best blowjob I've ever had. I untangle one of my hands from her hair and lean against the wall for some stability.

"I'm going to cum, love." The other night, I found out she was not a fan of swallowing so it's only fair I respect her wishes and give her warning. It doesn't bother me in the slightest. I know she'll happily wank me off and finish the job.

As she sucks harder, I can see her cheeks hollow. "Ahhh," I grunt out as the pressure builds some more. My hips move by themselves as they find their rhythm while I fuck her mouth. "Now!" I pull myself from her mouth. Jade stays crouched down, stroking my dick. The hot spurts of cum land on the wall behind her, while some dribbles down her hand.

When the last aftershock is done, she stands and kisses me. "You better clean that up," she says, pointing to the wall behind her. I laugh. Not because she's right, but let's face it, no one wants to walk into a public toilet and find the remnants of another bloke's pleasure as evidence on the wall.

Jade hands me a bunch of tissues, and I quickly clean the wall as she washes her hands. We're in a unisex bathroom at the back of a restaurant that's located in a hole in the wall. To be honest, it's not what I'd call my preferred choice but it has the best clam chowder in the area and we'd be fools not to try it. That was our thinking when we ordered it, but we've been notably absent from our table for quite some time and I have no doubt the soup will probably be stone cold by the time we sit back down again.

I stand behind Jade as she fixes her hair in the mirror. I'm taller than she by a full head, my skin is more tanned compared to her lighter, almost pale colouring, but her tan lines are visible and I have the urge to lick along them until I reach the place on her body I dream of the most.

She's so incredibly beautiful with her green eyes, long lashes, and pink cheeks. Jade watches me as I look at her in the mirror. I like seeing us together like this and once more, I find the words suggesting we stop this charade on the tip of my tongue. I so badly want to us both to come clean about who we are, but I have too much to risk. Losing her would ruin everything.

"They probably thought we dined and ditched." I hear what she's saying, but I can't take my eyes off her. She turns around to face me, her fingers brushing over my stubble. "Jackson, are you okay? Wasn't it good?"

Her voice is full of worry and I know it's due to her toad of an ex, making her believe she's frigid. He's a fucking bellend. Jade's so far removed from frigid it's ridiculous. I know it's easy, though, to believe the negatives than the positives. Those criticisms stay in your mind long after the harsh words are said.

My lips brush softly against hers. She falls into my embrace as I draw her into my arms. The last thing I want to do is let her go, but I know I should answer her questions. Thing is, I don't know which one I want to answer truthfully.

"I'm fine, love." I kiss her nose to reassure her, and then realise men hate it when women say they're fine; we all know it's code and they are anything but fine. "Actually, I'm really good. I'm here with you and that blowjob was bloody amazing. Best I've ever had."

She looks at me warily; probably because she's about to tell me I'm full of bollocks. Jade opens her mouth to say something, but closes it quickly.

"Come on, let's go see if we still have our table."

As soon as I open the door, I find a woman standing there. She rolls her eyes and mumbles something in Italian I can't understand. In fact, as soon as we walk out of the bathroom, I notice there's quite a queue of people waiting in turn. One man slaps me on my shoulder when I walk past him, but it's the women who snigger.

The table we previously had now has people sitting at it. I feel a little bad we ordered our food but didn't eat it, but I don't regret a single second of it. It was totally worth it. Jade and I pay the bill, taking an ear bashing from the owner about doing "stuff" in the bathroom and leave with our tails between our legs.

"That was the first time I have ever done something like that in a public place," Jade tells me as she puts her helmet on.

"Technically, we really weren't in public." I climb onto the scooter. Before I start it, I turn and look at her from over my shoulder. "But if you want to scratch it off your bucket list, I'm more than happy to take you somewhere public and shag you senseless."

She slaps my shoulder, but it's the look in her eyes that tells me she's not too opposed to my suggestion. She may be trying to be coy, but I know her better than she thinks.

"Why don't you think about it?"

"I don't want sand in... well, in places it shouldn't be," she tells me. I'd normally agree, but there are ways to avoid it. Plus, who said it had to be a beach? I'm sure I could find plenty of other public places that would suffice.

"We can get a cabana. Wait until the sun sets. We don't even have to be naked, if you're not comfortable with the idea."

Her cheeks turn rosy red with a furious blush and I know I'm going to get lucky under the stars tonight. That thought alone makes me want to head back to the hotel, but the day isn't done and I have other plans for us. First, given our last attempt of eating wasn't successful, we need to find food, and I'm really hoping word hasn't gotten around there are a couple of tourists who have a thing for having sex in bathrooms, otherwise we may be out of luck. After we've eaten, we're going to get the Bermuda train. I overheard the concierge telling another couple about it and I thought it would be nice for us to learn some history about the country we're in, not to mention it will give us an opportunity to see the sights.

Traversing through the roads, we find a food stand near the train stop. We sit along the fence while we eat and people watch.

"About the cabana."

"Yeah, what about it?" I pretend it's not a big deal, but

my dick is saying otherwise. He's totally up for some outside fucking.

"We can't get into trouble?"

I shrug. "I don't know. I mean, we probably could, but it's not as if we're going to be out in the wide open with our white arses on display for everyone to see."

"Your ass isn't white. Mine is. It's blinding. The reflection from the sun would probably bounce off my ass and blast someone in the face, making them lose their sight forever."

I laugh so hard I have to put my food down for fear of choking. Jade doesn't seem put off by the fact that I'm cracking up either. "First, love, your arse isn't that white. Secondly, if people are seeing your arse it means you're on top and I like the idea of that. And thirdly, I said we could use a cabana so you don't get sand in that pretty white arse of yours." I wink at her, which makes her laugh. "Sex in the cabana could be fun."

"Yeah, I think we should do it."

"Yeah?"

Jade nods. "Why the hell not? We have nothing to lose, right?"

Nope, nothing at all.

"I'll make the arrangements as soon as we get back to the hotel."

THIRTEEN

Jade

—————

*J*ackson said to meet him in the lobby, telling me I had to be dressed and ready for the day. Two days ago, he promised me cabana sex, but has yet to deliver. I don't know if he's playing some game or what, but the more I think about having a public sexcapade, the more excited I become.

Except, my excitement wanes when I think about my time here coming to an end. Not because my vacation will be over, but the bubble I've been living in will burst and it'll be back to reality for me. The person I am at home is nothing like the persona I've created. Here, I don't care who judges me because the likelihood is I'll never see them again, especially Jackson.

"Good, you're ready," Jackson says as he rushes into the foyer of the lobby. He looks winded, like he's been out running.

Ah, the sight of him running is probably a glorious thing. I often stare out my office window and watch men run down the streets. During the summer, they're kind enough to take their shirts off to give us lonely hearts a nice show.

I used to think about joining a gym to meet someone, but the thought of getting up at the crack of dawn doesn't appeal to me and by the time I'm off work, I'd rather go home and eat dinner. The winters are the worst though. I've been known to pack on the pounds, my winter fat, because I can barely find the energy to get on my treadmill.

"Yes, of course, I'm ready. Why do you look so peaked?"

"Peaked?"

"Your cheeks are flushed. Either you've been exerting yourself or you're up to no good."

Jackson chuckles and takes my hand. "I'm always up to no good where you're concerned. Come on, let's go. We have big plans today."

Do those plans happen to include a cabana? I answer my own question when he slips my helmet on. Once he's on the scooter, I climb behind him and hold the bag he told me to pack between us. I hate the bag. It's preventing me from feeling him pressed against me, which honestly has become my favorite thing about being with him.

All right, I have many favorite things. If I had to make a list, it would be about a mile long. Jackson embodies everything I would look for in a man, if I were looking, and if he was real. It's easy to be everything someone desires when you're pretending.

I used to play make believe when I was younger. I think almost everyone did, but sometimes I took it to extremes, creating a whole new family because I was ashamed of my father's business. I regret ever having those thoughts like and if my parents knew, they would be hurt. Now, as an adult, I know my family was doing whatever they had to do put food on the table. I also never understood why we lived in such a small apartment until my parents paid cash for my college education. It all made sense then.

"Where are we going?"

"You'll find out soon enough." He pulls away from the hotel and into traffic. When I arrived, I hadn't made any plans to sightsee. I thought I would sit by the pool or on the beach and read, maybe do some people watching, but Jackson had other plans. Honestly, I'm thankful I met him. Not because of the sex, but for the companionship of having someone to hang out with. Even if we hadn't taken our relationship to the next level, my time here would be amazing.

Jackson pulls up to the docks where ships in all sizes are stationed. He parks and waits for me to get off the scooter. Still, he doesn't say anything as he leads me down the pier. We come to a yacht. It's not the biggest on the ocean, but larger than others.

"Ladies first." He holds my hand as I step onto the dock.

"What are we doing?" Jackson follows behind on board and motions for me to walk toward the back and directs me inside. The small space is open with a kitchenette, dining room and living room with a television. It's cozy and welcoming.

"Good, we have everything we need," he says, opening the refrigerator.

"For what exactly?"

He comes over to me and takes my bag, setting it down so he can pull me into his arms. "I was thinking there were things I wanted us to do together, but haven't had a chance yet, so I rented this boat for us. We're going to sail around for the day. Maybe drop the anchor and go swimming." He leans in and kisses me. "And most important, find somewhere secluded so I can give you the things I promised." He whispers into my ear.

"Sex on the beach with no cabana?"

"And on the deck, in this room, in the bedroom. Most important of all, if you want to walk around naked, you can do so because we will be out in the middle of the sea and no one will see you."

"We won't be the only ones out there." I point out.

"That's true, but unless we're right next to them or they have binoculars, they won't see anything." He tucks my hair behind my ear and tilts his head a bit to the side. "Besides, if I have my wicked way, being worried about walking around naked will be the last thing on your mind."

"I didn't bring condoms," I tell him. We've been very safe and made sure to always stay protected.

"It's a good thing I did then. Don't worry, love, there isn't any danger we'll run out." He winks.

"Well, I'm out of arguments." I throw my hands up with a smile. "I win no matter what if I get to watch you walk around naked."

"That's the spirit. Oh and in case I didn't mention it before, I'm planning on having sex with you *everywhere*."

"So you've said."

Jackson smiles and rubs his hands together. "You'll never look at the captain's chair in the same way once we're done." He disappears outside before I can even fathom a response. I do like the thought of lying out without my suit on though, but walking around naked on the deck really isn't appealing, although I'll do it because he's asked me to.

"Do you need any help?" I call out as he passes by.

"No, love. Make yourself comfortable."

I do as he suggests and make us a quick breakfast. I'm starving and unless he ate while he was making arrangements, he should be too. In the refrigerator, I find a few bottles of wine and champagne, but also a mix of other beverages and a huge assortment of food. There will be no going hungry on this trip, that's for sure.

I whip up some eggs, sausage, hash browns, and toast to go with a pitcher of mimosas. Might as well start our morning off right. With it all stacked onto the tray, I carry it out and find us floating away from the dock. In fact, we're floating away from the island.

"Jackson?" I call out, hopeful he's on the boat.

"Up here, love."

Leaving the tray on the deck, I climb the steep steps to the top and instantly get lost in the view. "Oh, wow."

"Takes your breath away, doesn't it?"

"It's gorgeous, but shouldn't the motor be running?"

"It is running."

"I guess I expected to feel it."

Jackson motions for me to come over to where he is. He positions me behind the steering wheel and places my hand on the shifter-looking thing. "Pull it down gently," he says, guiding my hand. We start to go faster, putting more distance between the island and us. People wave, and I find myself waving back.

"I made breakfast. Let me go get it." I move as fast as I can down back toward the steps. Carrying the tray up is more difficult than I thought, but I manage to get everything up there after a few trips. After I get everything situated, I pour us both mimosas and take a seat next to Jackson.

"This is delicious, thank you for this," he says, between bites.

"Thank you for it all," I reply. "Seriously, this has been the best vacation of my life."

"It's not over yet."

Except I already feel like it is. Like this is the climax and when we step off this ship, we will have one day left. I can already feel the melancholy seeping in. Our last day will be somber and will end too fast.

"Which way are we heading?" I stand at the steering wheel, looking out over the horizon and the vast sea. Jackson positions himself behind me and starts massaging my shoulders. My muscles loosen almost immediately.

"Towards America. I think one of the Carolina's if I'm not mistaken."

I nod and roll my head back as his finger start kneading the muscles in my neck. "How far until we stop?"

"It shouldn't be too long. We aren't too far from Bermuda." Jackson pulls the two knots on my bikini top and lets it fall to the ground. "Keep going straight," he whispers in my ear as his hands slide through the gaps of my cover-up. He cups my breast and tweaks my nipples, sending shivers down my spine. I lean back into him, rubbing my ass over his hard-on. He groans, nipping and kissing at my neck.

His hand slides down my abdomen and into my swimsuit bottoms. I part my legs slightly to give him better access. Jackson toys with my clit, rubbing it softly. The sensation causes me to rest my body against the steering wheel for support. His other hand tugs at the strings holding the pieces of fabric in place. It falls easily to the deck, making way for Jackson to push his fingers inside of me.

I cry out, only for him to remind to keep the boat straight. Easier said than done, but I'm doing my best, even if I may not be on course anymore.

"I never knew this was one of my fantasies until this moment," he whispers. "This is fucking hot."

His fingers withdraw, causing me to look over my shoulder. His shorts are undone and he's rolling a condom over his shaft. The sight of him excites me, makes me hungry for what we're about to do. The sexual drive I'm experiencing is only because of him, and I can't imagine anyone will ever compete with what I've had. Jackson has ruined me for others.

Jackson guides himself into my core. The feeling is different from our previous times. I feel fuller while he seems to be thicker, harder. My mouth drops open as he pumps into me slowly, as if he's trying to savor the essence of what we're doing. I'm tempted to ask him if can we video-tape us so when I'm alone and missing him, I can watch and pleasure myself. I'm hoping the memories will be enough.

He grabs my hair and increases his rhythm. I'm not quiet and neither is he. The grunts and groans he makes turn me on more and more. I love that it's because of me. That because of what we're doing he feels this way.

"Fuuuuck." He draws the word out as he moves in and out. I can no longer hang on and slip my hands to the ledge in front of me. I can now bend over and the new position has me close to the edge.

"Jackson!" I scream out as my walls constrict around his shaft. "Yes, yes..."

"Fuck, yes," he echoes. He leans into me, growling as his hips move faster, slapping into my backside. He stills and his body shakes before he collapses on top of me. "Christ, that was amazing," he says, out of breath.

"It was." Truly, I'm at a loss for words. It was beyond hot and he's simply the best I've ever had. He knows this and there's some small part of him that loves that fact.

He slips out of me and laughs. "Whoops, we've gone off course, love."

I look him squarely in the eyes and shake my head. "I was doing just fine until I was intruded upon. Damn pirate came on board and took advantage of me."

"This pirate can't resist his beautiful wench."

"The pirate will lose a limb if he's not careful with his wording." I stand there with my hands on my hips.

He steps forward and places his hands over mine. His eyes turn serious. "As long as it's not the limb in the middle, I don't care what you do to me."

"Is that so?"

"It's a fact." He kisses me quickly before turning his attention back to the boat. I stand there for a moment, contemplating what I should say or do, but the possible rejection of telling him how I feel is too much for me to handle.

FOURTEEN

Jackson

I'm fucking shattered. I shouldn't have told Jade I wanted her to walk around naked all day because that's exactly what she's been doing, using her sexy as fuck body to her advantage. Not that she needed to be stark naked; she only had to flutter her eyelashes and that would have been enough for me to succumb to her every wish.

The problem is I can't keep my hands off her. And when my hands are on her, my dick is rock hard. I have never shagged this much in one day. It's a dream come true, except I have absolutely no energy left. I'm pretty sure there was one time when I was just lying on the bed while she did all the hard work. What kind of man does that make me? I should be ashamed of myself, and to be honest, I am. I had a stunning woman on top of me, her gorgeous breasts bouncing up and down, and all I could do was replicate a statue. I deserve to be dumped there and then, maybe thrown overboard and left as food for the sharks.

But sod it. I don't have the willpower to say no to her and I don't even want to try. I only have a few days left with her and I must make the best of it. I want this to be a holiday she remembers for a long time, something she can tell her friends, saying she had the time of her life, even if it wasn't the type of holiday she envisaged when she booked it. It wouldn't surprise me if being with her has ruined any future relationship I may hope to have, she's so unbelievably perfect. I know I don't *know* Jade, but it feels like I do. So what if she hasn't told me what her real name is, and she's not told me what she does for a job. I know everything else about her, right down to what food she does and doesn't like, without her having to say anything.

I've been tempted to have a sneak peek through her belongings, to see if I can find identification like a passport or driver's license, just so I have a means of contacting her in a few months' time. I'd make out that it was a freaky coincidence we ended up at the same supermarket or theatre. At the same time, though, I know I'd be pissed off if she did the same thing to me, and went snooping around in my stuff. I know it's double standards on my part, and I don't know where to start explaining it, especially since keeping in contact with her is something I want. Plus, let's not forget going through someone's belongings on the sly has all the signs of being a stalker written all over it.

I should just bite the bullet and ask her for her details. I should tell her I've an amazing time with her and I don't want this to be the end, and I would love to keep in touch. Of course, that's all good and well except that having a long-distance relationship is the last thing on my mind now and even instigating the possibility of that, especially when I know it's not something I want, would just leave us in a very difficult place in a few months. The fact is, if I'm not able to make a full commitment, I run the risk of the other person resenting, and ultimately, hating me, ruining whatever we have between us as a result. The last thing I want to do is to ruin all our memories from our holiday together. So, I'll keep my mouth shut, my thoughts to myself, and continue along with the plan. So far, it's been working effortlessly, aside from the time we both ran into one of the triplets.

The thing is, though, if I called time on this plan of ours earlier, I wouldn't be sitting here watching Jade as she attempts to do a spot of fishing. I should've known better, by now, to assume she's happy to just hang out and have sex all day. On the contrary, she searched around the cabin and stumbled upon a fishing rod and instruction booklet. Personally, I have absolutely no intention of fishing and am more than happy to sit here and watch her. It's not exactly a bad way to spend my time. So far, she hasn't been lucky enough to catch anything, but it hasn't stopped her from trying.

We've sailed around the entire island, which we've found out doesn't really take long and have found a nice little cove where we dropped the anchor and relaxed for a while. There are a few other boats near ours, which means we're dressed in our beachwear, although Jade's tiny bikini doesn't do anything to curb my imagination. I know every curve of her body. I've committed it to my memory and know exactly what's under the skimpy bit of material. Of course, watching her bend over the railing slightly doesn't do anything to help my imagination from running riot.

When I rented the yacht, I had grand plans for today. We'd sunbathe, shag, eat, shag, swim, shag, sleep, shag, eat... you get the idea. I can confirm we've done the shag part. In fact, I think we've pretty much become experts at it. Besides being completely exhausted, I'm also famished. It feels like I haven't eaten in days, which is probably the reason why my energy levels are at an all-time low.

With some effort, I finally move my arse from the sun lounger and walk towards Jade, kissing her on her golden shoulder when I'm near and tasting the sun lotion I've helped her apply repeatedly today. "Mmm, you taste just like the sun." I skim my nose along the back of her neck, inhaling her scent as I go. "And you smell like summer. My favourite," I murmur against her skin.

She leans her head back into mine and sighs. "I thought you were taking a nap?"

"I was trying to, but you were distracting me."

Her hand suddenly moves franticly as she reels in the fishing line until it is dangling in front of her then puts down the rod and pulls me into her arms. "I'm sorry, we can nap together."

"I like the idea of that." I lead her downstairs, below the deck. It's cooler down here but more importantly, there's a bed. The quarters are small with the king-size bed taking up much of the space. Normally, I'd be happy to have one, but our hotel rooms have queens, and it's been nice having her close to me.

Jade and I both undress and crawl into bed, her lying on one side and me on the other. We stay like this for all of two seconds before I'm pulling her towards me. She rolls onto her side and slides right into the curve of my body, fitting perfectly and allowing us to spoon. Of course, my dick rests in the crack of her arse, but thankfully it isn't ready for any action. I nuzzle her, trying to get as close as possible, so desperately needing to feel every inch of her body against mine. Our imminent separation from each other and this island at the end of this holiday will be sheer torture, and it's something I am absolutely dreading as the end draws near.

～

AT SOME POINT, Jade awoke, leaving me to sleep. I know

I shouldn't be mad, but our time is limited and I want to spend every single minute I can with her. If it means we spend the rest of our days here merely sleeping side by side, then so be it. I get up and put on my shorts before going in search for her and find her sitting on the deck wearing a white sundress. Music plays softly, creating the perfect ambience as the sun begins to set. She looks like a goddess, sitting there in the golden rays of the sun.

She turns around and smiles, taking a sip from her wine glass. "I found the wine," she says with a laugh. I pick up the bottle and shake it. There's probably enough left in there for a sip or two, but other than that, it's empty.

"You've started without me, love." I kiss her lightly, tasting the sweet juices of the wine on her lips.

"There's plenty."

Before I can protest, she slips past me and down into the galley, returning with another bottle and a second glass. Handing the bottle over to me, I see she's already opened it, and she holds my glass so I can pour some for myself.

"While you were sleeping, another couple came over."

"Oh yeah? What did they do, swim?"

Jade laughs. "No, silly. They were out sailing and pulled up near us. Anyway, there are fireworks tonight. Did you know?"

I shake my head. "No, I didn't. Do you like them?"

"I do. I don't get to see them often, but I always enjoy them."

"Perfect. Well, in that case, why don't I make us some dinner so we can finish in time to watch them?" I give her a kiss and it doesn't take long for it to turn into something more frenzied. It kills me to step away from her, but I really want the night to go as I had planned. Not that I have any grand plans, but it would be lovely to share a nice meal with her under the moonlight and if there are fireworks going off in the distance, then it really can't get any more romantic.

The music Jade was playing comes through the speakers in the galley. Knowing she's there dancing without me spurs me into action. Usually I would take my time and make sure everything is done meticulously, but I can't wait. Being away from her right now is killing me. There's a proverbial knife stabbing me in the heart—one stab for every second we're apart.

I know when I get on the plane in a few days' time, this is how it will feel. Like my heart is slowly being stabbed to death with the knowledge I won't see her again and once more, I refuse to let my feeling show. The last thing I want to do is to let her know I stopped playing our charade days ago and my feelings are developing into something real. No, in a few days' time, it's going to be business, as usual, the minute I've checked in and boarded my flight.

Dinner takes me forty-five minutes to prepare and during that time, I've set up a table for us, made us a salad to go with our food, and Jade and I have emptied our wine bottle. When she opens a third, I grow weary. I don't want her to be drunk off her head so she can't function. I don't want our night to be ruined.

With the table ready, Jade sits down. I've made sure there's water on the table, hoping she doesn't get upset. When she drinks it, a sense of relief washes through me.

"This looks amazing," she says, of the steak and boiled potatoes I've prepared. I thought about maybe making some kind of vegetable dish, but they always tend to get left to one side.

"Thank you. I did the best I could with the ingredients I could find."

"Honestly, Jackson, everything you've done has been

amazing. You could've made grilled cheese and I would've been happy."

"Ah, so now you tell me you prefer the simple things in life."

Jade smiles, but her expression quickly turns serious. "I am simple. If you saw me outside of here, you wouldn't give me a second glance. When I look at you, I see a man who has the finer things in life. Someone who has the most gorgeous woman on his arm always. That's not me. I'm not glitzy or glamorous. I'm not someone who gets asked out on dates by men who look like you. This week..." Jade pauses. She angrily swipes at her face, wiping away some of her tears. I immediately get up and rush to her side, pulling her into my arms.

"You don't see yourself the way I do, Jade. I saw you in reception when I was checking in and I was insanely jealous of the lucky guy with you. And then I looked around trying to find him and lo and behold he wasn't there. You were standing by yourself. I promised myself I would try to find you later in the day. It was nothing but sheer luck you happened to be in the room next to me. And when I saw you across the swimming pool, I knew that was my chance and I had to make a move. You are exactly the type of woman I want to be with." I kiss her once, pulling away before it gets any more heated, and move back to my side of the table.

I hold her hand as we finish dinner. The silence between us is awkward, and it makes me curious as to whether she would have said all those things if she hadn't been drinking and a little tipsy. Alcohol seems to bring out the best and worst in people, depending on what their trigger is. Clearly, me talking about simple things was enough to send her over the edge.

After dinner, I clear up while she gets the sun lounger ready for the fireworks. When I re-emerge from below deck, I have another bottle of wine in my hands along with two fresh glasses. Jade moves over, so I can slide behind her, and she makes sure my legs are covered with the blanket she picked up downstairs.

"Are you cold, love?"

"I'm perfect." Jade doesn't understand the magnitude behind what she has just said. I think she's flawless and not just on the outside. There isn't one thing I don't like about her.

Well, there is one and it's the fact she suggested this stupid game in the first place. I guess I understand why she did it. She's put me on a pedestal, thinking a guy like me would never be with her. I don't understand it and I'm not even going to try to figure it out.

The firework show isn't one of those twenty-minute ones. Once they start, they end up going on for an hour with the odd break here and there. Occasionally, Jade tells me which ones she likes. I haven't been watching them because all my attention has been focused on her. And because I've been drinking, I can't keep my hands off her. They're every-where. Stroking her thighs, tugging at the straps on her dress, cupping her breasts. She doesn't seem to mind and seems to be happy enough to return the favour by rubbing her hand up and down the front of my shorts.

Boats cruise past us, with horns honked and hellos shouted out as they head back to the docks. We raise our glasses to each one as they pass us by. I've lost count of how many bottles we've had, but I'm aware we've both got up at least twice each to get some more. I'm far too drunk to drive the boat back, but I should ask her anyway. "Do you want to stay on board or go back to the hotel?" I pull the top of her dress down, uncovering her back, making sure my hands cover her breasts.

"Stay here," she mumbles, shifting so she's facing me. Her breasts are exposed now, and although it's dark here, I don't want anyone to see her.

"Let's go downstairs, love." Even as the words leave my mouth, I have no intentions of moving. My hand slips under her dress to find she's not wearing any knickers. "My God, woman, what are you trying to do to me?"

"Nothing, just making things easier." Her hand pushes its way into my shorts. I lift my hips and help her pull them down. The cool night air causes me to gasp when my dick springs free. Jade strokes me and then sends me over the edge when she rubs herself against me. "Do you want me?" Her lips hovering over mine while her hips move back and forth and that, together with the location, must be possibly one of the most erotic things I've experienced.

"You know I do."

She continues to move against me, sliding her body up and down. Each time she does it, my cock jumps in anticipation of being buried inside her. I let her be the one in control, to have the power over me she desperately needs right now.

My eyes roll back when I feel myself enter her. "Jade..."

FIFTEEN

Jade

---

*M*y head is pounding, and I feel like shit. I don't remember coming to bed, but we must've because Jackson is passed out next to me. I sit up slowly and look down at my crumpled dress. It's obvious I was too drunk to even take it off or put it back on considering my boobs are hanging out. Pushing the sheet back, Jackson hasn't fared much better. His shorts are on, but they're definitely not covering him.

Any other morning and I'd slink down and wake him with my mouth, but I have awful cottonmouth and am in need of a gallon of water and a bottle of aspirin. Slowly, I get out of bed and pull my dress back up. The bathroom on the boat is tiny, but bigger than on the airplane. At least I can move around somewhat freely.

I start the shower and strip out of my dress, not caring I don't have anything to wear. Jackson won't care if I walk around naked, besides that's what he wanted while we're on the boat. For being a yacht, the water pressure is okay, but it's not doing anything to relieve my tense muscles. It doesn't matter which way I roll or knead my neck. The ache is still there.

If Jackson weren't in the other room, I would make myself throw up. I drank far too much wine last night, but once I started, I couldn't stop. While he is sleeping, I think about what life will be like next week when I'm back to work and Jackson is whoever he is wherever he lives. I don't know how I'm going to get over the feelings I have, but I have to find a way. I can't let my heartache tarnish the memory of this week. He has given me the best gift with his companionship, and I really can't ask for more.

"Jade, love," his voice carries over the shower. "Mind if I take a leak?"

"Not at all," I tell him. "I wish you could get in here with me. I need a massage."

The shower door opens and he apprises me. I'm wet, soapy, and sick to my stomach. "You look a little worse for wear."

"I feel it. I drank too much," I whine.

"So did I." He leans into the shower and gives me a quick kiss, not minding that the water is spraying his hair. "We'll head back soon." Jackson closes the door in time to miss my face falling. Heading back anywhere is the last thing I want to do.

I rinse off, only to realize I didn't bring a towel. When I open the shower door, right there on the hook is a white fluffy one just waiting for me. Knowing Jackson did that really sends my heart into overdrive.

With my towel wrapped around me tightly, I head up to the top deck where Jackson is drinking a cup of coffee. I need some, but the smell is making my stomach roll.

"Feeling any better?" he asks. His eyes are bloodshot

and he looks a bit rough around the edges. I lean into him and shake my head.

"I'm so sorry. I'm ruining our last day."

"Don't be daft, our day isn't ruined. Once we get back to solid ground and get some greasy food into our stomachs, you'll be right as rain in no time." With that, he starts the boat and presses whatever he needs to get the anchor up. I never asked how he knows all he does about the yacht or how he could afford to rent one. I think if he were to tell me he was a millionaire, I'd cry. Right now, I imagine him being a schoolteacher like his mother, even though I know it's not true.

It doesn't take us long to get back to port. Once the boat is docked, Jackson and I pack up our belongings and head back to where our scooter is locked up. The ride to the hotel is bumpy, but he does what he can to keep the jostling to the minimum.

Back at the hotel, we walk hand in hand to the elevator. Of course, because I feel like shit, this would be the time we run into the triplets. They smile and do the stupid little finger wave at Jackson, and don't make eye contact with me. I'm tempted to pull him away when the door opens, but he follows them in.

"Rough night?" one asks.

"Nope, far from it. In fact, it was pretty much perfect," he says.

"Doesn't look it," another one says. "If she's not giving you what you need, here's where you can find us." She slips him a piece of paper or something that likely has their room number on it. I wait to see what he does with it, and when he slips it into his pocket, I have to fight to keep my temper in check. It's clear now he's called an end to the game. As shyly as possible, I take my hand away from his and rummage through my bag, pretending to look for something.

The interaction with them does nothing for my mood nor does it help that I'm on the verge of tears. When Jackson opens the door to his room, I immediately walk into my side and attempt to shut the door between us, but he's hot on my tail.

"Hey, what's the matter?"

"Nothing."

"Really?" he asks with one eyebrow raised. "It doesn't look like nothing to me." I try to walk away from him, but he grabs my wrist and pulls me to him. "Talk to me."

I shake my head and try to pull away, but he hangs on tighter.

"Jade, come on. Everything has been going great and now... now, I'm sensing some tension between us."

"I said nothing's wrong." This time I'm able to free myself. I try to bypass him, but he blocks my path. "What the hell? Don't you get it?"

"No, I don't, which is why I'm asking." He rubs his hand over his face. "Look, I know we drank a lot last night and our time is coming to an end, but—"

"But what?" I step back and cross my arms over my chest.

"You're being a bit of a bitch."

"Screw you." I push past him.

"I think you've already done that, Jade. Or whatever the fuck you call yourself."

"Really? Like your name is Jackson." I throw my hands up in the air.

"What the actual fuck? What's wrong with you? We were having the time of our lives right up to around twenty minutes ago. What's happened to change that?"

I stand there, facing him, fighting back the tears. I point to the wall, as if the triplets are on the other side of us. I don't want to cry, but the tears come and there isn't anything I can do about it. "You took their number. You put it in your pocket while your pretend wife was standing right next to you."

"What was I supposed to do with it?"

"Oh, I don't know, tell her no. Tell her you don't want it. But I get it. I leave in the morning and you leave tomorrow night. Why not have a back-up plan."

"Is that what you think?"

I nod and tear my eyes away from him. I watch his feet retreat into his room and jump when his hotel room door slams shut. The tears come down frantically and my only coping mechanism is to start packing. This is probably for the best, ending it like this. I'm paying the emotional price of not being able to say goodbye to him. I should've bottled it all up and told Jackie about it when I got home, venting her to instead of ruining my last day with Jackson, but I couldn't. Why did he have to take her number? Why couldn't he just push her hand away or ignore her?

"Because what you have isn't real," I tell myself very loudly. Maybe my heart will listen now that I've said the words aloud.

I throw my clothes into my suitcase haphazardly, not caring if they're folded or not. No one at the laundromat will care whether my clothes came back from vacation wrinkled. When the drawers are cleaned out and the closet empty, I crawl onto the bed and try to make the hurt go away. This isn't how I wanted to spend my last day in paradise, but I have no one to blame but myself. It shouldn't matter what Jackson does after I leave.

I don't know how long he's been gone when I hear his

door open, but the smell of food has my stomach growling. I wish now I had closed and locked the door between us so I don't have to deal with... well all of it.

The side of my bed dips and his hand rests on my shoulder. I should push him away, but I don't. "Jade, I'm sorry. I shouldn't have taken her number. I only did it because I thought it would be better than getting drawn into a conversation with them. If I had declined, they only would have persevered until they followed us right back to our rooms."

I only nod because I'm afraid to speak out of fear I'll become a blubbering mess again.

"It was wrong of me to do that, especially in front of you." Jackson sighs and shifts away from me. I chance a look over my shoulder and find him with his arms resting on his knees. He turns, catching me staring. "I'm sorry, love." He wipes away at my tear-stained face and kisses me softly. "I was so pissed off after our fight earlier, but you were right. I shouldn't have done that. I promise you, I'm not that kind of man, Jade." He pauses, as he places a hand on my shoulder. "Look, I changed my flight. You told me you leave in the morning and now my flight leaves at eleven. We can go to the airport together."

I don't know if it's because he's sorry or concerned for my feelings that he changed his flight to show that I mean something to him. Either way, I'm falling for him and I don't think tomorrow will go very well for me. My name and phone number are sitting on the edge of my tongue. I want to tell him everything, but it's a game changer. He may be willing to spare my heart while we're on vacation, but reality might be something different.

I pull Jackson to me and kiss every part of his face I can until I reach his lips. He's hesitant at first, but finally gives in. There's an urgency in his kiss that sends the pit of my stomach into a wild swirl. Jackson grips my hip and moves me down the bed until he's pressing against me. His hard cock pushes into my thigh as a stark reminder of what he has to offer.

Jackson trails kisses down my neck and over my chest while I work to get his shirt off. He sits back on his knees and removes the fabric and slides his shorts off, letting his erection spring free. I sit up and do the same, with his help. He tosses my dress onto the floor and attacks my mouth with so much vigor I can feel it in my toes.

My hands are everywhere with my nails dragging slowly across his back and my hand stroking him, spreading his pre-cum all over to slicken my hold. Jackson rocks his hips while nibbling from my earlobe down to my breast. His lips touch my nipple with tantalizing possessiveness as his eyes seek out mine. He likes me looking at him, watching him as he pleasures me.

I reach for the bedside table eager to get a condom so he can take away the ache I'm feeling. It's as if he knows I don't need the foreplay, at least not right now, and sits up to grab one. I expect him to plow into me, but he doesn't.

Jackson hovers, kissing me softly as he glides in. My mouth drops open from the pressure, but I never take my eyes off him. Each thrust of his hips has me bringing my legs up higher, spreading wider to accommodate him. Still, he looks me in the eye, watching me intently.

I cup his face, and bring my mouth to his. Our tongues dance in rhythm to our bodies. Each cry, he swallows, and freely gives me every moan. He presses down on me, our bodies slick from sweat, moving against each other easily. I hold him. I grab at him. Anything I can do to keep him going. I don't want him to stop. I never want him to stop.

"Jade," he whispers my fake name over my lips. My

back arches and my toes curl. "Yes, love," he says. "Let go, sweetheart."

Jackson speeds up, slamming the headboard into the wall. The bed squeaks loudly over the slapping of our skin. He grunts out his release as mine tumbles through, milking him for everything he's willing to give.

He slows down, but the aftershocks are enough to keep him hard. Jackson still moves in and out of me, and I can feel him getting hard again.

"Ready for round two?"

"As if I'd ever say no."

SIXTEEN

Jackson
_____

*J*ade and I are at the airport, sitting in a café just past security. We haven't spoken much since we awoke earlier this morning. Everything about today is heavy and uncomfortable. I catch her crying a few times, which makes me immediately stop what I am doing so I can hold and comfort her. I thought about secretly slipping my name and phone number into her suitcase, but chickened out each time I went to do it. I don't want to be disappointed if she doesn't call or alternatively be stuck in a meeting or otherwise engaged and not speak to her as frequently as I would wish. With the family business expanding, my priorities lie elsewhere.

We decide in the taxi on the way here that once we check in our luggage, we'd sit somewhere neutral so there is no chance of either one of us guessing the destination of the other. What is clear, though, is she's flying back to the States, and while, initially, I was also heading there, when I changed my flight, I decided to head back home. I need some downtime before moving across the pond, so I can get my head back on straight. Some time with my folks will do the trick.

I'm sitting as close to Jade as I can, to try to keep her by my side for as long as possible. When she looks at the clock on the wall, I know it's time for her to go. I desperately want to walk her to the gate, but doing so goes against the agreement we made.

Outside the café, we stand amongst the other travellers who are either going home or just arriving. I pull her into my arms and inhale the smell of her shampoo, trying to commit it to memory.

Jade pulls away and takes a hold of my cheeks, bringing my mouth closer to hers. Our kiss is full of emotion, but oddly lacks everything else I need it to be—a promise, a declaration, a 'see you soon;' anything I can take and lock away safely.

"I have so much to say. I don't know where to start. Yesterday, I never got a chance to tell you how sorry I am for overacting and assuming you were going to meet the triplets. Not once during the week did you give me any reason to believe you're that type of man. This week..." she pauses and shakes her head. "Nothing will ever live up to this vacation. I'm not sure I even want to try. I hope someday we run into each other again and if we don't, I hope you at least remember the time we had here. Thank you for an amazing week, Jackson."

She slips away from my grasp before I can reply. "Jade, wait..." but she's gone, lost amongst the hordes of other holiday-makers moving around the terminal. I could probably follow where she went and find her easily enough, but we agreed it had to be this way.

I stand there on the off-chance she comes back, hoping to

catch a glimpse of her, and praying she's going to burst through the crowd and jump into my arms, tackling me to the ground. Yet, she never does. I don't know long I stand there, listening to the announcement for flights to North Carolina, South Carolina, Florida, and finally New York. Originally, New York was where I was going before I decided I needed to fly back to London. In fact, my original flight was due to leave around the same time as hers. Initially, I lied to her about when I was leaving in case things didn't work out between us.

At my gate, I stand looking out the window and watch the planes land and take off. My mind is on Jade, and I hate that she's now in the air and leaving our island of paradise. I hate that our week is over and I have nothing to show for it except for a huge gaping hole in my heart. I let her take a piece of me with her when I should have protected myself. I should have kept the wall up and been the cocky bastard I normally am. Instead, I let Jade get close and it's all because I thought that this time, I had nothing to lose and everything to gain. How wrong I was. At the end of the day, I did lose something—myself *and* Jade.

∾

ON MY WAY TO MY PARENTS' house, I stop off and buy some flowers, the morning papers, and some breakfast from the coffee shop. They're not expecting me, but I gave in my notice on my flat before I left for Bermuda, thinking I wouldn't need it again for a long time. I park my hire car and quickly rush to the front door so they don't think it is some door-to-door salesman trying to get them to sign up to some ridiculous offer.

"Mum? Dad? Are you here?" I open the door and walk in. My mum greets me with a surprised expression. She quickly puts her arms around me and gives me a comforting hug.

"Jackson, what are you doing here? I thought you were flying straight to New York after your holiday?" she asks as she kisses me on both cheeks.

"Small change of plan," I tell her. "I brought us some breakfast." I hand her the bag of goodies and her eyes light up. "Where's Dad?"

"Playing golf." She waves her hand dismissively. "Although, between you and me, I don't think he's actually playing. It's more likely he and the boys are sitting around at the club and reading the papers."

"Sounds about right." I follow her into the kitchen. She takes out three plates from one of the cupboards, setting the variety of muffins and croissants on one of them before offering it to me so I can take my choice. She then places it on the table and pours me a strong cup of coffee.

"Having second thoughts?" she asks.

I shake my head. "No, I'm ready to move to the States and expand the business. The timing is right and we're getting a good deal on the premises in Manhattan. It's a prime location and I've looked over their accounts with a fine-tooth comb. It's a good investment. They're in good shape and so, hopefully the transition should all go smoothly. The construction has already started on the new manufacturing plant as well. Everything's going to the plan." Everything except I might have fallen in love while on holiday and that wasn't in any plan at all. It's something I'm having a hard time getting my head around.

Not even when Sian's mum was pregnant with her, did the idea of being in love pop into my head. My ex and I barely dated for a month before we realised we were better off as friends. I love her because she gave me Sian, but I was never in love with her.

"And then where will you open stores?" she asks.

"Los Angeles, Atlanta, Chicago." I list the major cities in the United States. "I think once we're fully established in New York, the others will be pretty easy."

"And what happens when other, similar retailers have to close because they can't compete with you being in their neighbourhood??"

I shrug my shoulders and pick at my food. That's the nature of the beast when you're in direct competition with other brands, which are similar. Some businesses grow, while others stay at the same pace. My father cornered the market in sex toys, creating one of the largest manufacturing warehouses in England. Our warehouse operates twenty-four hours a day, with our employees working shifts so they can meet the orders we receive from around the country. But it's our physical shops, which are the success stories and bring in the bread and butter. If one was to stand outside, one would assume we're just like any other retailer, but inside, we strive to offer a first-class service to all our customers. There's nothing dirty or sordid about what we sell. No one judges if a customer decides to take home a three-foot vibrator or have a personalised life-sized doll made to your exact specifications. We do it all. We have it all. Our motto is everyone is welcome, everyone is valued, and everyone is treated to their satisfaction, both during their visit and long afterwards.

"We'll do everything we can to work with them before it comes to that. If it means we must buy out their stock or offer some of them a job, then we'll have to look at what we can do for them. The last thing I want to do is leave anyone high and dry."

"You're a good man, Jackson."

I'm glad my mum thinks so because right now I don't. Right now, I must concentrate on the business, but I can't help regretting that I let Jade slip through my fingers.

"Thanks, Mum."

"Did you have fun in Bermuda?"

"Yeah, it was good. I had an amazing time."

"You look nice and tanned." She taps my bicep.

I lean back in the chair and fiddle with the handle on my coffee mug. "I met someone when I was out there. A girl. We ended up spending the entire week together."

"Jackson..." she hedges, but I shake my head.

"I was stupid. I pretty much used her to get out of a sticky situation and it's backfired on me. She suggested we should lie about who we are so neither of us could get attached."

My mum looks at me as if I've lost my mind. I have. There's no doubt about that. "And now you're attached?"

I nod, and take a sip of coffee. "I know absolutely nothing about her and yes, I wish I knew everything."

"And what does she know about you?"

"My name," I tell her. "But only my first name. And she knows about Sian. She asked me about my tattoo one morning and I told her everything. I treated her as if she was my girlfriend or wife. I rented a yacht, hoping she'd open up to me and we'd forget all about the silly charade we were playing, but she stuck to her guns. I tried to woo her, show her what a good man I could be to her, but she still kept this wall up and no matter how hard I tried, I just couldn't get through it."

"Oh, Son." My mother walks over and sits down next to me. I rest my head on her shoulder and let her comfort me.

Coming home was the right thing to do. "What are you going to do?"

I hadn't thought about doing anything until now. But what can I do? Take out an ad in every newspaper in America looking for Jade? I don't even have a photo of her to post on social media so I can't ask if anyone knows her.

"Nothing. There really isn't anything I can do."

Mum doesn't say anything. I know she won't pressure me to try to find Jade, especially since I told her I have nothing to go on. It's frustrating though because I should've tried harder to quit the game when I could. From the moment I kissed her, I was being real with her.

The front door opens and my dad's bellowing voice echoes throughout the house. "Sylvie? Are you cheating on me? Whose car is on the drive? Oh, hi, Jay. I thought you were... Wait, where were you, I can't remember?"

"Hey, Pa." I stand up and give him a hug. "I was in Bermuda. Did you get many hole's in one today?"

"None, but my golf game is the best it's ever been," he says.

"And so is your drinking," my mum adds with a smirk.

My parents kiss and while I used to think it was gross, I quickly learned I want the kind of love they have. The kind that makes you want to come home at night, makes you want to sleep in on a Sunday morning, and have an early night on a Friday. My parents have had their ups and downs, no one is perfect, but the love they share is pretty much perfect, at least it is in my eyes.

"How long are you staying? Is everything okay with our expansion?"

"Yeah, it's good. I just needed to come home after my holiday and get back to normal before heading over to the U.S."

He looks at me with concern, but I shake my head. While I can confide in my mum about Jade, I won't tell my dad. It's not because he won't understand, it's more that he'll tell me to get over it and focus on the business. While my mum is sweet and emotional, my father is stern and all about the company. They're like night and day. Almost like my feelings for Jade. She was a bright light in my dark, lonely world and I want her back.

SEVENTEEN

Story

_____

From the moment I leave Jackson standing outside the coffee shop to now, the point where my plane is about to touch down, I've been a crying mess. I feel bad for the lady sitting next to me on the flight. She keeps handing me her tissues, while I blubber my way back to the U.S. To make matters worse, she tries to console me, telling me he isn't worth it. But he is. He is worth all this and more. All I can do is nod, which only induces another round of tears, snot, and gross amounts of saliva. Honestly, I'm surprised I wasn't booted off the plane mid-flight with the amount of crying I've done. It's rather embarrassing, but I can't stop. It doesn't matter what I try the tears won't stop flowing. And of course, my shirt is a bit low cut and I can see the faint bruising from the hickey Jackson had given me, and that right there causes another round of tears.

When I get off the plane, I happen to turn and look at the reader board. Bermuda is in bold letters. The seats are full with people waiting to board. I imagine some of the people are single and heading off to their own sexcation. I should warn them. Tell them whatever you do, don't make the same mistake I did. But I don't say anything because a fresh wave of tears streams down my face. Honestly, I'm surprised that I'm not dehydrated and in need of medical assistance.

Thankfully, the terminal is jam packed, meaning by the time I get to luggage claim, my suitcase is already going around the conveyor belt. I get in the long line and wait my turn for a cab. The man behind me seems anxious. I stare only at his feet and the ground. No need to let him think I'm willing to strike up a conversation.

"Excuse me, I don't suppose you have the time, by any chance?" he asks in a British accent. My body freezes and my heart starts racing a mile a second. Ever so slowly, I raise my head until I look at him. I swear my heart deflates like a balloon with a hole in it. I must stare at him for a long minute or so because he cocks his eyebrow at me and taps his wrist. Cocky bastard. My British man would never do such a thing.

I hold up my phone and tap the screen viciously. "It's not on. I don't know," I tell him. He could've easily looked at the million clocks inside the airport to figure out what time it is. Surely, he has a cell phone he could turn on, which no doubt updates to his time zone. I look at him and shake my head. I think he mutters something like bitch, but I don't care. What businessman doesn't know the time in this day and age?

When it's finally my turn for a cab, he taps me on the shoulder. "Would you like to share a taxi?" he asks after I turn to look at him. He's smiling and while it's nice, the fact that he has an English accent turns me off. No one could ever compare to Jackson. Ever.

"No thanks."

"Come on. We can save the earth."

I shake my head. I've been duped into sharing before from the airport and always get stuck footing the bill because I always seem to be going farther. When the cab pulls up to the curb, I wait until the porter has loaded my luggage in the trunk before I rush into the backseat and pull the door closed. "Brooklyn," I tell the driver. I feel like sticking my tongue out at the man, but refrain.

It makes me wonder if Jackson is like that, rude and insolent. I want to say no, but we were pretending for a week and he could very well be a complete jackass and I would never know. I refuse to believe he is anything but perfect. If I start thinking he's an ass, my memories will be tainted.

The driver pulls up to my building and instantly, I miss the vibrant colors of Bermuda. Still, as he drives away, I stand on the sidewalk, with people walking past me in a rush. Each one of them has their face in their phone or looking at the ground. Everyone is always in a hurry here. No one ever stops to smell the roses or just take in everything around them. They have no idea what they're missing.

As luck would have it, the elevator is out of service, leaving me no option but to lug my suitcases up ten flights of stairs. A few of the guys who live here, breeze past me, without stopping to help. Every time this happens, it makes me miss Jackson more and more. Not once, during our week together, did I have to carry anything. Or pay. Jackson paid for everything even under protest.

Rummaging through my purse, I finally find the keys to my place. Three locks and I can finally pull the door open on the loft I share with Jackie.

"Oh, my God, you're home," she squeals loudly and rushes toward me. The tackle hug almost knocks me off my feet. "Why didn't you text me when you got here? I would've met you downstairs to help you with your luggage?"

"I haven't turned my phone on." I drop my bag onto our kitchen table and walk into the living room where the couch waits for me. "I didn't want to check my email until I could boot up my laptop."

Jackie sits down in the chair opposite of me. "What'd you do, party last night?"

"Something like that."

"Details. I need details!"

As if on cue, tears start up once again. Her face falls and she comes over to me, pulling me into her arms. "What happened, hun?"

"I don't even know where to start."

"The beginning is usually the best," she says, jokingly.

"Right... the beginning."

"Wait," Jackie says. "I have a feeling this calls for wine." The thought of wine makes my stomach twist. I still can't comprehend how I drank so much when we were on the yacht and then let my hangover get the best of me. Jackson was right to leave me in the hotel room. I'm surprised he came back. I don't know if I would've.

"Okay, first things first... is he hot?" She hands me a full glass of what I'm guessing will be a rosé she loves. Jackie found this little winery in the middle of Vermont last summer when she went on a trip with her then boyfriend. She's been back many times since Vermont is one of the few states who aren't allowed to ship alcohol. I told her she should buy stock in their company. She's promised to take me, and maybe now would be a good time to take her up on the offer. I'm going to need an escape from my vacation.

"So hot, and British."

She gasps and squeals. "Did you sleep with him?"

"Yeah."

"Like how many times?"

I shrug. "I stopped counting after the first time or round. Whatever you would call it. Once we started, we didn't stop. Hotel room, hand jobs in the ocean, sex fest on a yacht."

"He has a yacht?"

"No, he rented one for us."

"Holy shit, British and rich? You lucked the fuck out, girl. Big dick?" she asks as if it's an everyday question. I suppose when one is single and with her best friend, nothing is off the table.

I nod, feeling slightly embarrassed. Jackie slaps me on the shoulder, causing my wine to jostle. I can't even bring myself to take a drink.

"Where is he? Is he coming here? When can I meet him? Does he have any single friends?"

"Geez, Jackie." I get up and go to the window. We have somewhat of a view, but there's more and more construction going on, diminishing what we can see. "I made the worst mistake of my life." I look over at her and she nods for me to continue, so I do. I tell her about how Jackson and I met, and the stupid game I suggested. I speak about the type of man he is, how he was attentive, sweet, and seemed to genuinely like me despite the fake marriage we had.

All while telling her, I fiddle with the ring he placed on my finger. I tried to take it off on the airplane, but it was stuck. Likely because my hand is swollen due to my inability to stop crying, but now that I'm home, it moves freely, yet the thought of taking it off makes me physically ill. This is the only piece I have of Jackson.

"So you don't know anything about him?"

I shake my head. "Other than he had a daughter named Sian who was stillborn."

"Did he say when?" she asks. I look at her oddly and she shrugs. "I don't know much about England, but maybe Sian is an uncommon name and you can search for her obituary." Jackie has a point, but doing so would be an invasion of Jackson's privacy. As much as I'd love to see him again, we had conditions for a reason.

"I'm not doing that, Jackie. If he wanted me to know who he was, he could've told me."

"But you didn't tell him about yourself either. You could've told him your name is Story Cavanah."

I shake my head and continue to look out the window. "And say what when he asks me why my parents named me Story? It's the most convoluted thing my parents could've done to me. Besides, I thought once he knew my name, other things would come out."

"No one cares about what your parents do or what your grandparents started. The world has changed so much from when we were younger. Hell, I bet if we were to go to a reunion, people would flock to you with questions. Everyone is more open, sexually. It's like the new norm."

"It doesn't matter. It's not like I can call him."

Jackie sighs. It's heavy and completely over-exaggerated. "I can't believe you had crazy monkey sex for a week with some hot guy who happens to have a monster cock and you didn't leave him your number!"

I look down at the top of my breast, wondering if the faint bruise is visible at the moment. It's not and by tomorrow, I'll barely see it. I have more, on the insides of my thighs and pelvic area. To the outside eye, I probably look like I'm diseased and need to be quarantined.

"He definitely didn't make monkey noises," I say, trying

to make light of the situation. "But when he moaned..." I pause and shake my head. "That was enough to make me come undone."

"So Bermuda will be forever known as a sexfest?"

"Sexcation." I correct her. "That's what I'm calling it."

Jackie comes over and looks at my ring. "It's beautiful. Never know, I guess. Maybe he'll walk into the hotel someday."

I smile, liking the idea. But knowing my luck, he'd walk in with his fiancée and ask me to coordinate their wedding. That would be enough to break my heart. Men like Jackson don't stay single for long. I should know because I've looked for one a time or two in my life. I always seem to find the one that comes from an affluent family and once they find out about mine, I'm no longer good enough. I made it a year with my ex before I told him what my parents do for a living, but once he found out, that is when things went south.

EIGHTEEN

Jackson

---

*T*he only thing wrong with waking up at my parents' house is Jade isn't here with me. I know my folks would love her and I hate they'll never meet. I think she would love London as well. She loved my accent well enough that being surrounded by people talking like me would probably turn her on, and that would totally be to my benefit.

Last night, I did the last thing I said I wouldn't do—sit on various social media sites, trying to find Jade's profile. Of course, it was fucking hard looking for someone I know nothing about, and I don't think technology has mastered the ability to search for someone by the curve of their body, or the shape of their lips or how perfectly our hands fit together. Maybe in my next life, that's something I should consider patenting. I also hit a blank when I searched for her name even though I knew it was a long shot. I rub my hand through my five o'clock shadow, remembering how much she liked it, especially when she was sitting on my face. I thought about shaving every day while I was there, but I only trimmed it so it was the perfect length for her.

In hindsight, if I could do it again, I would still play along with her game, but I'd make sure I take a load of photos so I had something to remember her by. During the time we were together, I never saw her with a camera or a phone and it may well be she's not a social media addict like most people. I don't blame her, social media nowadays can really be a brutal place with online trolls thinking they know everything. Taking a break from looking for her, I open my profile page and quickly change my name so it says Jackson. Only my mum calls me by my given name; to everyone else, I'm known as Jay.

Putting the word 'Bermuda' in the search field doesn't help much either, instead bringing up a plethora of random images and related links. Neither of us thought to take any photos while we were on the island, instead enjoying the limited time we had with each other. Normally, I'm not someone who insists on having my photo taken, but I must admit this time, I'm sorely regretting not getting Jade to pose for a few. If I had, I wouldn't have the problem I'm having now in finding her.

Of course, the thought has crossed my mind that maybe she doesn't want to be found. Why else would she want to play the fake name game? Maybe everything she told me was part of the charade, and she wasn't single after all. For all I know, she may be happily married with 2.4 kids and a dog. I absolutely don't want to believe that though. We were together for the whole week, apart from the few times I went down to speak to the concierge about booking some restaurants or organising some day trips. The day we hired the yacht, I didn't tell her we'd be staying out overnight. Surely, if she had someone at home, she'd want to call them to check in? No, I'm sure she was telling the truth when she said she was single. If she belonged to someone else, she wouldn't have been so ready to do the things she did with me. Unless she's an incredibly good actress.

A week before I left, my best mates threw a going away party for me. I've known Tommy Carpenter and Maxwell Locke for most of my life. Tommy's dad gave me my first pint long before I was old enough to drink. To this day, I still haven't told my mum about it; chances are, if she found out, she would blow a gasket and threaten that I couldn't hang out with them anymore.

Tommy and Maxwell were far from happy that I'd made the decision to move to the States. From the time we were all legally old enough to drink, it had become our ritual to have Friday night drinking sessions, and I was ruining that by moving across the pond. Tommy is an England boy through and through and will never leave the Motherland. Maxwell though? He's hinted that he may well pay me a visit once I've settled in.

I walk into The Old Man's Goat, the pub Tommy owns and stand in the doorway until my friend looks up in my direction. His face pales, but quickly morphs into a smile. "What the fuck are you doing here? They kick your arse out already?" he asks as he walks around the bar. I meet him halfway and give him a hug.

"Haven't exactly made it there yet." I take a seat at the bar while Tommy pours me a pint. Sitting here now, I still must give kudos to Tommy and how he came to own his pub. As a kid, he was always a chancer, and was the cocky kid in the school playground who would bet his lunch money on something ridiculous and win, no matter what. At sixteen, he bought a lottery ticket and the lucky bastard managed to win a substantial amount of money. Thankfully, his parents persuaded him to put it all in a savings account while he finished school and then think about investing it when he was older. They did everything they could to prevent him from blowing the lot on something ridiculous that he didn't need. Seven years later and with a business degree under his belt, he bought this building at an auction and completely gutted the inside, choosing to refurbish it with some modern touches. I must admit he's done a great job. On the outside, this is a traditional ye olde pub, but on the inside, its modern enough to appeal to the younger crowd. Plus, as it's a Freehold, he's not tied to one brewery and is able to choose which beers he sells. The story of how he named it is what I love the most, though. His dad owned a goat, which he kept in his back garden and Tommy loved that animal. As a tribute, he named his pub after it. All of this is how I know that Tommy is a Londoner for life. He'll never leave this place behind.

"How was Bermuda?"

I smirk and take a sip of the cold pale ale. It tastes good, but doesn't really quench my thirst. Something tells me only Jade can do that. Dammit, I wish I knew what her real name was.

Tommy puts another pint in front of me. He must sense I'll need it once I tell him all about my holiday, but before I have a chance to start, the sound of Maxwell's voice fills the room.

"What the fuck, mate? I thought you left?"

"That's exactly what I said," Tommy adds. "The moron missed us too much though so he came crawling back."

Max gives me a brotherly hug before sitting down on the stool next to mine. He's still in his suit, clearly having come here straight from work. That's what being a lawyer does for you though. Late nights and long hours, and for all the times he gripes about having to work through the night on some acquisition deal, I know ultimately, Max has his eyes on making partner in the long run. He grabs my spare pint and drinks half of it before I have a chance to protest.

"Oh, that was for unlucky Jay-Jay here," Tommy reprimands him playfully. "There was trouble in paradise."

"It wasn't..." I start to protest but quickly stop. Tommy is pretty much right. Everything was great until it was time for us to leave.

Max slaps me on the back. "Spill the beans, man. What happened that gave you grief?"

I roll my eyes, but know I'm about spill my guts and tell them everything. "I met a girl."

"How did I know you were going to say that?" Tommy immediately replies.

"Was she hot?" Max asks.

"Incredibly so."

"Did you stick it on her?" Tommy follows up.

I raise my eyebrows "Stick it on her? What, are you twelve or something?"

Tommy shrugs, "Hey, I own a bar. I pick up things from the people who come in here. But for you, old man, let me ask you again in a way you'll understand. Did you shag her?"

I can't help but laugh at Tommy and his reasoning for talking like someone who likes to think he's trendy with all this modern lingo, but I give him credit for trying to keep up to date. "Repeatedly." I finally admit.

"You lucky little shit. You would think because I'm a barman I'd get me some action, but nope, nada. I'm lucky if a tourist looks in my direction and even then, they're asking for directions on how to get to Tower Bridge or the West End."

"That's probably because you need to sharpen up your image a little," I jokingly tell him. I know women like the shaggy hipster look, but they'd probably draw the line at a hairstyle that looks like it hasn't been washed or brushed in three weeks. They want someone with sex appeal and a haircut can play a big part in that.

Tom runs his hand through his hair and laughs. "Stop trying to change the subject and tell us about this girl that's got you all hot under the collar."

I shake my head and reach for a few peanuts. I normally wouldn't eat them, because let's face it, how do you know whose hands have been digging around in there? I'm a guy. I know some people don't wash their hands after taking a leak. However, I need a distraction—the nuts will have to do. "So, I saw her when I was checking in at reception and as luck would have it, it turned out her room was next to mine and we had adjoining rooms. We literally bumped into each other on our patio but I thought I'd play it cool, so instead of speaking to her, I gave her 'the look.'"

Tommy and Maxwell burst out laughing before I continue and I know I'm about to get some grief for what I've just said.

"The look? What, did you smoulder at her and hope she'd become weak at the knees? Poor girl didn't have a chance if you turned on the Jay-Man charms!" Max teases as he almost chokes on his beer.

"Ha ha, very funny." I continue, "It didn't work anyway because she pretty much ran away and hid, but I didn't let that deter me. So, I went down to the pool for a swim and ran into these three birds. They were hot, but not as hot as my neighbour. Anyway, I spotted her sitting on a sunbed on the other side of the pool, so I made up some crap excuse about her being my wife and I went over to her. Fucking laid one on her right then and there."

"And she let you? Didn't knee you in the balls or

anything??" Tommy asks.

"Nope, in fact she kissed me back. I told her what I had said to the girls on the other side, and suggested we pretend it was true to save me from being pounced upon."

"Okay, so what's the problem?" Max asks. "You met a sexy girl that you shagged all week, and you pretended to be husband and wife, so you basically had a honeymoon without gaining a wife for life. Bob's your uncle! What am I missing?"

I finish off my pint and signal Tom for another one. He pours it and puts it on the bench in front of me, then resumes his position with his arms crossed, leaning on the bar and eyebrow raised, indicating for me to finish regaling my story.

"It was her idea to lie and use fake names. Thing is, I really like her, but I don't know a bloody thing about her apart from the fact that she's American."

"Ah, shit, mate. I didn't think of that. Yeah, that totally throws a spanner in the works," Tommy says.

"So, throughout your entire week together, there wasn't an opportunity for you to tell her your name and give her your business card, or sneak it into her bag?" Max asks. "What about a photo? If you have one, I have colleagues in the New York office that could probably help. At least they'll know of someone who's an expert in all this high-tech stuff and hopefully can find her."

I sigh and down my pint, needing the courage to tell my friends I completely messed up that part. "Nope, nothing. I thought about leaving my card in her suitcase, but then I didn't want to piss her off. And what if I did manage to leave it and then she never called? I may act all tough, but you guys know, even I couldn't handle the rejection." It was something I didn't want to think of.

Max and Tom are quiet on the subject after that. Max nurses his pint while Tom splits his time talking to us and serving the other customers that come and go. As for me, I continue to drink, drowning my sorrows in beer. Football is being shown on the TV and it makes me want to get on the pitch and hammer some balls into the goal out of frustration, only the last time I did I ended up breaking my leg and my mum lost her head both with worry and anger because I was so stupid. Plus, the fact remains, in a couple of days, I'm still leaving England once more and flying over to the U.S. I've delayed my meetings for too long and can't keep doing that if I want to take this business seriously and establish a presence over there.

"What's her name?" Max asks, I look over at him to see he's on his phone, typing rapidly.

"Doesn't matter, it's wasn't her real one."

"You may think that, but if people lie about who they are, then unless they are professional con artists, they generally tend to use the same fake profile so as not to slip up on remembering the facts. After a few times of doing it, they probably become a little careless and leave some clues," he tells me.

"She's not a con artist, Max. She's a woman that I pretty much pounced on and persuaded to spend her entire holiday with me."

"Yeah, and it sounds like she didn't put up much of a fight when it came to falling into bed with you."

I scoff. "Like you've never heard of a holiday romance? Come on, we were in a foreign country, in some fancy resort. You can't tell me you wouldn't have done the same thing if you were in my position." Except, for me it was much more than a casual week of sex. The one time we had a fight, it resulted in me making love to her and I can't remember any other time I've done that with a girl. Emotionally, I felt connected to her in a way I have never experienced before.

"You keep telling yourself that," he says, still looking at his phone. He is in complete lawyer mode right now and not paying attention to a single thing I'm saying. "So, are you going to tell me her name or not?"

"Jade."

"Jade what?"

"Just Jade. I don't know. We never told each other our surnames."

He looks at me like I have two heads. "You only knew each other's first name? Nothing else?"

"Do you blame me? I mean, have you seen what I do for a job?" I ask. "I dabble in sex for a living, so shagging a stranger really isn't an impossibility for me. I have been known to have the odd one-night stand when I'm at various conventions. Even I know you don't get attached when you do something like that. This wasn't exactly out of character."

Max shakes his head. He's the sensible one out of the three of us. Tommy has always been the go with the flow type, while I've been straight down the middle.

"I just worry about you, mate."

I finish my pint and ask Tommy for another. Max continues to search for Jade on his phone, and with any luck, I'm hoping he'll find her. If he does, I won't be ashamed to admit I'll probably kiss him with gratitude, but I'm trying not to get my hopes up. Something tells me there's a reason why Jade doesn't want to be found and has taken every step there is to make sure her identity is kept a secret.

NINETEEN

Story

---

*R*eturning to work after the most amazing vacation and most devastating heartbreak isn't my idea of fun. Every co-worker bombarded me with questions the moment I stepped into the hotel. Even the morning valet crew. Right now, I wish I hadn't told anyone I was taking that stupid trip.

One of the things I made sure to do was leave my laptop here and keep my phone off. When I arrived back home, I had no desire to touch either of them. I only wanted to talk to one person, and speaking to him wouldn't happen.

My laptop stares at me, waiting for me to slide it into the docking station. Once I do, the screen comes to life. It only takes a few seconds for my name to appear. I type in my password and leave my desk, letting my emails load. In a perfect world, my assistant, Foster, took care of everything while I was gone. Unfortunately, I don't live in a perfect world and I have a feeling she didn't do anything while I was away.

Foster is the definition of spoiled, but she works hard,

especially when I'm around. If I take a day off, she tends to slack and spend most of her time on social media or making her hair and nails appointments. When she was first hired to work the front desk, the poor girl had no idea how to fill out her paperwork because her parents catered to her every need. I don't think she has a driver's license yet because she has a car service. Honestly, I'm not sure why she even works, but I like her and am glad to have her on my team. She's resilient and learned the ropes. When the position as my assistant opened up, she applied. I was leery, but it's worked out for the best.

"Morning, Foster."

"Ms. Cavanah. I'm so happy you're back. We have eight brides looking to book the hotel for their wedding and I made the mistake of telling one of them the date she wants could be taken, she yelled and offered to pay double."

The one thing about Foster is she stresses easily. It would've been nice if she could've had the week off when I did, but someone had to stay in my office. I stand at her desk and watch as she piles my mail and messages into a massive stack for me. The one thing I was adamant about was that no messages were sent to my voicemail. It'll be bad enough to clean out my email. I didn't want to have to listen to a hundred messages as well.

"We have a wedding this week, right?" I ask her, wishing I had my phone.

"Yes, the Barker-Holt wedding. I've confirmed with the florist and musician. The bride is bringing her own hair and makeup staff."

"Perfect. Is that our only event?" Please say yes, but as luck would have it, Foster shakes her head. I sigh. "All right. I'll be in my office. Please try to take care of as much as you can before handing them to me. I need some time to get caught up."

"Yes, Ms. Cavanah."

Since taking over the event coordination at the Grand Plaza, a lot has changed. My predecessor had a policy stating the hotel could only hold one event at a time or one a day. Our hotel is massive, taking up an entire New York City block and we have ample space to accommodate different functions. Weddings are a different story. When I took over, I changed outdated policy and booked every room possible. It took three, maybe four months, before we started seeing mass capacity, which resulted in us hiring a full event staff. For the weddings, we max out at four a day. They're more intricate with decorations and seating, and my staff needs more time for set-up and take down.

I love my job, and am grateful my parents saved to put me through school. I think my father thought with my degree in business I would take over for him, but I minored in event coordination as well, driving home that I would never carry on the legacy that the Cavanahs have built. It's not that I'm unappreciative, it's the stigma that goes along with what my family owns and the guise they used to hide it.

Pressing the icon that will open my email account, I take a deep breath and watch as the number count continues to increase. I should've timed it to see how long it would take until they all finished loading.

The first email is one from the hotel I stayed at in Bermuda. I open it in anticipation that Jackson has sent a message to them to reach out to me. Only, it's a survey, asking me how I enjoyed my experience. I rarely fill these out, but make a note to do it later. I have to ask myself if the hotel was amazing or did Jackson make it feel that way?

Starting at the bottom of the list, I go through each email, responding to the ones that need my attention or forwarding them to Foster to answer. I'm hoping some of these inquiries read my out of office assistant message and emailed her.

The ones asking me when I'll be back get deleted. It was clearly stated on the auto return. The emails that need more attention get printed out so I don't forget about them. I keep a tidy desk and any clutter will drive me insane.

My phone rings, tearing me away from my computer. Because I can spend hours on the phone, I wear an earpiece, which is also part of our intercom system in the building.

"Yes, Foster."

"Ms. Cavanah, the bride I told you about, the one willing to pay double is on the line. Her name is Glenda... and I don't think she's the good—"

"Thanks, Foster." I cut her off even though I find her joke funny. "Story Cavanah."

"Finally," she sighs. "I have been trying to reach you for weeks."

"Technically one week as I was on vacation. What can I do for you?" I already have my massive events calendar pulled up so I can assist her.

"We want to book the Grand Plaza for our wedding, but your assistant told me the date I want is already booked!" She ends her sentence so much exaggeration that I find myself smiling.

"First, tell me your name and your fiancée's name."

"Glenda Baum and Mark Kin."

"Okay, one moment." I put her on hold and cover my mouth as I laugh. Maybe I'm the only one who notices the similarities or maybe it's because I'm lacking sleep and nothing is making sense in my world. It could be Glenda is related to L. Frank Baum and that is how she was named after his character. Of course, only with someone with the name of Story would pick up on that I suppose.

"Sorry about that. What date did you have in mind?"

Glenda tells me the date, which is in fact booked. We have four weddings that day and there is no way I can do a fifth. "I'm sorry, Glenda, but the day you want is booked. The night before is open."

"I'll pay double. Triple even."

It's not the first time a desperate bride has offered a higher fee. "Unfortunately, I can't take that offer. Like I said, the night before is open. Many couples get married on a Friday night. It allows their out of town guests a little extra time to visit our beautiful city, maybe catch a Broadway show."

"I'm supposed to be the show," she screeches.

This is probably the only part of my job tI don't like, the bridezillas. Sometimes I luck out and don't have any, but I'm guaranteed to have one per weekend. Normally, they wait until the week before to unleash their fury on me, not before we've even signed the contract.

"How about a different weekend?"

"You don't understand..." It's clear she's crying. I'm relieved this is happening over the phone and not in my office. Brides are hard enough to deal with when they're not crying, but add in the emotions and we're all done for.

"Ms. Baum, I can help with another day, but the date you're looking for is booked. I can't, in good conscious, bump another bride. Friday night is open or there's Sunday afternoon. But Saturday is booked."

"You'll hear from my lawyer." Those are the last words she says before hanging up. I lean back in my chair and cover my eyes.

"Welcome to freaking Monday," I mutter.

"Rough day already?"

Pulling my hands away, my ex is standing in the doorway. "What are you doing here, Kevin?" I took our break-up hard. He on the other hand did not. He didn't start dating or anything, but acted like it was no big deal that our long-term relationship ended.

He comes into my office and sits down. I find myself staring at him, comparing him to Jackson. Kevin wears corduroy pants and a tweed blazer. Something tells me Jackson would never be caught wearing these fabrics. No, Jackson is all about designer labels. He wants the best quality in everything.

"I heard you went on vacation."

"Really? Who would've told you that?"

"I stopped in to see your father. He said you went to Bermuda. That was very risky of you."

I'm not sure I want to know what he's doing in my father's shop or why he felt the need to go there. And it's not likely I'll forget my dad is sharing my personal information with my ex. He really ought to know better.

"Kevin, I'm really busy here." I wave my hands over my desk so he can see the pile of work I have to contend to. "What do you want?"

He reaches for my hand and studies the ring on my finger. I make the mistake of trying to pull my hand back, but holds on tighter.

"A gift?"

"No, I bought it myself." I finally pull free and tuck my hand under my desk so he can't see it.

Kevin looks at me, probably wondering if I'm lying. I honestly don't care if he does. What I do now is none of his business. He sits back down and crosses his ankle over his leg. "Story, I thought I'd come here in person to tell you I'm getting married."

I push my lips together to keep my mouth from dropping open. I couldn't get him to commit to me, but months after we break up, he's ready with someone else. Maybe he's right and I am frigid.

"Well, thanks for that."

"We'd like to book the hotel. I know firsthand what type of events you put on, and we want the best."

Shoot. Me. Now.

I paste a fake smile on my face and nod. "What day?" I pray the day he tells me is booked, but of course it isn't. It's free as can be. I work through the motions of putting together a packet for him and his... I can't even say it. "I will only hold the day for twenty-four hours. Look through the packet and give me a call tomorrow, and you can pay the deposit over the phone."

"Aren't you at least curious as to whom I'm marrying?"

I stand and motion for him to leave. "Because it's my job, yes. But because I know you and we have a history, I really don't care, Kevin. I'm glad you found someone to put up with your mundane life."

He looks at me with shock. If I could call Jackson and thank him for this bit of self-esteem he gave me, I would.

"Furthermore, I rarely deal with grooms. It'd be best if your bride stopped in with the paperwork tomorrow. Have her call and make an appointment with Foster."

I slam my door in his face, which feels amazing. The large picture window I have in my office faces Fifth Avenue. Lucky for me, people can't see in, which helps my people watching tremendously. I stand there, looking down at the front door, waiting for Kevin to leave. Just as he walks out, a runner crashes into him, knocking him down, but the runner never loses stride. I fist pump, point and laugh at him, sad and yet thankful he can't see me.

TWENTY

Jackson

I'm two weeks behind schedule. I should be in the States already, but when I went back to the office, I ran into a little hiccup. The company we're acquiring—the one that has already agreed the terms in writing—has decided to up the price. But it's not only the price that has kept me here negotiating with them, but also they want to retain their distribution rights "in the event" they decide to open another shop elsewhere.

I had no choice but to agree to the new price, but I was adamant they were not going to retain any rights. After much to'ing and fro'ing, we finally agreed on new terms, verbally, and now they're waiting for me to fly over so we can sign on the dotted line.

Apart from that, everything else in the States is moving along swimmingly. The refurbishment we're doing on the building we bought to use as our distribution centre is almost done and we should be ready to go by the time the deal is finalised and ownership of the store transfers over to us. I'm planning on closing the store for a couple of days and will reopen with new signage, including one advising the public that it's has new owners. We'll have to take the rest of the rebrand slowly, though, as the last thing we want to do is lose any business. Plus, once the news gets out we have taken over, hopefully there'll be a flock of new customers and we'll be dealing with an immediate increase in sales. Once our products are on the shelves, I expect them to fly off there like hot cakes, with people queuing up to buy them before they sell out.

"So, when are you actually moving?" Max asks. He hands me a bottle of beer. We're sitting on the rooftop patio of my old place, which overlooks the London landscape. I had one of the nicest flats around and I still regret having to give it up. It didn't make sense keeping it on when I was moving abroad. Luckily, Max snagged it before the landlord put it out for rent.

"I don't know yet," I tell him.

"Please tell me you're not thinking of staying here and commuting."

I shake my head. "Fuck, no. Can you imagine the commute? Seven hours on a plane together with a five-hour time difference. No thanks. I'm moving. I'm just delaying it a little."

"Because of the girl?"

I nod. I know it's stupid, but I half-hoped for some reason Lady Luck would be on my side and Jade would turn up here or maybe she'd call. I know it's a farfetched notion, she's in the same boat as me—she doesn't have any of my information.

"I still can't believe you didn't follow her to the gate. At least you'd have known where to start looking for her."

"We made an agreement. Besides, I'm not looking for her. I have nothing to go on."

Max sits down on the chair next to mine and kicks his

pasty white feet out in front of him. One of the side effects of working long hours behind a desk is the inability to get out and about and making the most of the good weather, when we have it. The only reason I had a bit of tan before I went to Bermuda is because we had a few weeks of hot weather and I took advantage of it and played a few games of footie before I left.

"Dude, you need to book yourself in for a tanning session. Are you auditioning to play a vampire or something? You're blinding," I tell him. We both laugh, but he does nothing to cover up. "How's work? Are you going to make partner?"

He shakes his head. "No, not for a long time, at least. This new girl started, and let me just say rumour has it she's shagging her way to the top. Our boss has already given her three of the most high-profile cases we have now." He takes a long sip of his beer. "To be honest, I'll probably be better off looking somewhere else."

"You could always work for me. Try out New York. I need a good lawyer in the company. Plus, I hear the women in the city are fucking hot!"

Out of the three of us, Max is the youngest, and on his twenty-first birthday, I gave him a blow-up doll. Tommy and I set her up so she was sitting at the bar in a bra and knickers, and paid a few blokes to pretend to talk to her. For a minute, Max thought she was real. When he found out she wasn't, he was so pissed off, but eventually saw the funny side. I'm pretty sure Anita Little is still in the storing cupboard at the back of Tommy's bar.

"The last thing I need right now is a woman."

"I thought the same thing and then I met Jade, and man..." I shake my head. I don't know if I can hire a private investigator to find her or not, but I must do something. I must know if what we had on holiday is worth pursuing in the real world. I think it is. And I think she knows it too, but is too afraid I'd reject her now our holiday is over.

"Hey, dickheads!" Tommy yells from behind us. I turn around and see his arms are full of beer and he has a couple of shopping bags hanging precariously on his fingers. I get up to help him, taking the beer of course.

"What are you doing here? I thought the plan was that we were meeting you at the Goat?"

"I've got Simon managing the bar for me tonight, because we're hitting the town," Tommy says. I glance at Max, who shrugs.

"Hey, hey, hey, we're all here."

I look over Tommy's shoulder to see a string of people walking through the door. They all stop and shake my hand, welcoming me back and wishing me a good trip. Most of them are people who live close to us or the pub, but there are also a few we know from Max's Uni days.

"All right, what's going on?"

Max comes over and puts his arm around my shoulder. "We couldn't let you come home and then leave us again without a proper party."

"Man, you didn't have to do this."

"Any excuse to party," Tom says. "So, you're going to have to deal with it, and drink up."

Getting drunk is the farthest thing on my mind right now. There are far too many people here and I've already spotted an old flame of mine. She's already giving me the eye and there's no doubt she has something very specific in mind. I'm not in the right frame of mind to entertain anyone, unless it's Jade.

Christ, I would give anything right now to see Jade walk through the door, or even show up at my office. My office would be ideal. I could play out another fantasy of taking her on my desk and having my wicked way with her. Just thinking about her gives me a hard-on, and being in among a bevy of people isn't the best place to get one of those.

I try my best to mingle and avoid any questions on why I'm back here already. My go-to answer is I had some remaining business to take care of. They don't need to know about Jade, and that I had to come back home to get my head straight. I'm still not quite in the right frame of mind, and it's probably not going to sort itself out until I get over her.

As the night goes on though, my former flame moves close to me until she has me cornered. Try as I might, I can't remember her name. Clearly, it wasn't important to know it when we were getting it on, but I feel like an arse not knowing it now.

"Hey, Jay, remember me?" she asks as she stands so close she's almost invading my personal space.

I nod. "Yep, of course."

"How have you been?"

"Good. Getting ready to move to the States."

"Oh, I love it there." She places her hand on my arm. I want to shake it off, but don't want to be rude. "Where are you going?"

"New York. I have business over there."

"Oh, New York is on my list of places to go. I've been to Florida. It's gorgeous there. You should go sometime."

"Good to know, I'll add it to my list."

One would think my stilted answers would hint that I was not in the mood for conversation, but instead, she slides next to me and leans back against the wall of the roof. There is no way she's going anywhere soon.

"So..."

166

"So," I say back. I don't usually get lost for words but I haven't a clue what to say to her. Having a one-night stand with her is the furthest thing from my mind. I'm not interested in the slightest.

"You don't remember my name, do you?"

I shake my head while trying to keep eye contact with her. "I'm sorry, I don't. I've been trying to think of it since I saw you walk in." It's not the truth, but she doesn't need to know I've been thinking about another woman all night.

"Ashley," she tells me. She doesn't seem too upset that I don't remember her.

"Yes, that's right, Ashley. Now I remember. What have you been up to lately?"

"Well, I've graduated from university and have started working. Being a responsible adult sucks though. I had to work through the summer, which means I couldn't go on holiday, when I wanted to. I'm dying to go to Ibiza."

"It's beautiful there."

"Have you been?" she asks, touching my arm again.

"A few times. It's definitely worth it."

"Maybe we should go sometime and you can be my tour guide"

I start to shake my head, but hold off. "I have a fairly full plate now, what with the move. I don't know when I'll go on my next holiday."

"Well, maybe I can come over and see you in New York once you've settled in?"

How do you turn someone down nicely? I'd normally feed them some white lie, tell them I'm busy, and that I'll call them as soon as things settle down. Try to be a vague as possible, but I get the feeling Ashley won't get the hint.

"Sure. I mean if you do find yourself there, then give me a call. I'll see if I can find some time to show you around."

The smile on her face tells me she's heard what I said and absolutely got the wrong impression. I only hope that by the time she can visit, I won't be in New York anymore, or if I am, I'm so busy I don't have time to meet her.

My night continues much the same as it started. I stand leaning against the wall and watch people mingle. Every so often, Tommy checks on me, making sure I'm okay. He's probably wondering why I'm such a miserable sod. I can't explain it. It feels like I've gone through a massive breakup and am heartbroken. It was one week and I'm acting like it was years.

That's because in that one week, I fell in love with a girl and don't see that changing anytime soon. It's stupid to think I can love someone after one week, but I do. I need to figure out a way to find her once I get to New York. I must see her again. Even if it's just so I can get closure.

After a few hours, I bid my friends goodbye and head back to my parents. Max offered to let me crash on his floor, but nothing beats the home cooking I know I can get when I'm with my mum. When I get home, they're both awake and watching a film.

"Hey, son," my dad says as I walk in.

"Dinner's in the oven," Mum tells me.

"Thanks. Sorry I didn't call. The guys threw a surprise party."

My mum gets up from the sofa and follows me into the kitchen. She takes out the food from the oven and serves it up on a plate, even though I tell her I can do it myself.

"I want to. In a few days, you'll be gone and I just... well, I'm glad you've been here these past couple weeks."

"Yeah, me too." I take a seat at the table and wait for her. She puts my plate down in front of me, along with a piece of freshly made apple pie. I'm tempted to start with pudding

168

first, but know that'll earn me a telling off. Coming home was the right thing to do. I needed to be here, back with my family where I feel grounded.

"I think I'm going to leave at the end of the week."

Mum nods. "I thought as much. And what have you decided about Jade?"

I put down my fork and sigh. "Once I've settled in, I'm going to put an ad in the papers. One of those seeking a connection type of things."

"Where will you put it?"

Shrugging. "I'll start with the major cities and hope for the best."

Mum puts her hand over mine. She smiles. "You'll find your Jade. I can feel it."

For my sake, I hope my mum is right. Having Jade back in my life will change my current outlook.

TWENTY-ONE

Story

---

*A*s soon as I step into my office, the anxiety I have been feeling over today sets in. I'm meeting with Kevin's fiancée, the woman who he committed to after a few months, when I couldn't even convince him sex on a daily or every other day basis is part of a normal relationship or we should live together to save money. I spent half the night, tossing and turning, wondering if he cheated on me with her, and ran a list of questions through my mind that would tell me as such when I meet her today.

Foster smiles when she sees me. She knows what today will bring. It's the catalyst for what is surely going to be a shitty week. Not only is the hotel booked solid with guests, but also a majority of those guests are here for five very large weddings and two conventions.

"Your nine o'clock is here," she says quietly, as if to soften the blow that Kevin's choice is right behind me, likely throwing daggers into my back that are etched with ridiculous sayings like, "I won" or "He's mine," except she has no reason to. It's not like I'm going to fight her for him or go running back to Kevin, begging for him to take me back. She can have him fair and square.

So no, she's probably some sugary sweet woman who is unbelievably excited to be getting married and it's my job to make sure the venue she has chosen is exactly what she wants. I turn and grin. There are two women, both with beaming smiles on their faces.

"Diane?" I'm moving forward with my hand extended, praying that one of them will stand up and shake it. When she does, I'm taken back by how beautiful she is. Not that Kevin doesn't deserve beautiful. I just remember him taking blatant jabs at the money I spent on lotions and cosmetics.

"It's nice to meet you, Story. Kevin has told me so much about you."

Cue awkward pause. What on earth would he say to his new love about his former ex? It's not like our break-up was amicable. It was messy, dirty, and a lot of hate was spewed both ways. Mostly from me because of the way he made me feel worthless and undesirable.

"You too, Diane."

The woman next to her stands and reaches for my hand. "I'm Nita, Diane's maid of honor."

"It's very nice to meet you both. Now come with me and let's get started." They follow me into my office and take a seat on the other side of my desk. While my computer boots up, I pull out the portfolios I have built over the years to give brides some ideas. Most come in knowing what they want while others haven't a clue. "Can I get you ladies some coffee or tea?"

"We'll take coffee," Nita says.

"Perfect. Why don't you start leafing through the books, and I'll be right back." Normally I would ask Foster to bring in what I need, but this is the perfect time for me to take a quick breather and gather myself.

Foster's eyes are wide when I step out of my office. I motion for her to follow me into our kitchenette area.

"She's not hideous," she says as she reaches for a serving tray.

"Nope, she's not. And she seems nice, if not a bit timid, but that's to be expected. She's about to design a wedding. No pressure or anything."

"And her friend?"

"Same, although she did speak for her, but I'm chalking it up to nerves. It can't be easy sitting in your fiancé's ex's office. I don't know what the fuck Kevin was thinking."

Foster puts her hand on mine. "He's thinking the Grand Plaza is the best place to get married and knows the event coordinator will do an amazing job."

I smile at her compliment and take it to heart. While she's accurate that the Grand Plaza is the best, I don't know if Kevin was thinking the latter about me. Foster opts to carry the tray in. She also puts a few pastries on there and adds a small vase of flowers I didn't realize we had.

When we walk in, expectant eyes greet us, along with cheerful smiles. I don't know if these two women are trying to put me at ease or what, but it's working. Taking my seat, I log into my computer and pull up our price chart. I have it memorized, but I like it for reference.

"Okay, Diane and Nita, let's get started. First thing, when do you want to get married?"

Diane gives me her date, which surprisingly is open. I try not to let it bother me that it's in two months, but it does sting a little.

"Do you know what you want?"

She looks at Nita, who implores her to speak up.

Diane's body sighs, as if she's giving into her friend. "I'd like purple, and I know it's your favorite color, but—"

I hold my hand up, stopping her. "This is *your* wedding, Diane. You're marrying Kevin, not me. Believe me, I'm over him and very happy he's found someone." I have found someone too, except I don't know his real name and the memories I have of him are fading. I have found myself making things up just so I can think about him.

"See, I told you she'd be amazing." Nita bumps her shoulder into her friend's. Diane nods, almost as if she needed the both of us to reassure her everything will be okay.

"Are you thinking lavender?" I ask.

Diane shakes her head. "Dark velvet, almost black."

My eyes go wide, wondering if Kevin realizes this. He hates black, refuses to own anything of that hue. I thumb through the color samples we have for linens and show her the darkest one, but she shakes her head. "Do you have a sample? We can always have linens ordered."

"Is there an additional cost?" Diane asks.

"There is, but it won't be much since we'll keep the linens. Do you have a florist in mind?"

Diane shakes her head again. "Kevin said that you could do it all."

Of course he did. "We can, sort of. How it works is I will contact all necessary vendors and you will meet with them. The fee you pay us will be distributed to cover the others."

"What services do you offer?" Nita asks.

"Everything," I tell them. "Dress, tuxedos, bridal gifts, photography, flowers… anything you would consider part of the wedding. Each package is tailored to your specifications.

The one caveat is our dresses are rentals and I know a lot of brides want to keep theirs."

"Oh yes, I definitely want to keep mine."

"And my dress. I'd like to keep it," Nita adds. I've never met a bridesmaid who wanted to keep their dress. In my line of work, I have seen some repugnant creations and have often wondered what brides are thinking when they pick them out. Research shows brides do this so the guests aren't fawning over the bridesmaid dresses, but only hers. There's a lot of truth to that.

"Completely doable. Like I said, we can do whatever."

I spend the rest of my morning with Diane and Nita, going through details. From what I can tell, Diane is a bit goth when it comes to her color choices, but I like them. Her dark velvet and cream-colored night ceremony will be beautiful, even if she's marrying my ex.

The worst part is I like Kevin's fiancée. Like *really* like her when I want to hate her. Diane is everything I'm not, and perfect for Kevin. She's a librarian, a lover of the written word when I'd opt for the film version of a book any day. In spending time with her, I also found out she loves math. I mean, who the hell loves math? It's complicated and half the time doesn't make sense with its ridiculous rules, but Kevin is an accountant and was always spouting mathematical terms I had no understanding of. But Diane... ugh. I hate-hate-hate that Kevin has someone and I've only found, and subsequently lost, the most amazing man I have ever met.

I keep telling myself someone will come along, that Jackson showed me that I'm worth it. Kevin had really done a number on my self-esteem, but in a matter of days, Jackson changed the way I look at myself. I only wish he was still here because I could really use him right about now.

"Ms. Cavanah, Silver from *Babes, Inc.* is on the line," Foster says, interrupting my thoughts. My head hangs as I audibly groan. I'd rather deal with Kevin than with anyone from *Babes, Inc.*, the biggest convention company for adult sex toys. This week starts four days of hell for me. I love my job, but some of the companies who use our facility for their events are less than desirable in my professional opinion. The Grand Plaza is an upscale hotel. The best of everything, and yet the Board of Directors won't discriminate against who is allowed to book our conference rooms. I know... discrimination is bad and all that, but I feel as if our clientele deserves better, and hosting the ninth annual sex toy convention isn't my idea of better. People like Madonna who stay at our hotel don't really need to see "titty-tassles." Okay, bad example. But there are others, more distinguished like our president... the point is, it's not for me and I shudder at the thought of thousands of people walking in and out of the hotel after having touched the same phallus-shaped objects all day. I think that should be done in private, at a store where there isn't a ton of people staring while one examines the battery-operated boyfriend to see if it's to your liking. And don't get me started on the men. I think they're sometimes worse than horny women.

Of course when we hold these types of conventions, the atmosphere at work is boisterous. Everyone here gets a free sample from the distributor. In fact, they love it when a popular convention is held here because they get free stuff. Not to mention any food which is leftover.

As much as it pains me to answer this call, I have no choice. "Story Cavanah."

"Story, darling. It's Silver from Babes. You remember me, don't you?"

"Of course." Not that I could ever forget a name like

Silver or the fact that she offered to demonstrate the Anaconda 3000 in my office when she arrived to sign the contract which could've easily been done through our web portal. "What can I do for you?"

"I wanted to let you know Jay Collins will be in attendance and wanted to make sure he's booked at the hotel, in the penthouse suite."

Um... who? "Unfortunately, Silver, I don't handle the hotel reservations. I'll gladly transfer you."

"Oh no, I've already spoken to Rene and she insists you're booked, and frankly that just won't do."

Please grant me the serenity I need to get through this call. "I understand, Silver. I do, and I wish I could help, however my hands are tied. There isn't anything I can do if the rooms are booked. I'm sure Mr. Collins will be happy at one of the many hotels within walking distance of the Grand Plaza, or perhaps a different room?" I push my fingers into my temple to ward off the impending headache.

Silver laughs. "Clearly, you don't have any idea who Jay Collins is?"

"I'm sorry, I don't. His name doesn't ring any bells."

"He's only the owner of the largest and oldest manufacturer in sex toys."

"That's great," I say, and I don't really care. "But like I said, my hands are tied when it comes to reservations. Now, is there anything else I can help you with, Silver?"

"It'll be a mistake for the Grand Plaza if he's not booked there."

And one we're willing to take.

"I'll take that to my staff meeting and if anything changes, I'll give you call." I hang up and lay my head down in my desk and repeat my mantra, "I love my job. I love my job."

TWENTY-TWO

Jackson

*S*tanding outside the building I'm minutes away from owning is surreal. This moment has been a long time coming. It was my vision to expand to the States, and take over existing businesses in a bid to build a massive manufacturing facility here, employing hundreds of people as a result. My father thought I was insane, but gladly handed the reins over and wished me good luck. Of course, now that the day has finally arrived, he's called me multiple times to make sure everything is "okay." I placated him during each call, knowing deep down he wanted to ask if I was having second thoughts about investing our hard-earned cash into this business. This deal will roll over into the next and so on until I have at least one shop in every major city, all except for Vegas, which is known to be a hard market to crack. We don't sell sex or allow it in any of our stores. I'm not sure our standards could live up to those in Las Vegas.

But my dad could never bring himself to bite the bullet and ask outright if I was having second thoughts and I respect him for that. It doesn't matter who I am or what I do, with every investment comes a bucket load of worry, not only in my own mind, but also from everyone around me. Even Max, who gave the terms of my purchase and the contract with the Cavanahs the once over, was a little hesitant to tell me that this was a good idea. I get it, they just have my best interests at heart, but they also know I can sniff out a good investment when I see one and this is definitely a bloody good investment. Sure, there's a lot of money being exchanged today, but it'll be worth it. I'm determined to ensure this venture is a success.

I've toyed with knocking down the existing building and rebuilding it, but my engineer pretty much put the kybosh on my plans right from the start, telling me it would take months, if not a year or longer, of standing in front of various boards seeking the approvals and building permissions I would need to have in order to get the design I wanted. He also said something about the business being grandfathered and I shouldn't mess with what's already there unless I want to open the "can of worms" and face the people who are trying to clean up the city. There are also the current owners and the people I'm buying out who live in the building and the sales agreement stipulates they have a two-year period to find a new place to live.

To be honest, the sooner they move, the better. I have big plans for the flat they occupy in the building. It'll become part of the business: an office space for the shop manager together with ample space for a boardroom to conduct business meetings. I haven't decided if my office will be here or at the warehouse, but I imagine I'll spend quite a big chunk of my time here. My parents think I should also live here, but I prefer my loft space I found in Brooklyn. The character of the old building and the newly refurbished interior won me over. The biggest selling point, though, was having access to the roof. During my first few nights here, I think I stayed up there until the sun rose, just watching the city as it came to life and completely ignoring any advice given to me on the best way to get rid of jet lag. It was worth it though. After all, America is the land where dreams come true and I was finally here living mine.

From the outside, no one would know this quaint little bookshop is a disguise for one of the oldest sex shops in New York. The underground shop used to take up the entire block and was three levels below ground, stocking every product made, except for ours. Up until now, we didn't distribute to the U.S. Over the years, this business has hit hard times and has had to continuously downsize, meaning valuable business space is going to waste. It's my plan to change all it.

The cute little bookstore storefront convinced me to make an offer on this business. I have no intention of getting into the book business, but it was very like the shops we have in Europe. They all look family friendly on the outside, but our name is synonymous with sex toys, so people knew when they found our shops, they were not child friendly. Here, though, we'll have a full-time "babysitter" on hand who will read the kids books and entertain them with arts and crafts and video games, so their parents can do their private shopping downstairs. It sounds all kinds of wrong, but it'll bring in the customers and sales will rocket.

The alarm on my phone goes off, indicating that it's time for me to walk into my soon-to-be newly acquired venture. The bell above the door rings and an older woman glances up at me. I stumble over an imaginary line once I see her. She looks familiar almost like we've met before. I don't know if it's her lightly coloured hair or her green eyes remind me of Jade, but something doesn't feel quite right. Shaking away the cobwebs, I walk towards her, with my hand held out.

"Hello, I'm Jay Collins." I introduce myself and shake her hand.

"Gwen Cavanah," she replies with a light, but firm handshake.

"Gwen. Is that short for something?" I know I'm laying it on a bit thick, but it's the businessman in me that needs to know these things. Sometimes when a deal is about to head in a direction I don't want, I normally use my charm to bring it back to a good place. In this case, knowing this woman's name is my secret weapon.

"Actually, it's Guinevere, but no one has ever asked me that."

Works every time.

"Guinevere, as in King Arthur?"

"Of course. My mother is Welsh and was rather put off I didn't marry an Arthur or even a Lancelot, although she wasn't a fan of his as much."

"No, I suppose waiting for a man to come along that fits a specific description would be rather tiresome."

Gwen laughs. "You have no idea. Anyway, let me lock up and I'll take you to the office. My husband Conway should be waiting for us." As she locks the door, I look around the shop. I'm planning on spending a good amount of time here on weekends, learning all about the books we will sell and how we can increase our stocks with new titles.

"Follow me." Gwen leads me to a curtained area at the back of the shop, which has a sign hanging overhead which says, "18 and older." I make a note to change that to make it more appealing and professional. We walk downstairs and through another door and enter the "Cave," as it's known.

"You must be Collins," the man behind the counter says. He looks years older than Gwen, with grey hair and glasses perched on the end of his nose.

"Please, call me Jay," I say, shaking his hand. "Will your lawyer be joining us?"

"Not needed. I think we've hammered everything out, unless you think we need one here?"

I shake my head. "I think everything is in order." I open my briefcase and pull out the papers. Each page is tabbed, showing us where to sign. As we flip through, I notice an additional signature is needed to complete the documents.

"Will Story be joining us soon?" I don't have any idea who this 'Story' person is, but they need to counter-sign the agreement so the sale can be finalised.

Gwen sighs. "Sorry, Story is our daughter. We thought she'd be here. Let me call her." Conway gives her the telephone, and she smiles as she waits for her daughter to pick up. *"Hello, dear. Are you on your way? Oh, okay. I'll tell him."* She hangs up and her grin turns into a frown. "I'm sorry, but she's tied up at a conference right now, but says she'll swing by tonight to sign the papers."

I'm trying not to let this delay bother me, but it does. It's Thursday, I have other places I need to be and I wanted to get the papers filed so the ownership can be handed over. Now I must wait until their daughter shows up and signs on the dotted line.

"Where is she? I'm happy to take the papers over to her. I'd really like to get them finalised and filed with the relevant authorities as soon as possible, so the transfer of money can take place, which I'm sure is also your preference?" Conway's eyes light up at the sound of money being mentioned and he nods once before looking at his wife. I knew the subject of cash would be a sure-fire way of getting things moving along. Besides, he was the one who put the price up when I decided to go home and nurse my broken heart.

"She's the event coordinator at the Grand Plaza," Gwen tells me.

I can't help but smile. "That's perfect actually. I'm heading there next as I'm a guest speaker at a conference going on tonight. I'm surprised you're not attending, to be honest," I say to Conway, who shakes his head.

"Our daughter... she doesn't appreciate the business side of things."

"She's embarrassed," Gwen adds with a shrug.

I nod with understanding, but I far from understand. There is nothing to be embarrassed about when it comes to sex. It's the most natural thing to experience with someone, and whether one's other half isn't around, or one's single, there isn't any reason why one shouldn't pleasure one's self. Of course, thinking about sex and masturbation brings back the memory of pleasuring myself in front of Jade. I would give anything to do that again. This, however, isn't the time or place to have such a memory, and of course, doing so has left me with an awkward situation on my hands.

"Do you mind if I have a look around?" I excuse myself before either of them can give me an answer and peruse the shelves. As soon as the deal is done and I have the keys in my hand, my builders will come in and knock down the walls. The empty room behind us will be repainted and have new shelving units installed. All the stock will move into there and the front of the shop will be refurbished and serve as the 'welcome' area for the customers. The goal is to return this shop to its former glory, ensuring it's done sympathetically and aesthetically in line with the style of the building. If I change it too much, it could result in the business taking a hit. Too little, however, could mean I don't garner enough interest to keep the current clientele and gain new ones. My plan next week is to find the right balance in the rebuild, and finding the right toys to stock once we re-open.

Walking around a sex shop with a growing hard-on isn't my idea of fun, far from it in fact. Gwen and Conway speak in whispers behind me as I try to imagine every gross thing I can to soften the problem I have in my pants.

"I must go back upstairs," Gwen says behind me and I take a deep breath and turn around to face her. Her hands are clasped together, twisting nervously. "It was nice meeting you, Jay. We'll be good tenants. I know it's in our contract that you can't evict us for two years—"

"I have no intention of violating our agreement," I tell her, hoping to calm her down a little and put her worries at ease. "I'm a man of my word, Gwen. As I told Conway many times over the phone, he still has a job here, as do you, if you'd like it. I'm not here to toss anyone out on the street."

"Thank you, that is very kind of you." She smiles at me and turns away. I lock eyes with Conway, who looks like he's about to tear our contract to shreds. I can't let that happen.

"I best get going," I tell him as I gather the papers together. "Once your daughter signs these, I'll drop them off at the clerk's office for filing and drop the cheque off."

"Okay, sure."

I pause before I reach the door. "I meant what I said, there's a job here if you want it." I don't wait for his answer and walk up the stairs and out the door without making eye contact with Gwen for fear of seeing her cry, which is the last thing I want. I'm not ruthless, but I am a businessman and this sale is all about business.

Hailing a taxi in the city is easy and with one quick whistle, I'm in the back of a speeding yellow cab and on my way to the Grand Plaza hotel. During the drive, I look over the papers and my eyes linger on Story's name. I laugh, thinking how funny it is they've called their daughter Story and own a bookshop. I suppose, in hindsight, they couldn't have called her after another product they sell.

The Grand Plaza is luxurious, if not a little ostentatious. Everything is marble and in black and gold. Whoever built this hotel spared no expense when it came to details. To think that *Babe* is having a toy convention here is a bit ridiculous, but I guess even the big wigs like their toys.

"Hello, I'm looking for Story Cavanah," I tell the young receptionist at the front desk.

"May I tell her who's calling?"

"Yes, it's Jay Collins."

She picks up the phone and dials a number, whilst I continue to look around on the pretence I'm not listening to her conversation.

"Hi Foster, there's a Jay Collins here to see Ms. Cavanah. Okay. Sure. Oh, okay." She hangs up and clears her throat. "I'm sorry, but Ms. Cavanagh's assistant said she's not in her office right now. May I take a message and have her call you?"

"No, it's fine. Can I assume she'll be back shortly?"

"Yes, she's in the building, but tending to the conventions going on right now."

"Thank you, I'll come back again in a few minutes." I walk towards the lifts with my phone pressed against my ear. "Silver, I'm here and in the lift."

"Perfect, I'll meet you there. Just wait until you see the crowd."

"Can't wait." I met Silver years ago at an event I held.

She approached me with a business idea of doing these types of conventions all over the place. This is the first time my company has participated with her, though, and the timing couldn't be any more perfect.

As soon as I get out of the lift, Silver is there, waiting for me with her arms open wide for a hug. I walk towards her and suddenly stop dead in my tracks because out of the corner of my eye, I see her...

TWENTY-THREE

Story
———

The sheer amount of people at the sex convention is mind-boggling. As with any event held at the hotel, I peek in on them, making sure the organizers are doing okay and don't need anything. If my job is stressful, the organizers must be at their wit's end by the time the doors open, praying they've crossed every T and dotted every I. Their businesses can easily flounder with a bad showing. I suppose ours could too if we were to receive a bad review, which is why I'm here. I may not agree with this type of display, but as the customer of what surely is a booming business, it's my job to make sure they're happy.

I'm thankful my parents are getting out of the sex toy business. It's been hard on them and us as a family. Growing up, Jackie was my only friend. Her mother worked for my parents so it only made sense she wouldn't care about Jackie being my friend, but others didn't see it that way. I wasn't raised in the "sex" world, so to speak. I wasn't one of those children who went to their parents' work after school with the exception of the bookstore. One mother accused my father of ruining her marriage. I thought for the longest time my dad had cheated on my mother, but it turns out this woman's husband met another woman in my dad's store, which honestly could've happened at Starbucks. And that started it all off. From that point forward, no one could be or wanted to be my friend. They were all taught that pleasuring one's self was taboo. No one stopped to consider many people bought toys to help with dysfunction or to spice up their bedroom lives. I hated school. Being teased and ridiculed every day made me hate my parents and their professions.

Babe has rented out our largest space and by the looks of it, they could've used more room. Silver spots me and comes rushing over. Despite our tempestuous phone conversation the other day, she's been absolutely lovely.

"Story," she says as she places her hands on my upper arms and proceeds to give me air kisses. She's as American as sliced cheese, but wants everyone to think she's from Europe. It's my job to play along. I'm grateful she doesn't have a British accent because I don't think I could handle that right now.

"Good afternoon, Silver. You've really packed the place."

She looks around and smiles. "This is nothing. These people all paid double to see the products first. General admission starts at five."

"I'm impressed."

Silver claps her hands. "I must show you the Anaconda. It's every woman's dream." Her head falls back, almost as if she's recalling her own adventures with it.

I shake my head. "Thanks, but I'm not interested."

"I know you keep saying that, but I'm not giving up." She winks. "You must meet Mr. Collins when he arrives. He's our guest speaker."

"You have a guest speaker?" I should've grabbed a brochure when I walked in, but I would've never thought this was a symposium. What's he going to talk about? How to properly insert the Anaconda?

"We do. He's the leading developer in toys."

"Unbelievable," I mutter, hoping she doesn't hear me over the loud volume in the room. "Hopefully you were able to find him a suitable room?"

Silver's face morphs into something I can't accurately describe. There seems to be some irritation coupled with an eye roll, which all turns into regret? I can't be certain. "He told me not to worry about it, but this is Mr. Collins we're talking about and I…"

"I get it, Silver. You want to make sure he's fully accommodated."

"Yes," she says, grabbing onto my arm. "His support means everything, which is why I scheduled an escort for him while he's here." My eyes go wide, and she shrugs. "You know to take care of his needs. I mean I would love to be the one to fuck him, but he doesn't mix business with pleasure."

I nod, but keep my lips pressed together.

"No one can expect the Sex God to come to a convention like this, with all these women and toys, and not feel the urge, right?"

"Right." My stomach rolls and a very forced smile tries to take shape. Silver has singlehandedly reminded me why I have shunned my parents' business. "Sex God, huh?" I don't even know why I'm asking her, but the fact she called him this has me wondering. Is this a self-proclaimed title or one that has been given out by his many conquests?

"Oh, yes," she says. "He's the personification of the perfect man and he knows what it takes to make a woman feel amazing—"

"Right, well, if you need anything—"

"No, you must meet Mr. Collins. He'll want to thank you for all of this." She spreads her arms out over the room. "He will be so impressed and thankful. Even if you don't realize it, you're helping us bring pleasure to the men and women of the world."

Somehow I doubt that, and I honestly have no desire to meet his man. I have visions of him screwing half of Manhattan, and using my hotel to do it.

"I'm sorry, but I really must check on the other conventions in the hotel, not to mention the pile of work I have. These rooms don't book themselves, ya know." I laugh at my own stupid joke that she clearly doesn't get.

"Yes, I need to book for next year."

"Great!" The fake smile of mine is back. "I'll stop by later." There's a slight pout, but it changes quickly when her phone rings. She puts her finger up, motioning for me to wait, and while I have other things to do, it's my job to appease the client.

She squeals after hanging up. "Mr. Collins is here. Please stay?"

I nod, and wait while she moves the few feet into the hallway where the elevators are. I take this time to go through my messages and see one from Foster telling me the Sex God known as Mr. Collins asked to see me earlier. I roll my eyes as my imagination takes over. He probably needs a suite for the harem of women likely following him around or Silver has tasked him with giving me a demonstration of the Pocket Pussy Pro.

Of course, now all I can think about is Jackson and the first day we met, and the triplets and how they were hanging all over him. I suppose I wasn't much better. Once I got a taste of him, I wasn't about to let go.

People bustle around me, bumping into my shoulder and muttering apologies as they do. I look up, wondering what's taking Silver so long, only to have the wind knocked out of me. Perfect blue eyes stare into mine and I know it's an illusion. That my mind is playing tricks on me. I turn and survey the crowd before glancing back in his direction. He's gone and just like that, I feel a rush of tears I fight to keep at bay.

Except, I can smell him. I close my eyes and pray this sensation goes away. I have worked hard to forget him, although I never will, and this is a major setback for me. I can't believe that I can't even think about Jackson, without imagining him. I pocket my phone and turn around, only to run into...

"Jackson..." My breath catches as my hand twitches with the desire to touch him. "Are you real?" I have to ask because right now I don't trust myself enough to separate fiction from reality.

"Jade?" His eyes search mine for confirmation even if that isn't my name, I'm still the "me" he was with in Bermuda. How can this be happening? We weren't supposed to cross paths even if I had hoped we would. I never thought it would be so soon.

"I'm as real as you are," he says in his smooth accent.

My arms fling around his shoulders as I crash my lips to his, plunging my tongue deep into his mouth, desperate to taste him, while he wraps his arms tightly around my waist and moans. He pulls me tighter against his body to remind me of everything I have missed since our last time together. My dreams haven't done him justice. I'm tempted to drag him to my office and mount him, feeling his need press into me.

"Wait, you know each other?" Silver says, interrupting

us. I pull away, and hide my face, ashamed for what I have just done.

"We met while we were on holiday," Jackson says as the realization of why he's here hits me hard.

"I... uh..." I step away and when he reaches for my hand, I cross my arms. I look around the room at the nearly thousand people and shake my head. I can't even look at Jackson, knowing he's this Sex God Silver has been talking about, and knowing he's here with an escort. Without another word or shared look, I bolt from the room and head for the stairs, as I hear him call after me, using the fake name he only knows me by. Right now, I'm thankful because any one of the employees who are working could stop me for him, thinking that I can't hear my name being called. It's not hard to get lost in the mass of people and by the time I'm behind the cinderblock wall of the stairwell, I finally breathe.

And the tears flow.

And my heart breaks.

It's different this time though. When I left him at the airport, I left knowing I'd never see him again, and if we did, it would be amazing. But this... seeing him here, especially after Silver went on and on about him, I can't. I can't fathom being with him, knowing he screws anyone that comes his way.

That thought makes my stomach wrench. I cover my mouth until I can walk the few feet to the trashcan where I expel my recently eaten lunch. I know we used condoms while we were together, but I feel dirty and am probably riddled with a disease that will fester.

Rushing down the stairs as fast as I can in my heels, I head toward my office. Thankfully, Foster isn't there to see what a mess I am. I grab my purse and laptop, and leave her a note, telling her I'm working from home for the rest of the day. It's really unprofessional of me, especially with the events going on, but I can't be here, knowing Jackson is here, and likely making appointments for his next sexfest to take place.

Outside, I think I hear the name Jade being yelled again, but I ignore it. I ignore him, the man I fell in love with, as I climb into the back of the taxi. Tears stream down my face as I ask the man to drive. I normally take the train to save money, but not today. I need to get away.

Jackie is home when I arrive. One look and she's off the couch, pulling me into her arms. I tell her everything, hiccupping my way through my nightmare. She holds, consoles and offers me wine. Apparently wine fixes everything. When I finally take her up on the offer to get drunk, she hands me my own bottle.

"At least you know his name now," she says after sitting back down next to me.

"I wish I didn't. I was content thinking he was this flawless man who rocked my world, and while he looked, smelled, and kissed perfectly, knowing what I know about him makes me feel disgusted."

I get up and carry my bottle of wine to my window. "I was wrong to suggest we fake name each other, that we lie about our lives. Had he told me what he did for a living, I wouldn't be standing here right now, drowning my sorrows in wine. I wouldn't have been nursing a broken heart for weeks because my vacation would've been just that, but instead—"

"Instead you fell in love and now reality is showing you love is blind."

I scoff. "Love is stupid. I should've known better."

"I have nothing nice to say," Jackie adds. "Except—"

"Don't." I warn her. She knows how I feel about what he does. If I couldn't accept my parents doing it, there is no way I'm dating a man who is considered a Sex God, especially one who sells sex for a living.

"All I was going to say is there's a bright side."

"What's that?" I ask.

"We have a smoking hot newbie upstairs. I'm talking GQ status. I would bang him, but maybe you should."

I shake my head. "Go for it. I'm not interested."

TWENTY-FOUR

Jackson

*H*ow the fucking hell does something that's running so seamlessly turn into a bloody nightmare within a matter of seconds? I haven't been feeling completely whole since the day Jade left me at the airport to fly home. Yet, seeing her again. Kissing her again. Feeling her body pressed against mine and knowing she wants me as much as I want her? It felt like I could finally breathe, that my dark, grey world had been flooded with colour again. Only, our moment was interrupted by Silver, and I could only watch as Jade's face morphed into complete horror, and it's a feeling I don't understand.

Getting through my presentation yesterday was painful. I wanted to chase after Jade, but Silver pretty much disallowed me from doing so, blocking my view until I could no longer see where Jade had disappeared to. If I wasn't surrounded by the buyers I plan to do business with, I would've had very little hesitation in pushing her to one side so I could run after the girl that I'm one hundred percent in love with. But as always, I put the business first and let Jade slip through my fingers. In the best-case scenario, I'll hire a private investigator to see if he can find her. I also plan on sitting Silver down after the weekend and ask her exactly how she knows Jade. I need every single detail and piece of information I can get to enable me to find her again.

After my speech, I walk around the floor of the exhibition, and meet with the manufacturers of different products, setting up times where we can discuss their products in more detail and which ones I'll be interested in selling in our shops. As I anticipated, most of them were eager to do business with me and some were shocked to learn I'm in the process of buying the Cave. Many of them mentioned they were surprised the owners weren't at the exhibition themselves, but I didn't indulge them with any other information.

And now? Now I've parked myself in one of the most uncomfortable chairs I've ever had the misfortune to sit in, as I wait for Story Cavanah to arrive for work. Her assistant has assured me she'll be in today and there was an emergency which she had to deal with yesterday. I must've gone down to the front desk at least once an hour looking for her, until I was eventually informed she had left the building. I should've left a message with the receptionist first thing, but I didn't. Maybe if I had, Ms Cavanah would've been able to meet before leaving. I don't really have a good excuse to feel as frustrated as I am. I want to finalise this deal, pay the Cavanahs the money they are owed, and start the rebuild. In my business, time is money, and if the amount of people flocking to this convention is any indication, there are a lot of people who have a lot of money to spend and I want them to use their hard-earned cash in my shop.

"Ms. Cavanah should be here any minute," Foster informs me. "She's rarely late."

"Thank you," I say, before turning my attention back to the newspaper I bought from the seller on the street corner. My attention span is second to none, though; every so often, I hear people mentioning Story's name, yet when I look up expecting to see the elusive Story, she isn't there. On the fifth or so time I hear her mentioned, I look up to see Jade is standing in front of me.

"What are you doing here?" she asks in a clipped tone. The girl I know from our week in paradise stares back at me with angry eyes.

"I have a meeting—"

"He's here to meet with you, Ms. Cavanah."

I look back and forth between Foster and Jade, and the realisation slowly dawns on me who Jade is. Jade is Story. Jade is Story Cavanah. I stand up to greet her, but she looks far from impressed. Instead, she walks straight past me and through a door, with me following closely behind. She throws her bag onto a chair in the corner and sits down with a huff.

I had planned everything I wanted to say to Jade, but now that I'm facing her, I'm standing here like a bloody moron. My mind went completely blank. I can't get my head around this situation. What are the chances the bloody gorgeous girl who I spent one of the best weeks of my life with, who I shagged senseless six ways from Sunday, is the daughter of the same couple I'm buying a business from? If this means the odds are in my favour, then the first thing I need to do when I leave here is buy that frigging lottery ticket I meant to get weeks ago and hope I'm in with a chance of winning the jackpot.

I walk over to her window and look out over the city.

Jade, or rather Story, types furiously away on her laptop, clearly deciding that ignoring me seems to be the best policy. I repeat her name again and again in my head, only to be met with images of her withering under me as I say her name, except I'm no longer saying the name Jade, and the bed we're in, is mine.

"What do you want?" she asks me again. I turn around to look at her, but her eyes are focused on the screen of her computer. "I'm very busy and you're wasting my time."

Her snarky attitude catches me off guard. This isn't the woman I know. Instead of answering her, I walk over to her door and shut it, catching Foster smiling at me before I do so.

"My name is Jackson Collins, but almost everyone calls me Jay," I tell her, taking a seat on the chair in front of her desk and hoping we can start a clean slate.

"Right, figured that much out yesterday." She still refuses to look in my direction and I'm beginning to think the time we spent together meant nothing to her. Maybe she was playing a game all along and I was the poor bastard who fell for it hook, line, and sinker. Thinking about it, I guess that's exactly what happened. She was the one who wanted us to use fake names and even though I know I was telling the truth, I know she was playing a game. And now the game is over, it appears that whatever we had is too, but I refuse to accept that. One doesn't kiss someone the way she kissed me yesterday if there are no genuine feelings there. "Again, is there a reason you're sitting in my office?"

"Is this the way you want to play this? With you pretending you don't know who I am?" I ask her. At the very least, I would have imagined her parents would have told her the details of our business agreement.

She leans back in her chair and purses her lips together.

This dominant, sassy side of her I'm seeing now turns me right the fuck on, and doesn't help the perpetual hard-on I've been experiencing since I saw her yesterday.

"Sure, I do, you're the Sex God Silver filled me in about. Tell me, do you like your escort?"

I'd like to think there's a hint of jealousy in her words, but by the look on her face, I can't be sure. There is a definite hostility running through her.

"Why, are you jealous?"

"Not in the slightest, but as you can see, Mr. Collins, I am very busy so if you could tell me why you're sitting in my office without an appointment, I'd really appreciate it."

I nod slowly and bite the inside of my cheek. The girl I met in Bermuda isn't the same girl sitting across the desk from me. In fact, this one is being a complete cow, and is apparently hell bent on trying to forget I know every curve, line, divot, and valley of her body. She can pretend all she likes, but we both know we have an amazing history between us, no matter how hard she tries to forget it. But if she wants to play this game, then so be it. I open my briefcase and take out the papers that she needs to sign, placing them on her desk.

"I need you to sign these documents where indicated."

She looks up and narrows her eyes at me, and if looks could kill, then I'd be on my way to being six feet under. "You're the one putting my parents out of business and their home?"

Fuck my life.

~

I THOUGHT that the next time I walked into the bookshop, I'd be doing so with a cheque in my hand, but sadly this isn't the case. I don't even have a signed contract and I have no idea if I will soon. After my meeting with Story went tits up, I found myself sitting inside the hotel reception, making various calls to my contractors. Story left me with no choice but to put everything on hold when she vehemently declined to sign the purchase and sales agreement.

And by vehemently, I mean violently. I've never seen a pile of papers come flying at my head so fast, until earlier this morning. Add to that her stapler, various amounts of pens and, guaranteed to do some serious damage, her tape dispenser. This was all accompanied by her effing and blinding at me like a bloody sailor. When I saw her taking her shoes off, I knew I had to admit defeat and left her office as quickly as I could, closing the door just as her stiletto became airborne, flying straight towards my head.

Of course, Foster smiled as I walked past, making me wonder if this was an everyday occurrence in Story's office. The thing is, I know it's not. Something has set her off, and it's not that I'm buying her parents' business. Besides, according to them she's embarrassed so you'd think she'd be chomping at the bit to sign the papers and be rid of it once and for all.

I've been trying to figure out why she's had this sudden change of heart about us and find it hard to believe it's because Silver told her about me having an escort, which, by the way, I don't have. I told Silver I didn't want one. Ever since I slept with Jade, I mean Story, having sex with someone else is the last thing I want to do. Even though I'm sure she hates my guts now, Story must know I would choose her above anybody else any day of the week. No, her attitude towards me must be about the business and not about what happened in Bermuda.

"Hello, Gwen," I say as I walk into the shop. I haven't

spoken to her or Conway about their daughter's actions and thought it would be a better idea to sit down with them both. Currently, I'm at a stalemate and I haven't got a bloody clue what to do about it.

"Mr Collins, what a surprise. Are you ready for your keys?" Gwen asks me and it's as if she can't wait to hand them over to me. Apart from the fact that they upped the asking price when I failed to show up the first time, they've seemed to be on board with selling. Conway even mentioned that he'd like to finally take his wife on a well-deserved break. Are they telling Story something else or is she doing this to piss me off?

"Unfortunately, Story didn't sign the papers like we hoped she would."

"Oh?"

I shake my head. "I'm don't know why exactly, but your daughter threw me out of her office and told me never to come back."

Gwen blanches. "That doesn't sound like Story at all. She's very level headed and has been ready for us to sell for a long time."

"So, I thought. You said she was embarrassed?"

"Oh yes," she says with a nod. "She had a rough go of it in high school, blamed us... well, her father mostly for not having a reputable job."

"Aha. So, her not signing the contracts doesn't make sense, then?"

She shakes her head slowly. "Not at all. I will speak to her though and give you a call?"

"How about this." I pick up a scrap of paper from the counter and write down an address. "I've made some dinner reservations at this restaurant tonight, for four people. Bring her along, but please don't tell her I'll be there. Maybe if the three of us can show her that this is a good deal, she'll come around?"

Gwen takes the paper from me hesitantly. "If you think so."

"Trust me, I do." Gwen doesn't need to know that I have carnal knowledge of her daughter, and I'm resorting to dirty tactics. It's obvious Story is willing to forget about our time together in Bermuda. I, however, am not. It's not even an option for me. What is, though, is giving up on this deal if it will make her happy, even though something tells me her parents could do with the money.

As soon as I walk out of the shop, I'm on the phone, calling my mum. When I left England, we said we'd video chat every Sunday, making use of the WIFI so I don't run up an extortionate phone bill, but that's the last thing on my mind now. I need her motherly words of wisdom.

"Jackson," she shouts into the phone. "How is America?"

"The land of opportunity. I have something to tell you."

"What's that?" I can hear the excitement in her voice.

"I've found her, mum. In the most unbelievably twisted form of irony, I've found her."

"Oh, son, that's amazing. Tell me all about it."

I spend the next hour, pacing up and down in front of the shop, filling my mum in on everything. At one point, she offers to fly over and knock some sense into Story. According to my mum, I'm the most amazing man there's ever been, and mums always speak the truth. I'm not about to disagree with her.

"So, what are you going to do?"

"Put the deal on hold and woo the ever-loving shit out of the girl."

I can hear her clapping on the other end. "That's my boy!"

TWENTY-FIVE

Story

_____

*T*he last thing I want to do is go to dinner with my parents, but when my mom called... well, she didn't leave me much choice. It's never a good sign when either of my parents use my full name to start off a conversation, and when she sternly used mine, I knew I was in for it. I expected it, but was unprepared to be on the receiving end of her demands.

Thankfully, she allowed me enough time to go home and change; only, now that I'm home, leaving is the last thing I want to do. Jackie has stocked the refrigerator with wine and every bottle is tempting me. Unfortunately, the new man who moved in has blocked our roof access. Technically, he pays for it, but we all used it while the loft was vacant.

Nothing in my closet looks good. My clothes seem drab, old and barely hanging on by threads. None of this is true. It's my way to stall the inevitable. My parents will want to know why I didn't sign the papers today and I don't know what to tell them. For most of my life, I've wanted nothing more than to have them sell the stupid store and now they are, I don't want them to, at least, not to Jackson Collins. They can sell to anyone else in the world, as long as it's not Jackson.

I crawl onto my bed and bury my face into my pillow. The tears come easily and the sobs cause my body to shake. I dreamed of the day when I would run into him again, but not like this. Not being some sex toy guru who has been labeled a Sex God by some chick named Silver, although he was a god when we together. I suppose it makes sense though. Jackson knew his way around my body. He made me feel things I didn't even know existed. He made me crave him, desire to be connected to him. It was all a game of some sorts for him. He probably saw me across the pool, looking lonely, and figured I'd be an easy conquest. Well, the joke's on me now, isn't it?

I'm tempted to call my mother and cancel. The mood I'm in is teetering between depressed and homicidal, not that I'd actually kill someone, but I'd like to ring Jackson's neck all while hugging him, kicking him, kissing him, and strangling him. I'm mad at him but on the other hand, I want to fall into his arms and make love to him until the end of my days. None of which can happen. His profession... I can't accept that.

"What are you doing?"

I turn to find Jackie leaning in my doorway. By the look of her hair, she's coming fresh from her shift at the hospital.

"Wallowing in self-pity."

"Why, what happened?" She comes into my room and sits on the edge of my bed. "I expected to have a text message telling me you fucked your gorgeous Brit all over your desk."

I wish.

"We both know that isn't going to happen." I sit up and

hug my pillow to my chest. I don't bother wiping away the makeup stains that are sure to be on my face.

"It's just a job, Story. One that earns him a shit ton of money."

"How do you know?" I ask.

Jackie shrugs. "I looked him up online. I gotta tell you, he's fucking hot, and I'm rather jealous you met him first."

I'm not sure hot is the word I'd use for him. He's fucking gorgeous, but looks can only get you so far. "I can't believe you looked him up."

"I can't believe you haven't," Jackie scoffs. "You're acting like he's scorned you. He hasn't. So what if he owns the biggest European manufacturer of sex toys? Hook a sister up!" She taps my leg. "That man rocked your world and for weeks you moped around here. Well, he's here, Story. He's in fucking New York City and walked into your hotel. If this isn't some form of kismet, I don't know what is."

"It's not that easy, Jackie. You know that."

"I know. It's his profession. I get it. I was there when the kids treated you like shit. When they taped condoms to your locker and asked if your mother had a strap on, but the world has changed. Porn is free on the web, and women are more into expressing themselves. Maybe if you tried—"

"I'm not trying a dildo or vibrator so I can get over my aversion—"

"Not even for Jackson? The man you fell in love with without knowing a single thing about him, except he's not a liar?"

"How do you know he's not a liar?" I ask.

Jackie throws her hands up in the air. "He told you his name, Story. While you said yours was Jade, he said Jackson. So what if he goes by Jay in the professional world? He told you the name his mother gave him. That says a lot to me about a person in this situation. He treated you like a queen. He never left your side, and now he's here and you don't want anything to do with him?"

I look past her and toward my closet. I don't know how long I've been sitting here, but surely I'm late or about to be for dinner. "I gotta go meet my parents." I slip off my bed and stand in front of my closet, and look at the same clothes I was earlier.

"You never told me why you're wallowing."

"Because Jackson is the man who is buying my parents' business, and that means—"

"That you'll never escape him or the Cave?"

I look at her and nod, before turning back to my closet and sigh.

"And what will you tell them?"

I shrug and pull out my black shift dress. "About what?"

"About Jackson?"

"Nothing. I'm sure he'll come back to my office and I'll sign the papers then. I doubt he will tell my parents he knows me. I don't think that's something you want to tell the parents of a daughter."

"Yeah, I suppose you're right." Jackie gives me a hug before leaving my room. I change quickly and freshen up my makeup. A quick glance at my phone shows me if I don't leave now, I'm going to be late. Being late isn't something my father likes.

"Maybe you'll meet the new guy," Jackie says as I rush to the door.

"No more guys, Jackie, at least not for a while."

"Whatever you say, sunshine."

I pause before walking out. Knowing Jackson is in my city doesn't change anything. At least that is what I'm telling myself. My heart and body say a whole bunch of other stuff. It's ridiculous how my senses knew he was in the conference room, and it felt so wonderful when he was in my arms. I didn't even hesitate or question what I was doing when I kissed him. It didn't matter I was at work. I had to feel him, to have the reminder of what he felt like when he was pressed against me.

Then my world closed in and everything shifted. Silver had to open her mouth and ruin the moment. In fact, she ruined everything, even though none of it is her fault. When I saw her today, she gushed about Jackson and asked me how I knew him. I lied and told her I thought he was someone else, but I don't think she believed me. I wouldn't. There was no mistaking Jackson and I knew each other.

The cab ride to the restaurant my parents chose takes longer than planned. Of course, they're in Manhattan while I'm across the bridge. Nothing is ever easy in the city, especially when it comes to traffic. The valet helps me out of the car, while another opens the door.

"Hello, do you have a reservation?" the hostess asks. I look over her shoulder, wondering why my parents would pick this swanky place. The prices are likely out of their reach, which means they have something to tell me. Thing is, I don't know if it's good or bad news, and by the way my week finished, I'm banking on bad.

"I'm meeting my parents. Cavanah."

She looks down the list and nods. "Yes, follow me and I'll show you to your table. Your party is already here."

My parents are always early. As soon as my dad sees me, he stands and pulls me into his arms. "Story, I've missed you."

"Um... I saw you last Sunday, remember?" I look at my mom and she smiles. "Oh, God! That's why you've called me here, right? To tell me you're dying? Do you have cancer? Is it Alzheimer's? Is that why you can't remember dinner last week?"

"Story, sit down. Your father had a bad choice of words."

I glance back and forth between my parents, and finally take my seat. The waiter appears, offering me a glass of wine. I take it, sucking it down greedily while I hold my finger up, asking him to wait. Only after he refills it, do I look at my parents.

"Sorry," I tell them. "Rough couple of days at work and I had a panic attack just now. I seriously thought one of you would tell me you're sick. You're not, right?"

"No, we're not. We shouldn't need a reason to take you out to dinner though." My mom points out.

"This place is like a month's salary, Mom. You know I would've been very happy coming home for dinner." I lie to her. I honestly can't remember the last time I stepped foot into their apartment.

She reaches her hand across the table and pats mine. "Story, tell me honestly. Do you like coming to the apartment?"

I look down at the table and shake my head. I know I shouldn't be ashamed of what they do, but I am. Even if my mom only works in the bookstore, she's still there. She still helps my dad buy products. There is nothing like coming home from school to find a dozen different dildos on your kitchen table because they forgot I got out early. Maybe this is why Kevin thinks I'm frigid. Jackson didn't think...

Speaking of Jackson, I can smell him or his cologne rather. I know he's not here, but I still fight the urge to look around the room to see if I can spot him.

"So why would we force you to come over when we

know it makes you uncomfortable?"

I clear my throat, and smile at the waiter as he heads toward our table. I open my menu and cringe because there are no prices listed. I'm going to have to find a way to pay for this because there's absolutely no way they can afford to treat me to dinner here, especially since I haven't signed the purchase and sales agreement.

The light bulb goes off, but I don't say anything until after I order. After the waiter has left our table, I lean forward and look at my parents. "I know why I'm here," I tell them. "It's because I didn't sign the papers today."

"Well, yes," my father says.

"And I bet you want to know why."

They both nod.

"I think..."

"Yes, love, why don't you tell them what you think?"

Before I can react, Jackson is sitting down in the empty chair. I should've known something was up. Ritzy places like this don't normally leave an extra water glass on the table.

Jackson looks smug, which pisses me off. "You want to know what I think?"

"That's exactly why we're all here, Story. Tell us what you think," he says. I try not to let his voice and the way my name sounds coming from him have any effect on me, yet it does. I push my legs together to ward off the building ache. From the moment I touched him earlier the longing has been building. It would be so easy to push aside my values and fall back into his arms, but I'm not a hypocrite.

"Fine. The reason I didn't sign the papers is because I think you're being taken for a ride. The offer on the table is weak, and surely Mr. Collins can do better than what he's offering." I make it a point to look at Jackson and smirk.

TWENTY-SIX

Jackson

'd really like to know what the bloody hell I've done to Story to make her act like this, aside from the profession I'm in, which mind you, is ludicrous it's even an issue. It's not like I'm a mobster or doing something illegal. When she told her parents I'm taking them for a ride, I pretty much lost my head. I could tell by the look in her eyes she only said it to be spiteful, but I'm at a loss as to why, exactly, she would do that. It's not as if I treated her like shit when we were in Bermuda. I know I treated her like a princess and showed her exactly what she meant to me. Maybe she really does think that I'm not offering them enough compensation in the sale, but they were getting a good deal before they upped the price and they're getting an even better one now. I'd really like to know why I'm the bad guy suddenly.

Right now, I'm standing on my balcony, listening to the people who live a few floors below me who are having a small get-together. The thought of meeting my neighbours in my new apartment block hasn't crossed my mind until now, but knowing Story is out there somewhere makes me feel somewhat lonely. Before knowing she was within reach, I was resigned that I would be a Billy no mates, whose daily routine consisted of waking up, going to the gym, going to work, and then coming home with takeaway. That went out the window the second Story placed a smacker on my lips.

Yeah, she kissed me. And believe me, I don't have any intention of letting her forget it. All I need is a plan, not only where the business is concerned, but with her as well. I want them both, her and my empire and I refuse to believe Story will keep me locked out of her life, especially after seeing the most recent offer I've put together.

The sound of a knock on the door interrupts me from feeling sorry for myself. For a split second, I contemplate ignoring whoever is out there but I was brought up not to be rude, so I walk over and open the door. On the other side is some woman who I've seen around and about in the hallway a couple of times when I've collected my post.

"Can I help you?"

"Fuck, your accent," she says, using her hand to fan herself. I can't help but smile, because let's face it; almost everyone in New York has an accent, just like they do in London. Surely, I'm not the only British man she's met. "We're having a soirée, two floors down. You should come."

"Do you always invite people you've never met before to your place?" I ask her.

She puts her hand out for a handshake and I take it. "I'm Jackie. I've seen you around and figured I'd extend a friendly neighbourhood hello."

"Pleased to meet you, I'm Jay," I say as she smiles. "Sure. Should I bring anything with me?"

She shakes her head. "We got you covered." She winks before heading back down the stairs. I stand in the hallway until the door opens and then slams shut, wondering whether I really want to go down there and join them. The thing is, I probably do, but I'm also not in the mood to be sociable.

"Fuck it," I say to myself, making sure I've got my keys before closing my door. At least this gives me an excuse to be nosey and see what the other flats in this building look like. I know I got lucky when I rented the loft space. It was the high ceilings, exposed beams, natural hardwood floors, and the full-length windows that attracted me to the place. Add the simple white colour scheme and it was just what I was looking for—a character building with all the mod cons in a minimalist style. Of course, being able to access the roof was a bonus and I offered well above the monthly asking price to ensure the landlord would not only agree to rent the place to me, but to also ensure I was the only one who could access the roof. Sure, it's a dirty tactic, but apparently, it's how I operate now.

I knock once and a "come in." is yelled out in reply. This flat has an open-plan kitchen and lounge and from what I can see, is decorated nicely. There are people hanging around various nooks and crannies and none of them seem to be bothered that a stranger has just walked in. For all they know, I could be a serial killer and they still wouldn't have paid the blindest bit of notice to me.

There is music playing, but it's not loud enough to drown out the various conversations going on. Some bloke offers me a beer and pats me on the shoulder, acting as if we've been friends for a while. I shrug and open the bottle, taking a quick sip before I move from the kitchen to the living room area. Its décor is like mine, with the exposed beams, large windows, and wood floors, only I have more ceiling height and the walls haven't been painted. Even so,

I'm impressed with the building and more than happy I can call it home.

"Are you fucking kidding me? Seriously, are you fucking following me?"

Ah, and there's the voice that's been haunting my dreams for the past few weeks. I turn around to find the love of my life standing in front of me with her hands firmly on her hips. If looks could kill, I'd be long gone by now, withering on the floor with blood seeping out from the wounds caused by the dagger she's thrown my way. Her cheeks are bright red instead of the endearing pink, and I swear I can see steam coming out of her ears. Any normal guy with any sense would probably treat an incredibly pissed-off woman with kid gloves to calm down the situation, but I'm far from normal. Instead, I raise my bottle of beer in a toast, and take a few long sips, maintaining eye contact with her.

Everyone around us is staring at our silent exchange, waiting with baited breath as to what will happen next and it takes them a few seconds to realise this is a one-sided argument so they quickly lose interest and move on. Thankfully, Story hasn't moved, still watching me like a hawk. I really don't give a flying fuck how angry she is, I could stay here and watch her for days.

"Oh good, you're here." Jackie walks into the room and that's when the realisation dawns on me. Story's best friend is also called Jackie. It was the one truth she told me, and it must have been at the back of my mind. I should remind Story I told her the truth about my name. I need her to know I never wanted to give her a fake name or play the stupid game she insisted on. The best thing about it was that we pretended to be married—that part I loved.

"How do you know him?" Story asks her.

Jackie looks between me and Story a couple of times. "He's the new guy upstairs."

Story's eyes catch mine, and the redness in her cheeks returns with a vengeance. "Is this some perverse joke?"

I shake my head.

"Wait, what's going on?"

"*That.*" Story points, making me feel about two feet tall. "Is Jackson or Jay or whoever the fuck he introduced himself as," she seethes. If I had any decency, I'd put down my beer and leave. In fact, I should probably leave New York and take the loss, but for some reason, I seem to have some serious self-esteem issues right now. I love the way Story is treating me. It's telling me that deep down she's clearly affected by me being here and I therefore need to work harder to remind her of what we had together.

Jackie's mouth drops open in shock. I'm smiling like an idiot because obviously it means she knows who I am. Clearly Story told her about me. I'd be happy dancing on the spot if I could, but instead, I settle for mentally patting myself on the back.

"So, you're the one?" Jackie asks me.

"The one?" I clarify.

"Yeah." She nods. "The one who rocked her world?" Jackie points her thumb over her shoulder towards Story, much to her dismay.

I laugh. "Guilty as charged. And just for the record, I loved every fucking minute of it."

Jackie once again fans herself, just like she did upstairs. "How the fuck are you not doing him right now, Story? His accent, those smouldering blue eyes, and we both know what's between—" Story slams her hand over her friend's mouth. I don't have to be a genius to guess Story told Jackie about the size of my package. Of course I'm grinning from ear to ear, not to mention it makes my dick ache in my jeans. I take a quick look down below and silently beg him to calm the fuck down, at least until I can get close enough to Story.

Story finally takes her hand away from Jackie's mouth. She looks completely embarrassed by what she did. To be honest it upsets me a little, seeing Story looking defeated. Jackie quickly makes her excuses, and leaves a very pissed-off Story and a slightly remorseful, if not a little smug, me in a staring competition. There are still a few people milling about, including one lass who has been giving me flirty looks from the minute I walked in.

Carefully, I walk towards Story. She does everything she can to avoid making eye contact with me, but she doesn't move out of my reach when I put my hand on her hip. Leaning in, I discretely inhale the scent of her perfume and my eyes close as the memories wash over me.

"I've missed the fuck out of you, love," I whisper into her ear. "And the woman over there is watching me and has been doing so since I walked in. Tell me you don't want me to go over there and talk to her."

"I don't care what you do."

I pull back and look at her. Those beautiful green eyes I remember seem so lifeless. She looks as if she's been crying, and I've no doubt I'm the cause of her tears. I gently cup her cheek, feeling the warmth of her skin against mine. "We both know that isn't true, Story."

She steps back and crosses her arms, resting them under her magnificent breasts. I want to bury my face between them, and fall asleep while holding one in my hand. "I thought I made myself clear the other day. I don't want to see you."

I nod and take another sip of my beer. "And I thought I made myself clear that I thought that was bollocks. We have something between us, Story, and you and I both know it, so the sooner you accept it and give in, the sooner we can get back to loving each other."

"Do you mean fucking? Are you looking to continue our vacation?"

"If it means you're back to being my wife and sleeping in my bed every night, then yes, that's exactly what I mean." That was the last thing she wanted to hear. Story storms away from me in a huff, leaving me high and dry to deal with the other woman who has been giving me the eye. I should probably leave, but I don't. Instead, I walk down the hall and stare at a door, which I'm guessing she's hiding behind. I'm tempted to open it so we can hash everything out. There's been a lack of privacy with every conversation we've had thus far. It would be nice to get everything out in the open without anyone being in earshot. Ideally, I'd like to take her back to my place, up to the roof, and hold her in my arms while we wait for the sun to rise.

"All in due time," I tell myself. I'm going to win her back, of that I am determined. Technically, I didn't do anything to lose her, but that stupid game we played in Bermuda has left us both high and dry.

I decide the best thing I can do is to give her space, so I move away from her door and turn around, coming face to face with the girl I've been trying to avoid. Judging by the smile on her face, she's been waiting for the chance to get me by myself. I'd probably feel the same if I was in her position. I mean, if a guy gets the opportunity to pull the girl he's had his eye on all night, then he'd jump at the chance. Why wouldn't she feel the same way? Unfortunately, I don't know the answer to that. I've never had to chase after a woman before, unless I count Sian's mother but for another reason entirely.

"I'm Robyn with a y." She holds her hand out as she introduces herself, and I politely shake it.

"Jay." I think about adding "with a y" but the last thing I want is for her to think is I'm flirting with her.

"You're new around here, right? I heard Jackie talking about her new neighbour coming down."

I nod. "Just moved here."

"Born and raised," she says, with a laugh. "I'd be happy to show you around, that's if Story hasn't staked her claim."

I turn and look at what I'm guessing is the door to Story's bedroom. When I turn back again and meet Robyn's eyes, there's an expectant look in them. "Things with Story and I are complicated now."

"But you've just met, right?"

"Not exactly."

"Oh, okay. We're all friends and well... if you want a tour guide, let me know." Robyn walks back towards the kitchen, leaving me standing by myself outside Story's door. A few of the guys look my way. One even shakes his head as if he thinks I've done something wrong. Given the way Story was shouting at me earlier, I don't blame them.

"Fuck this." I finish my beer and put the bottle down before walking straight into Story's room. Her head pops up and her eyes narrow. It's obvious she's been crying. I close the door behind me, locking it for good measure, and walk over to her.

I don't give her a chance to react, and without hesitation, I crash my lips to her, slipping my tongue into her mouth. She moans and grabs hold of my shirt, pulling me until I'm resting between her legs. I rock into her, creating the friction we need. Her legs squeeze around me as her back arches, pushing her breasts against me. It's all the invitation I need. My lips trail down her neck and towards her chest until my hand tugs on the V of her shirt, leaving her lacy blue bra showing.

"Fucking gorgeous," I say against her flesh. My tongue darts out and tastes her taut nipple. Her nails dig into my skin and I hiss at the sensation but enjoy every single bit of pain.

"Please, stop," she says. I do as she asks, but I don't move away, choosing to nuzzle her neck instead, and kissing her lightly to test her reaction. She leans into me and whispers my name, "Jackson." I could take this as a sign that she wants me to continue, if it wasn't for the tone of her voice telling me otherwise.

Instead, I move away, sitting on the edge of the bed and resting my hands on my knees while my hard-on presses uncomfortably into the buttons of my jeans. The throbbing is almost too much. Clearly, my dick misses the feel of her as much as I do. Story sits up and pulls a pillow in front of her chest. When I see the tears welling up, I wipe them away and kiss her gently on her cheeks. "You've asked me to leave you alone for weeks, you've avoided me, and you've shouted at me, you've called me every name under the sun. I should call it quits and give up, but I can't, Story. I can't give up on us."

"Why not?" she asks.

I shake my head. "You and I have something, surely we owe it to ourselves to explore and see where it leads."

"Jackson—"

"No, love. Let me finish."

"Okay." She nods. If I'm not mistaken, Story moves closer to me, so I do the same. I let my hand rest on her leg with my fingers dancing along her skin and it feels fucking amazing.

"The week we spent together in Bermuda was the best

week of my life. I've not been able to stop thinking about you from the second you walked away from me. The deal with your parents was meant to be finalised after our holiday, but instead of coming here, I had to fly home to get my head together. My mum, Maxwell, and Tommy all know about you. Maxwell even tried searching for you online to see if he could find you."

"Who is Maxwell?"

"He and Tommy are my best mates. The thing is, Story, we were only hours into our charade in Bermuda and I wanted to put a stop to it. I hated it. I hated not knowing anything about you and I hated not being able to tell you anything about me. I didn't once lie to you. Not about my name and not about how I felt about you."

"I hate your company and what it stands for."

"I know, love, and if I could change one thing, my job would be it. But I can't, it's what I do, it's how I make a living." I stand up and lean towards her until our lips are a whisper away from each other. "But I promise you, Story, I'm going to prove to you that I'm worth it. So, you better be prepared." I don't kiss her, and even though it kills me to walk away, I know it's what I must do.

TWENTY-SEVEN

Story

_____

Seeing Jackson, in my home, a place where I have imagined him over and over again... well, it set me off, and not in the way I wanted it to. Every time I've sat on my couch, gone to bed, or showered, I have pictured Jackson here, living with me, sleeping in my bed, eating at the table, and falling asleep watching television.

Every part of me wants to welcome him into my life, but I can't. The end result, be it a break-up or a marriage with children, leads to heartache because they would eventually go through what I did. It's stupid and trivial, but being bullied over what my father did for a living has always stuck with me, and I can't fathom having a child go through the same thing I did. It would be unfair and hypocritical. I have all but shunned my parents and their jobs, choosing to meet them for brunch on Sundays or have them to my apartment for dinner. I've gone as far as to avoid the store. Even when my mother called to tell me the papers needed to be signed, I lied to her knowing full well she would send them over by messenger or bring them herself. Maybe my aversion is unhealthy and completely irrational, but to me, it's valid.

I can't tell Jackson though out of fear he would think I'm a total nut job. Hell, he didn't propose to Sian's mother, why would I think he'd do anything different with me? Because in my dreams, it's what I see for us, it's what I want, and I hate that I can't have it. After one week, he ruined me in the best and worst way possible.

The world is cruel. This is the only way to sum up what is going on. Jackie pushed me to take the vacation to Bermuda. To go let loose and have some fun, and I did. Meeting Jackson was by chance, pure dumb luck. I was in the right place at the right time. Sure, with him being my adjoining neighbor, we could've easily met, but I doubt we would've ended up the way we did. And now look at us. Fate brought us together, but it's reality that will keep us apart. His company... I can't accept it, and it breaks my heart into a million tiny shards, which are ripping through my body. I'll have to live with the pain of knowing the man I fell in love with, the man I don't deserve, is walking among the millions of people in New York City, and living upstairs from me.

When I finally emerge from my bedroom, everyone is gone. Jackie is picking up the stray beer bottles and singing along to a song on the radio. She sees me and smiles.

"You knew he lived here, didn't you?"

Jackie stops and empties her hands so she can turn the volume down. "I knew. I figured it out the other night after you told me his name and I looked him up. The pictures online are a bit outdated, but I knew the minute I ran into him earlier at the mailbox."

"Why didn't you tell me?"

She shrugs and motions for me to take a seat on the couch. "Would you have spoken to him?"

I shake my head.

"You would've freaked out though, much like you did tonight."

"Jackie—"

She turns, pulling her leg up underneath her other one and takes my hand in hers. "I love you, Story, but I'm going to be blunt. That man, he's in love with you."

"How do you know?" I ask.

She sighs. "Because I can see it in his eyes. I have spent enough time as an ER nurse to know when a man loves a woman. Do you know how many men bring their wives or girlfriends in, who can't even look me in the eye when I ask them a question because they're focused on their partner?"

I shake my head.

"Very few," she says. Jackie might be a bit cynical though; she sees a lot of overdoses, beatings, and death where she works. "But with Jackson, the way he looks at you even when you're yelling at him, he's got it bad. And frankly, so do you."

I start to shake my head, but she glares at me. "It doesn't matter."

"Bullshit," she says. "Who gives a flying fuck about his profession?" I blanch, but she continues anyway. "Here's the thing. Your father, he owns the store. I know the products were always spread around your house. I know your dad scolded you if you touched something. I was there for the bullshit at school. Jackson, he owns the company that makes the product. Something tells me he isn't going to have a closet full of monster cocks, likely because he has one."

"Jackie! I can't believe you almost told him I said that."

"Did you see him blush? He was flattered." She continues to hold my hand while I let tears fall down my face. My heart aches, both with desire and pain. I want

Jackson desperately, but don't know if I can get over this hurdle.

"Robyn thinks he's cute. She saw him go into your room."

Nodding. "He came into talk."

"Did you do much talking?" she asks.

Instantly, my cheeks feel hot. "He talked, I listened."

"After he...?"

I start to laugh and push her away. "I'm not going to kiss and tell."

"Um, why not? You did when you got home. I mean how else did I know about the schlong?"

"That was before."

Jackie stands and stretches. "I get it, before he lived upstairs and I could put a name, face, and body with the details you gave me." She walks toward her room, turning around before she gets to her door. "He seems like an amazing guy, Story. I'd really hate to see you lose him over this. You were both born into situations you have no control over. Where it's damaged you, his has been successful."

Her door shuts quietly, leaving me with my thoughts. I can't disagree with anything she has said. She's right, as usual. Instead of going back to bed, I decide to go out and sit on the fire escape. It's not a very big space, but Jackie and I do like to come out here every so often and just sit.

Stepping out onto the metal platform, I lean back slightly so I can look up to where Jackson's apartment is. When the rooftop came up for rent, Jackie and I looked at it, but it rented too fast. This whole time, the universe has been conspiring to bring Jackson and me together. Whether we met in Bermuda or the day he bought my parents' place, we would meet.

Rushing back in, I head for the front door and run

toward the stairs, climbing them as fast as I can until I reach the top floor. In hindsight, I should've taken the elevator, but this is by far more dramatic.

I knock on his door. At first, the taps are quiet until my heart takes control and I'm pounding. It opens, and he's there, looking confused until a smile spreads across his face. Of course, he's shirtless, barefoot, and his jeans are open, reminding me that for a week, he belonged to me.

"Are you busy?" I don't know why I ask him that. Maybe it's his appearance or what Jackie said about Robyn thinking he's cute. Not that I would expect Jackson to leave my room and go bed Robyn.

"For you, never." He stands back and holds his door open, inviting me in, but I don't move.

"I have a question."

"I'll tell you anything, Story."

"It seems you and I were destined to meet. Whether at my parents' or by chance when we picked up our mail."

"Seems that way, doesn't it?"

"Pretend for one minute that Bermuda didn't happen, and you're sitting across from me in some random office, signing the agreement with my parents. What do you see?"

Jackson steps forward, putting us toe to toe. "I see a beautiful woman who makes my heart race, someone who has my undivided attention, and has the power to make me forget my name, let alone the deal I'm about to finalise. Story, when I look at you, I see someone I want to spend all my time with, someone I'd follow anywhere and every-where even if it's only to convince her to have lunch with me." He holds my face softly between his hands. "I see a woman I can easily fall in love with."

"How do you know?"

"Because I have never, in my life, felt this way about

anyone. From the second I saw you in the hotel reception, Story, I had to know you. Just being with you sends the most amazing sensation through my body."

"So you're saying you'd chase me no matter what?"

"I'll chase you to the ends of the earth, if you'll let me."

I reach up and kiss him lightly, pulling away before he can deepen it. "Please chase me, Jackson. Please show me you're worth the risk of being labeled a hypocrite." I step away and rush back down the stairs. When I get to my door, I pause, wondering if he's going to come down. I hear a door shut lightly, and assume it's his.

~

I DIDN'T SLEEP WELL last night. My dark sunglasses hide the bags my makeup couldn't even come close to covering up. My head is pounding. I woke up late and didn't have time to take a shower.

"Good morning, Ms. Cavanah," Foster says, all bright and cheery like. One would think I have a hangover, but I didn't even drink. Maybe it's an emotional hangover, but I wouldn't know because I've never felt one before.

"Morning," I mumble as I pass her desk. Usually we chat, but not this morning. I open my office door and that's when the aroma hits me. Blindly, I reach for the light, flicking it on. I gasp. My office wall is lined with flowers of every kind. "Foster?"

"Yes, Ms. Cavanah," she says, coming to stand behind me.

"Where did these come from?"

"There's a card on your desk," she tells me. I walk over and pull off my sunglasses, and let my eyes focus on what's in front of me. The card addressed to me rests against a blue, wrapped box. The handwriting is unfamiliar, but I have a feeling it's Jackson's. Foster is still standing in the doorway, waiting. It makes me wonder if he's asked her for my reaction.

Carefully, I open the envelope and pull out the card.

Story,

I've never told you how much I love your name. Even though Jade was exotic and perfect for our vacation, Story means everything, and as far as I'm concerned, ours isn't anywhere near finished.

I know I went overboard on the flowers, but guessed you would place them around the office, share with your colleagues, or maybe even give one bunch to Foster; she seems to really care about you.

I noticed when we met again the other day that you're still wearing the ring I gave you. You have no idea what that did to me or what it continues to do. Knowing I put that there, as part of our game, and that it's stayed, proves something to me. I hope the contents of this box will match it perfectly.

This is me chasing. Please let me catch you.

Love, Jackson

I set the card down and wipe away the tears that have started to fall. Unwrapping the box, my mouth drops open at its contents.

"What is it?" Foster asks.

"Sapphire earrings." He's right. They match my ring perfectly.

"Excuse me, Ms. Cavanah. I don't mean to overstep, but if I may be so bold to say, I think that man likes you."

I look at her and smile. "I like him too, but it's complicated."

"Well, hopefully you figure it out before lunch. Mr.

Collins will be here at noon. He told me to tell you you'll be eating in."

I watch as Foster shrugs and shuts my door. It seems everyone is conspiring against me and in favor of him. Every part of me wants to be Team Collins, except that small nagging portion of my brain.

TWENTY-EIGHT

Jackson

It's been three weeks since I started trying to win Story back, and the adventure has been worth it. The only thing I'm not happy about is I've not been able to touch her in the way I've wanted to. Instead, I've respected her wishes and have kept my hands to myself. It's been the best three weeks of my life, and that's not even including the week we spent together in Bermuda.

Everything is different between us now. Whereas our holiday was based on lies and sex, the relationship forming between us now has a more solid foundation, even if we're still doing our best to ignore the gigantic elephant in the room. Since I sent the flowers and earrings, we've seen each other every day, and if I'm lucky, sometimes twice. I risked showing up at her office on the official first day of 'Operation Story,' as I call it, taking her something to eat, as opposed to taking her to a restaurant for lunch. After a long talk with Foster, I had a pretty good idea about how busy Story is and the last thing I want to do is add to her stress.

Ever since that day, I've done whatever I can to show her how much she means to me, and that I'm here for good and not going anywhere. I want her to know I'm worth the possibility of her being called a hypocrite because she's dating someone who works in the business she hates so much. Between you and me, I think it's complete bollocks for anyone to think that Story being my girlfriend would mean she's being hypocritical.

One of the best things with trying my best to win her back is I've managed to see some of the city's amazing sites, and we're not just talking about the tourist traps. I've picked up on insider's knowledge, like which hole in the wall cafés serve up the best breakfast at six in the morning, and that China Town is the best place to get food late, and if I had an urge to get some pizza, then Little Italy is the place to be, but I have to be prepared to wait to be served.

Every night, after our date ends and I give her a chaste kiss goodnight, I crawl into my bed and hope the next day will be the one when she finally tells me I've passed the test, won the marathon, and crossed the finish line. The thing is, though, if she tells me that day is today, or tomorrow, or one day next week, I'll never stop chasing her because she's worth every minute of it. I'm crazy for this girl, this sweet, unbelievably sexy, innocent woman who drives me wild just by being in a room with her. Every day since I've known her has been ten times brighter than before, and I find that not only am I not as stressed, I also have a more positive outlook on life. For once, it's not all work, work for me—I have something to come back to after my business day is done. Story pretty much has me under her thumb—she only has to smile at me and I'm weak in the knees and ready to do anything for her.

In the beginning, a small part of me thought she might give me a run for my money, but when she began calling me and inviting me to go for dinner, or join her at the park or catch a film, I knew she was having difficulty in fighting her feelings. I have never, in my life, felt this way about someone and a small part of me feels like a dickhead because I didn't feel the same way about Sian's mum.

I look down at the one photograph I have of my daughter and sigh. It's her birthday today and for the first time, I'm not in London and can't visit the cemetery to put flowers on her grave. I didn't plan on being away, though, and I can't help feeling guilty, almost as if I'm neglecting my daughter. Story is important to me though and I didn't want to leave her while we were in the middle of trying to get over our differences. I know Story would have understood if I told her why I had to fly back to England, but I just couldn't handle the thought of not being able to see her for a week.

I scroll through my contacts in my phonebook until I find the details for Maria, Sian's mum. She usually calls me, but I haven't heard from her yet. It only takes a couple of rings before she picks up. "Hello, Jay."

"Hi, Maria. How are you?"

"The same as I am on this day every year ." She sniffles into the phone, and I know my tears aren't far behind.

"I'm sorry I can't be there this year."

"Your mum told me this morning when I saw her. The flowers, as usual, are beautiful."

"I'm glad you like them."

"The ones for Sian though, those are a little over the top. People will assume she only passed away recently."

I take a deep breath and let it out slowly. "I'm feeling a tremendous amount of guilt for not being there. I guess I overcompensated."

"Who is she?"

"Pardon me?"

"Your mum told me you're seeing someone, and that you're in love. Are you?"

Even though my heart hurts for my daughter, I can't help but smile. "Yeah, I am. She's called Story, and we met while we were on holiday."

"Is she American?"

"Yes, she is. She actually lives in my building."

Maria jostles the phone, clearing her throat and coughing a little before coming back on the line. "Does she know about Sian?"

"Yes, I told her. I hope you don't mind. I think it was about two or three days after we met."

"Wow. I never thought I'd see the day Jay Collins falls in love."

I laugh because she's hit the nail on the head. "I'm hoping to bring her back to England soon, once the business settles down and we're not so busy. Maybe we can meet for tea?"

"Sounds good, Jay. Listen, I'm running late for an appointment, so I'd best go." Maria hangs up without saying goodbye and I find myself holding the phone to my ear, waiting to see if she comes back on the line. Our conversations are never great, but that one was awkward. I probably should've gone home and visited Sian's grave, but right now, Story is more important, although it pains me to say it.

A knock at my door brings me back to reality. When I open it, the woman I'm madly in love with smiles at me. She's wearing her usual work attire—a pencil skirt with a blouse—but today she's also holding two cups of coffee in her hand.

"Good morning," she says, walking into my flat. I don't give her an opportunity to get any further than the front hall before I pull her towards me, kissing her cheek before placing my head in the crook of her neck. Story tries to hold me, but the cups in her hand make it awkward and the hug is completely one sided.

When I pull away, she leans in and kisses me. It's not the first time she's made the first move, and I know I should keep it innocent. The last thing I want is for her to push me away, especially today.

"I'm surprised to see you." She hands me one of the coffees.

"My morning meeting was cancelled, and I thought—"

"That you'd come here and take advantage of me?" I waggle my eyebrows at her and she blushes. It's one of the most beautiful things about her. "Or," I say as I put the cup of coffee down and walk towards her. "Are you here because you can't control your desire for me and you've reached your tipping point?" It'll only take one look towards my nether regions for her to realise I have a very prominent hard-on in my trousers.

"What makes you think you turn me on?" she counters back at me.

I chuckle. "I know I turn you on. You seem to have forgotten the first time we met on the balcony and how you reacted when I licked my lips. As I remember, you went running at breakneck speed back to your room. I knew for a fact, right then, that you would be mine."

"You're so full of yourself, Jackson."

"And you could be full of me too. All you have to do is say the word."

Story shakes her head and pushes me away, playfully. I'm tempted to ask her the real reason why she's here, but I don't want to rock the boat. I was never a patient man until I met her, and I know she's going to be worth it.

"Actually, do you fancy taking the day off? There's something I want to show you."

"Let me look at my schedule." Story sits on one of my bar stools and crosses one leg over the other, immediately making me wish I was pinned between them. I've had dirty thoughts about her in every nook and cranny in this flat, at least twice over and then some. "Foster has moved my other two appointments. I'm free."

"Perfect." I kiss her on the cheek.

∾

THE DOWNSIDE of being new to New York and spending all my time on wooing Story is I've not had the opportunity to get myself a car. I chose the flat in Brooklyn because I loved the architecture, the size of the loft, and it was in a nice neighbourhood. It also gave me a good amount of space between the store and the manufacturing plant. The last thing I want to do is live and work in the same place. I don't want to feel like I work twenty-four hours a day, seven days a week. Of course, if I was being smart, I would have rented a penthouse downtown or even bought somewhere central, but I tend to be quite frugal with my money and don't normally splash out on luxuries. Having said that, I haven't held back where Story is concerned, either here or when we were in Bermuda.

We're in a town car, heading towards the suburb of Kensington. When I'm not with Story, I've been spending time with her parents, trying to find a way to finalise our deal. So far, Story still hasn't signed the contracts, and I still can't fathom why she's delaying the process. I've done everything she's asked me to do. I had the property revalued; the assets of the existing store looked at again, and even had a contractor come in to look at her parents' apartment.

When all the numbers came back and it turned out that my offer was far more than the value, I thought for a fact she would sign on the dotted line, but alas, we're still waiting. Maxwell thinks she's delaying because she's afraid I'm going to dump her once the deal is done and dusted. Of course, I can't exactly ask her if that's the reason, but I can try to prove I'm in this for the long haul.

"What are we doing here?" she asks me, as our driver turns into a long driveway. I get out of the car and quickly run over to Story's side so I can be a gentleman and open the door for her.

"I wanted to show you something. It's a different kind of business deal that I've been working on."

"Are you turning this into a brothel?" she asks. I wish I could say she's joking, but I have a feeling she's not.

As soon as the car drives away, I bring her into my arms. "Story, I don't sell sex. I manufacture the toys that bring people pleasure. That's all. There is no hidden agenda. I'm not into all that kinky shit. I don't have whips and chains and balls to gag you with hidden in my flat. You won't find me visiting sex clubs." I shake my head, hoping that I'm getting the message across loud and clear.

"Have you ever used any of your toys?" she asks.

I look around, slightly frustrated, wondering why we're having this conversation in public and in the middle of the suburbs, but I still answer her. "Yes. I've used a cock ring."

"What does that do?"

I take her hand and rub it up and down the front of my trousers, over my growing erection. The house we're about to go into is empty and could use a good christening, if she'll allow it. Maybe that's what she thinks we're here for, although I've not given her any indication to make her believe that. "You put it at the base of the shaft. The best part is there's a vibrator, which hits the clit perfectly. It's best when you use it for slow, rhythmic grinding."

"You sound like a commercial." Her hand still moves up and down my hard-on.

"I'd be lying if I said I didn't have good knowledge about all our packaging and the instructions for our products." I wink, but clearly I've done the wrong thing because she's removed her hand and stepped away from me, putting some distance between us. "Come on, love." I don't take her hand in mine, and she walks two steps behind me. Unlocking the front door, I open it and let her walk in first.

"Holy shit, Jackson. This place is huge."

I don't say anything, instead, letting her walk from room to room, admiring the décor and hard work that's turned this house into the masterpiece it is. The inside is painted a soft yellow and there are pillars throughout the downstairs space. There's a huge kitchen, with space for a dining area, in addition to a formal dining room and living areas. This house is probably far too big.

"Is this your house?" she asks me as she walks into the master bathroom with its en suite, dual shower, unit and separate soaking bath.

"Not exactly," I reply as I lean against the door and watch her, realising this could quite easily be her dream home. "Would you like to spend your holidays here?"

"Right, as if that would ever happen."

Walking towards her, I drop the deeds of the house on the dressing table. "I bought this place for your parents," I tell her. "I don't know what else to do, Story. Your mum and dad want to sell their business to me and I know you don't like it, but it's what I do. It's what my father and grandfather did, and while I know you suffered at the hands of those cowardly bullies, I didn't. My family has built an empire and I want to see it succeed both here and in other states. I want you to be there with me when it does.

"Your parents picked this place out. We must've looked at ten or so houses until they decided on this one. This isn't my way of trying to get you back into bed or to get you to give into me, but it is my way of showing you I'm not a complete dickhead. I'm not trying to steal from your family. This is for your parents, and so you can visit them whenever you want. That's one of the things your mum said to me. She wishes you'd come over and see her more often, and now you can."

"You bought them a house so I'd sign the papers?" she asks.

I nod. "And so you can spend Christmas with your mum and dad."

She rushes towards me and flings her arms around my neck so quickly she catches me off guard. I stumble back into the dressing table behind me. I expect her to kiss me, but instead, she looks straight into my eyes. "I love you, Jackson. I fell in love with you on the island, but didn't how to tell you. I wanted to leave my name, number, email, anything I could, so you could call me, but I was afraid of the rejection. I was afraid I couldn't fit into your world, and I still am."

I cup her cheeks and bring her lips to mine. I keep our kiss innocent because there'll be no holding back once I get started. "I love you, Story. I am completely and utterly besotted by you. Meeting you in Bermuda changed everything for me. I wanted to follow you, leave a note of my number in your suitcase, and bribe the assistant at the Information Desk to give me your details, but I was shit scared that you didn't want me to find you. I know you hate what I do for a living and if I could change that for you, I would do so in a heartbeat."

"You would?"

"I'd give it all up, but I can't. Please don't ask me to."

She shakes her head. "I would never ask you to do that. It's my hang up, and I'll learn to deal with it, but I have some requests."

"Anything you ask."

"Until I'm comfortable about that... stuff."

I laugh a little. "Maybe if you were willing to play around, you'll understand."

"Don't push it," she tells me.

But I do push it. I push my rock-hard groin into her. "There is something else I'd really love to push into you."

She slaps my chest. "Not in my parents' house!"

For the first time since Bermuda, I smile like the cat that got the cream. Like I told her, I knew from the moment I met her that she would be mine.

TWENTY-NINE

Story
_____

When Jackie and I moved to our apartment, we fell in love with the view from the roof. The only problem was whoever was renting the top floor could block access if they so choose. The tenant prior to Jackson didn't care if anyone used the roof because he worked nights and was never home anyway. When Jackson moved in, it all changed. Of course, at the time, I didn't know he was living there, and while access is still blocked to the rest of the tenants, I at least get to take in the view. Sometimes, Jackie does too, but it's mostly Jackson and I lying on the chaise, watching the sun go down.

It's crazy how fast we fell into domestic bliss, almost like we were meant to be and it took a twist of fate to bring us together, and now that we are, we haven't left each other's side, except to go to work.

Once Jackson told me he had bought my parents their house, I had no more excuses left. In fact, it was long before that day I knew I was close to giving in, but I just couldn't bring myself to admit defeat, so to speak. After long talks with Jackie and my mother, they opened my eyes. Not only to what a great man Jackson is, which I already knew, but also to accepting that love should conquer all. It was my mother who suggested I lay down some ground rules. She was certain he would agree to anything just to have me.

The door to his apartment opens and he steps through with a bottle of wine in one hand and two glasses in the other. His black dress shirt is halfway unbuttoned and his hair a complete disarray. "Tough day?" I ask, taking both glasses so he can pour into them.

"You have no idea. I have a lot on my mind."

One of the rules, aside from the obvious, is we don't talk about work. I don't want to know how the toy business is. It's bad enough Silver is already calling about next year's show, and continues to gush about the Sex God, Jay Collins. Thankfully, she'll never know if it's true or not, but I can fully attest that yes, he is. Another reason we don't speak about each other's jobs is because I made the mistake of bitching about my ex Kevin and his wedding. Telling Jackson all about Kevin coming in to see me shortly after I went to Bermuda, where he dropped the bomb that he was engaged, wasn't a high point for me. To make matters worse, Kevin and Diane were in my office one day when Jackson stopped by, and in true Jackson form, he made sure to show Kevin I am not the frigid woman he proclaimed me to be.

And now they're friends. As if our relationship isn't already twisted with fate, Jackson and Kevin are golfing buddies and we've been invited to the wedding.

"I'd ask if you want to talk about it, but..."

Jackson pushes my hair off my shoulder, only for it to fall back into place. "I have something to ask you."

"What is it?"

He takes my wine glass and motions for me to follow him to the chaise, where I sit down. He takes the spot next to me and reaches for my hand. "Story," he says my name in a way that makes my heart race. I have a feeling he's about to propose and while I'm in love with him, I don't know if I'm ready for marriage.

But I know I am. I'd marry him tomorrow without second guessing my decision. The time we've already spent apart from each other has been torturous and I can't imagine my life without him.

"Yes, Jackson?" I clear my throat after my high-pitched question. I turn slightly so I'm facing him, making it easier for me to jump into his arms after he asks me.

"Will you move in with me? Will you live here and share my flat?"

My shoulders slump and I try to hide my disappointment by smiling. He's right to ask this first. We should live together before taking the giant leap of marriage. "Oh, Jackson. Yes, of course. I mean it makes sense, right? I'm already here every day, my stuff is here, I've taken over your closet, and honestly I don't want to give up the roof." I finish by winking.

He leans forward and kisses me. "I got this made for you." He sets a velvet box onto my lap. It's large enough for a necklace and knowing him, he's found the perfect match for my sapphire set.

I push the lid open slowly and giggle. The key to his place sits nestled on the black velvet pad. It's attached to a platinum keychain with... my eyes pop up, meeting his. Jackson is down on one knee, taking my hand in his.

"I know we haven't been together for long, but there is absolutely no chance in hell I'm wasting any more time. Story Cavanah, will you do me the absolute honor of being my wife?"

I start nodding before he even has a chance to finish his

question. My arms are around him, my lips pressed to his, and I'm pretty sure I'm sitting on his lap. "YES! YES! YES!" I say loud enough for people down on the sidewalk to hear.

Jackson sets me back onto the chaise and disengages the ring from the keychain. I slip off my other ring and hold my breath as he slides the platinum band and solitaire onto my finger. "Fits like a glove," he says, as he picks me up and carries me into the apartment. I thought I couldn't get enough of him in Bermuda but since we've rekindled our affair, we've been going at it like rabbits. My favorite though is on the roof, under the stars. It reminds me of the night on the yacht.

His hands have moved my skirt up and over my hips, and his fingers push into my flesh, kneading their way toward my core. He brushes his finger over my sensitive spot and I jerk in his arms, and continue to make love to his mouth.

Gently, I'm set on the bed. Jackson steps back to undress, smirking as I watch him, waiting until he's naked before I strip out of my clothes. As he hovers over, I use this opportunity to trail my fingers over Sian's name. The day he showed me my parents' house, he told me that it was her day. He didn't call it her birthday or the day she passed, but just her day.

Jackson nudges my legs wider and taps his cock against my clit. "Are you ready to try something new?" he asks, teasing me. Ever since he told me about the cock ring, I've been curious. I know it's in the drawer, but each time he's asked I've said no.

Not this time. I know he won't hurt me or do anything I'm not comfortable with. I nod and he doesn't hesitate to reach for it. I rest on my elbows and watch as he takes the purple ring out of the packaging.

"One second, love, I need some lube." One would think he'd open the drawer, but no, he thrusts into me, pumping his hips rapidly. The bastard has a wicked gleam in his eyes as he pulls out, leaving me dizzy and panting. Forget the stupid toy, I just need him.

But oh my God, his dick is vibrating inside me. My eyes roll back and my arms give out as the ring rests against my clit.

"Holy fucking shit," I scream. He laughs and continues to move in and out of me slowly. The pace is agonizing, I need it faster, and thrust my hips to meet his, to encourage him to speed up, but he doesn't.

Each pass over brings a new sensation. I can feel it all the way down to my toes. My body zings with pleasure as my insides tighten.

"Fucking hell, babe. You're so bloody tight, fits like a glove," he mutters into my neck, repeating the words he said earlier. While this feels amazing, I already know I miss seeing him. There is nothing sexier than watching him make love to me.

"Jackson, I'm coming...I just... I can't... Oh God, Oh God..."

"That's right, sweetheart, say it. I'm your Sex God." He grunts and finally picks up speed. I made the mistake of telling him what Silver said and he hasn't stopped calling himself since. He's earned it though.

My body freezes as my orgasm takes over. The pressure is intense, my toes curl and I gasp for air. Jackson pulls out and buries his face between my legs, lapping at my juices, before plunging back into me, but now it's different.

I open my eyes to find him staring at me. "It's just us now, love." He kisses me passionately and continues to make love to me throughout the night. There's a definite shift between us. I know it's likely since we're engaged, but it could also be because I gave him something I've never done with anyone else. It may be a sex toy, but it means something to me, and to him. I don't think I'd ever trust anyone else with my body, the way I trust Jackson.

Sometime in the middle of the night, Jackson finds me on the roof, staring out over the city. He holds me from behind, locking his arms around mine.

"We haven't talked about the future," he says.

"I want children," I blurt out. "But I don't want them to grow up like I did, being bullied because of what their father does. I know it's stupid, but—"

"It's not stupid, love. I understand. If you don't want to tell them, then we won't."

I turn in his arms and reach up on my toes to kiss him. "How many children?"

"As many as you want. One, two, a football team's worth. Whatever you want. After all, I'm the one who does the fun part, you're the one who has the hard job."

"Are you worried?"

He nods. "I won't lie, I'll be paranoid," he says. "I'll annoy you, and pamper you and wrap you in cotton wool. I'll ask you numerous times a day if the baby is all right and if he or she is moving. I know the effect Sian's death had on her mum. I don't want you to have to go through that."

I rest my forehead on his bare chest. I can't imagine carrying a child and not bringing it home from the hospital.

"So, when can we start?" he asks.

Leaning back so I can look at him, he's smiling like a Cheshire cat. "How about after we get married?"

"Next week, then?"

"Excuse me?"

Jackson laughs. "My mum and dad are flying out to

meet you. It'd be perfect timing, love. I can get my mates over and have a shindig at the hotel. I happen to know the coordinator there." He nods, as if this is the best plan.

Thing is, I don't see why we have to wait. Everything about us has been unconventional from the get-go so why prolong what we know is about to happen.

"I'll look at my schedule tomorrow after Kevin and Diane's wedding, and we can pick a date."

"Bloody perfect."

"And I'll get a room for your parents at the hotel."

He shakes his head. "No need. They're staying with your folks."

I roll my eyes. He and my parents are thick as thieves. But he's given me an idea. "How about we get married there, in the backyard?"

Jackson's smile spreads from ear to ear. "Now *that's* bloody perfect."

THIRTY

Epilogue

"*A*re you absolutely sure about this, mate?" Tommy stands behind me, watching as I straighten my bow tie in the large mirror. I'm standing in one of the five bedrooms in the Cavanahs' house. They call it the blue room and it's where I slept last night after we had our rehearsal party. Falling asleep without Story was sheer torture, and I doubt I caught more than a few minutes sleep. It's daft when you think about how you become used to sleeping next to someone, and for me, it took no more than one night with Story. It makes no difference if that night happened however many months ago on some island. She makes everything one hundred percent better for me.

"Of course I am. Why wouldn't I be? I proposed to her, didn't I?"

"Yeah, you did. I have to admit for a minute there, I thought she might be up the duff or something, because you haven't known her that long."

I focus on my tie even though I know it's perfectly fine. Tommy's not the first person to bring up that Story and I haven't known each other for long, but their opinions mean jack shit. All that matters is I'm in love with Story and have been ever since Bermuda. I don't know about Tommy or anyone else, but I, for one, am not willing to wait around. When you know, *you know*.

"She's the best decision I've ever made."

"Your relationship started with a lie, mate."

I shrug my shoulders. "I don't look at it like that. Sure, it started out as a game, but at the time, that's all it was meant to be. I would have either met her on holiday or when she signed the contracts for her parents' business. The only difference is if I met her later, I'd be getting married next week instead of today," I tell him. "Although, with all these questions, I'm beginning to think you fancy her or something, with all those looks you were giving her at dinner last night."

Tommy says nothing, instead giving me the stink eye. I raise my eyebrow at him in return as I wait for his comeback. Instead, he breaks eye contact and shakes his head. "Guilty as charged. She's bloody fantastic. In fact, I was hoping you got cold feet so I could be her knight in shining armour and give her a shoulder to cry on."

"You little shit." I laugh as I punch him in the shoulder. He laughs too and we end up in an awkward man hug, which Maxwell interrupts when he comes bursting into the room.

"Fucking love hugging. We should make this a regular occurrence," Max says. I find my way out of the tangle and straighten my suit jacket. I can see that my hair is messed up in the mirror but on this occasion, I decide to leave it. It looks damn good and I know Story likes the messy look. I do too. It's another reminder about our holiday together.

"You never did tell us where you're going for your honeymoon," Max says.

"That's because we're not having one, at least not straight away. She can't get the time off work and I'm up to my eyeballs in the refurb on the shop." It was a decision we both made. It makes complete sense for us right now, and we both agreed we'd rather go somewhere tropical during the winter so we could escape the cold weather.

"She didn't fancy quitting her job then?" Tommy asks, but I'm shaking my head before he even has a chance to finish his sentence.

"Absolutely not. We both work long hours. I don't want her sitting home by herself going stir crazy. Story's really independent and I'm not going to take that away from her. Besides, she's fucking sex on legs when she's got her work suit on."

There's a knock on my door and we turn around to see my dad peeking his head around the corner. "Your mum says it's time for you to get your arse outside."

"Such a way with words, Dad."

He waves me off and then disappears down the hall. Maxwell stands in front of me with his hands on my shoulders. "If you're having second thoughts, I'm prepared to step in and take one for the team."

"Fuck that, mate. I got there first," Tommy argues with him.

"Fuck you both. I think you'll find that *I* got there first and she's all mine. Nice try though!"

"This is like a game of finders keepers," Tommy says.

I shake my hand and signal for them to get the hell out of my room. "Nah, mate, this ain't a game. This is the real deal. I'm about to be a married man."

"Least you'll get endless sex." Max jokes, which gains him a high-five from Tommy.

"I already get that, you knobs." They both snicker good-humouredly at my retort and I wish I had my phone with me so I can take a photo of this moment.

Gwen and my mum have been very strict about where I'm allowed and not allowed to go today. There are some rooms that are no-go areas and I know better than to cross them. Luckily for me, the main bedroom is on the other side of the house so there is little chance I could bump into Story, but it doesn't mean I'm not looking for her either. Even with Tommy playing bodyguard and preventing me from looking, I strain my head around him. It's not about me wanting to see her dress, or what her hair's like or anything; it's just because I want to see her. I need the reassurance she's not nervous or having second thoughts.

Outside, there's a newly built trellis surrounding a beautifully landscaped flowerbed, together with a fake fountain. Before we decided to have our wedding ceremony here, I had joked with Conway that they should've picked one with a frog pissing in the water. Thank God, he had the sense not to listen to me and went for something more sensible. Together with my dad, they've painted the wooden arch, which is currently covered with flowers and twinkling lights. They also put down a sandy path, which my bride will walk down. And in the corner is a cellist, playing music to keep the ambiance alive.

During the quick planning period, we decided to keep the ceremony as intimate as possible but we both knew we wanted the beach to play a part. It's not that we were opposed to a big wedding, we just didn't want our family and friends to feel like they had to fly across the country to be here for us, so we decided to just have our parents and our closest friends here today.

My mum spots me as I walk into the garden and rushes

over to me. Her eyes are full of excitement. "Story looks just breathtaking. Jackson, I simply adore her."

"She loves you too, Mum." I've barely said the words before my mum is kissing me on the cheek and then running off to do who knows what.

I knew my parents would love Story; after all, there isn't anything *not* to love about her. You only have to look at Tommy and Maxwell's reaction to see that. They've both told me that if I fuck this up, they'll be there to pick up the pieces. I don't doubt it either. As soon as I told my folks I would propose, they booked a flight over to New York so they could meet her. I told them they should wait a bit, but I also understood where they were coming from. Other than Sian's mum, I really didn't introduce them to any girl-friends. I think they were afraid she either didn't exist, or she wouldn't be around for long.

From the moment my mum, Story, and Gwen met, they've been inseparable. I won't lie, there's been an element of jealousy at the amount of time they've all spent together. Of course, I know it's because they've been talking wedding stuff. After tonight, everything will be back to normal. My parents are sticking around for a few weeks, though, so I'll still have to share my wife with them.

My *wife*. I still can't believe I'm doing this. Actually, I can. The part that's unbelievable is that marrying Story seems so natural. I've been to enough weddings in the past to know the groom is normally nervous as hell, and there's an element of cold feet going on, however fleeting. Me though? I can't wait to see my bride and I keep looking at my watch to see how much more time is left before she walks down the aisle towards me. I'm ready to be tied to her for the rest of my life.

"Places," someone shouts.

"Ready?" Maxwell asks. He's my best man and Tommy is an usher even though the only guests here are our parents.

"Let's do this." I walk towards our makeshift altar. I stand next to the justice of the peace and Max and Tommy stand next to me. The music changes into one of the three wedding songs Story and I picked out. My mum and dad appear, followed by Gwen and Conway, who kisses his wife, before heading back to where Story is waiting.

Foster is the next to appear. Her dress is a knee-length pale-blue, and she's holding a small bouquet of white flowers with some in her hair. Jackie follows her, dressed like Foster. She winks at me before taking her place.

"I think she was looking at me," Maxwell whispers into my ear. I contemplate telling him he's wrong, but maybe he's not. Maybe Jackie was giving him the eye.

The music changes again and my parents along with Gwen stand and look to the back of the aisle. When Story walks around the corner with her hand linked with her arm, both mothers gasp.

"Fucking hell, mate," Max grunts into my ear.

He's right. The woman who captured my heart only minutes after meeting her walks towards me in what she calls her mermaid dress. I clearly remember how excited she was when she found her "perfect" gown, and how she couldn't wait for me to see it. I can see now why; every curve I've spent hours paying attention to is highlighted perfectly, especially her magnificent breasts. It's almost as if this dress was designed with me in mind, and without being a cocky bastard, I'm dying to look at my watch so I can count down the hours until I can peel it off her.

She's wearing her hair in beachy waves, which is another phrase I've learnt since living with her. I prefer to call it the "Jackson shagged me senseless," look but she didn't like my suggestion. Story's bouquet is a mix of blue and white flowers, which matches the colour scheme she picked out. As for me, I'm wearing a cream linen suit that she chose for us, even though if I had my way, I'd be in shorts. After what seems like years, she is almost standing in front of me. So near and yet so far.

"Today we are gathered to witness the joining in matrimony of Story and Jackson. Who gives this woman to be wed to this man?"

"Her mother and I do," Conway answers. He kisses Story on her cheek, and places her hand in mine. I give it a squeeze, hoping it tells her that I am so fucking happy right now. She stands facing me with the biggest, brightest smile I've ever seen.

"Story and Jackson have asked that I skip the "mumbo jumbo" and get right to the good stuff." Everyone laughs, but the justice of the peace is telling the truth. We don't want a load of theories about marriage, like how to make it work or how to be the best partners for each other. And we definitely don't want the story of how we met to be brought up. Story has yet to tell her parents how we met and I respect her decision. I wouldn't want to know that my daughter shagged some stranger for a week either. It's for the best that they think we met because of them selling their business.

"They just want to shag," Tommy comments and everyone laughs, except for me. I mean, he's got a point, but my future father-in-law is sitting a few feet in front of me. He's bigger and could still tackle me to the ground if he wanted.

"With that said, Jackson and Story have written their own vows. I'm really here for the cake. Jackson, you may go first."

Story hands her bouquet to Jackie and takes my hand in hers. I clear my throat and look at my wife to be. "Story, you changed me from the day I met you. Marrying you today is quite simply the easiest and most satisfying thing I will ever do in my life, until you do me the honour of making me a dad. But until that day, I promise to trust and value your opinions, and stand by your actions. I pledge to always treat you as my best friend, as my equal, and as my priority in life. I promise you that I'll make mistakes like leaving the toilet seat up or eating the last chocolate chip cookie. I will ask for your help when I need it, and give you my help and support when you ask for it. Most of all, though, I promise to love you with everything I am, every second of every day, every day of the week, every week of the year, and then some."

She wipes away a tear I should've caught before it landed on her cheek. Story tries to give me a watery smile, but her emotions are already getting the best of her. "Jackson, I am proud to take you as my husband, my partner, and Sex God..."

My eyes widen, but everyone, including Conway laughs. "The day I met you, I thought you were out of my reach, yet you showed me we are equal in every way. You have helped me overcome a challenge, showing me... well, I'll just leave it at that."

I know exactly what she's referring to, but that's strictly bedroom talk. Nonetheless, I love that she managed to slip it in her vows.

"I vow to trust and value you, your opinions and I stand by your actions. I promise to always take an hour longer than needed in the bathroom. I pledge to walk around in yoga pants on Sundays and ask ridiculous questions about rugby, but most importantly, I promise never to refer to your soccer as football. I'm sorry I just can't do it."

That makes me smile.

"I pledge to always admire your huge..." she pauses and winks at me. "Heart, to always be your cheerleader, confidant, and sounding board. But most of all, I vow to be your wife."

"I love you." I mouth to her.

"Yes, my mumbo jumbo was definitely not needed. Rings?"

Unfortunately, we must let go of each other's hands at this point and I turn to face Max who puts Story's wedding ring in the palm of my hand. "You're one lucky bastard, man."

"I know."

Story smiles and scrunches her shoulders together when I face her again.

"Jackson, repeat after me," the justice says. "With this ring, I thee wed."

With Story's hand in mine, I place the ring at the tip of her finger and repeat the words slowly, sliding the band until it's securely in place. She does the same thing to me, slipping the platinum band onto my ring finger and holding my hand securely in hers.

"It's with great honour and privilege that I now present for the first time, Mr and Mrs Jackson Collins. You may—"

I don't wait a second longer for him to tell me I can kiss my wife. I cup her cheeks in my hands, pulling her towards me until our lips meet. Behind us, fireworks explode and our family cheers, and this becomes the second-best day in life because obviously meeting Story—the girl of my dreams —will always be my first.

Acknowledgments

Sexcation was planned out last year. I've been sitting on the title for what seems like forever, hoping that in the spring of 2018 I could finally release it. When a surprise date change my schedule opened up and I started writing, putting down anywhere from four to eight thousand words a day. This story easily moved up my list as one of my favorites.

Yvette: My dedication barely scratches the surface when it comes to how I feel about you. While we may live an ocean may separate us, you're my best friend, confidant, the one I bounce every idea off of and the one I can trust with my life. Thank you, not only for being the voice behind Jackson, but also for always being there.

Amy: Sending you every chapter is exactly the ego boost I need. If I can't get a reaction out of you, I haven't done my job.

Letitia: I don't even know what to say. Not only does your friendship mean the world to me, your vision when it came to this cover surpassed any expectation that I might have had. From the moment I saw the cover on my screen, I had goose bumps. You nailed it! I love it. And you!

Leslie: I love you to pieces. Thank you for always being there, listening, and helping.

Carey: You, my dear, I love with all my heart. We will conquer!

Briggs: You have quickly become one of my best friends.

Ena & Amanda: You ladies rock my world. Thank you for putting your heart & soul into Sexcation.

Homies: If posting equated to steps – you'd kick everyone's arse in Fitbit challenges. You ladies are amazing!

Amy, Natasha, Cara, Adriana, LK, Sarah, MJ, Rebecca, Molly, Chelsea, Katelyn and Meghan: You ladies are the best co-workers. I love working with you! And anyone else I've forgotten.

Readers & Bloggers: Thank you! Your support means the world to me. I know there are so many novels to choose from on any given day. The fact that you've read Sexcation will not go unnoticed.

Dad: You are my biggest cheerleader, and that is best feeling ever.

Girls: As I always say, being your mom is the best job in the world.

To my family: Thank you for your continued support.

About the Author

Heidi is a New York Times and USA Today Bestselling author.

Originally from the Pacific Northwest, she now lives in picturesque Vermont, with her husband and two daughters. Also renting space in their home is an over-hyper Beagle/Jack Russell, Buttercup and a Highland West/Mini Schnauzer, JiLL and her brother, Racicot.

When she's isn't writing one of the many stories planned for release, you'll find her sitting court-side during either daughter's basketball games.

Forever My Girl, is set to release in theaters on January 26, 2018, starring Alex Roe and Jessica Rothe.

Don't miss more books by Heidi McLaughlin! Sign up for her newsletter or join the fun in her fan group!

Connect with Me!
www.heidimclaughlin.com
heidi@heidimclaughlin.com

Also by Heidi McLaughlin

THE BEAUMONT SERIES

Forever My Girl – Beaumont Series #1

My Everything – Beaumont Series #1.5

My Unexpected Forever – Beaumont Series #2

Finding My Forever – Beaumont Series #3

Finding My Way – Beaumont Series #4

12 Days of Forever – Beaumont Series #4.5

My Kind of Forever – Beaumont Series #5

The Beaumont Series Boxed Set

THE ARCHER BROTHERS

Here with Me

Choose Me

Save Me

Lost in You Series

Lost in You

Lost in Us

THE BOYS OF SUMMER

Third Base

Home Run

Grand Slam

THE REALITY DUET

Blind Reality

Twisted Reality

SOCIETY X

Dark Room

Viewing Room

STANDALONE NOVELS

Stripped Bare

Blow